Praise for *Losing Face*

'*Losing Face* is a quintessential Australian story by a skilled and authentic storyteller. It's a confronting yet tender exploration of masculinity and sexuality told from within a community that holds rigid expectations of both … This novel gives readers a unique glimpse into a world often spoken about but rarely spoken for, a world beyond highways and shopping malls, a world of love, loss and self-discovery.' – **Jan Fran**

'In this gorgeous, gripping novel, George Haddad has imagined the lives of unforgettable characters, and examined what he's found in them with compassion and grace. Stunning and rigorous, warm, moving and sharp, this is a surprising story by a brilliant writer that contributes something new to the way we look at families, mothers, and boys.' – **Ronnie Scott**

'At a time when we need narratives that require more of us than comfort, George Haddad's writing delivers. His is a refreshing and challenging voice. Haddad is the remarkable storyteller I have been waiting for.' – **Tony Birch**

'I loved this beautiful book, and its richly realised main characters, Joey and Elaine. It's tough and it's powerful, but it is also joyful and, ultimately, hopeful.' – **Tegan Bennett Daylight**

'*Losing Face* showcases George Haddad's rich storytelling talents in this vibrant chronicle of three generations of one family coming to terms with the mistakes they've made in the past and learning how to live in the present. This novel is wide in scope, rich in the sharp telling details of everyday life, and Haddad is superb at evoking characters who are both unique and relatable in all their complex, layered humanness. *Losing Face* is a deeply affecting portrait of one family's engagement with the moral complexities of contemporary Australia.' – **Felicity Castagna**

 George Haddad is an award-winning writer and artist practising on Gadigal land whose work explores masculinities and the limitations of language in communicating truths. His novella, *Populate and Perish*, was the winner of the 2016 Viva La Novella competition and his short story 'Kátharsis' was awarded the 2018 Neilma Sidney Prize. Haddad is currently a doctoral candidate and sessional tutor at the Writing and Society Research Centre, Western Sydney University.

Losing Face

George Haddad

UQP

First published 2022 by University of Queensland Press
PO Box 6042, St Lucia, Queensland 4067 Australia

University of Queensland Press (UQP) acknowledges the Traditional Owners and their custodianship of the lands on which UQP operates. We pay our respects to their Ancestors and their descendants, who continue cultural and spiritual connections to Country. We recognise their valuable contributions to Australian and global society.

uqp.com.au
reception@uqp.com.au

Copyright © George Haddad 2022
The moral rights of the author have been asserted.

This book is copyright. Except for private study, research, criticism or reviews, as permitted under the Copyright Act, no part of this book may be reproduced, stored in a retrieval system, or transmitted in any form or by any means without prior written permission. Enquiries should be made to the publisher.

Where required, every effort has been made to trace copyright holders and to obtain their permission for the use of copyright material. The publisher apologises for any errors or omissions in this list and would be grateful if notified of any corrections that should be incorporated in future reprints or editions of this book.

Cover design by Josh Durham (Design by Committee)
Author photograph by Patrick McDavitt
Typeset in 12/17 pt Bembo Std by Post Pre-press Group, Brisbane
Printed in Australia by McPherson's Printing Group

  University of Queensland Press is assisted by the Australian Government through the Australia Council, its arts funding and advisory body.

A catalogue record for this book is available from the National Library of Australia.

ISBN 978 0 7022 6555 6 (pbk)
ISBN 978 0 7022 6682 9 (epdf)
ISBN 978 0 7022 6683 6 (epub)
ISBN 978 0 7022 6684 3 (kindle)

University of Queensland Press uses papers that are natural, renewable and recyclable products made from wood grown in well-managed forests and other controlled sources. The logging and manufacturing processes conform to the environmental regulations of the country of origin.

For my mum, Nawal, and my aunty, Inaam

Prologue

Long ago, before factories, churches, cars – before the city of Bankstown – when Arabs were summoning spells in the sand, there lived a djinn that terrorised the desert. She tormented the mothers and children of the camps when the men were away. Only when the men were away.

She'd bury the urns of rice and milk under a foot of sand so that when the men found the food, they would punish the women for being mischievous, for not watching the children. The djinn would conjure pools of fire, bubbling with flailing limbs, on the palm of her shimmering hand to terrify them. She would untether the goats and run with their leashes, her laugh slicing the dunes, then return the panting goats to their posts, collapsing on their knees.

Late at night around the fire, the women's tongues withered with complaints about the djinn, who they had named Ma'raka – The Battle. They told the men about her goat-liver skin, about her limitless speed. But, tired and horny, the men dismissed the nonsense over and over and ordered them all to bed.

The quashed women hatched a plan. The next time the men were away they would trap and kill her with the boiling blood of a goat. They figured something organic, hot and sacrificed was their best bet to vanquish something so otherworldly.

The morning came. They boiled the blood until it was a great sludge then moved all the living things into the largest tent so she would come looking for them. They waited. The children grew restless. The women searched each other's faces for answers. And then they heard her whipping over the dunes, humming her thunderous tune that rumbled up their feet and into their hearts. They spotted her shadow growing large against the skin of the tent. The bravest women stood at the entrance holding the pots of gurgling blood in their dancing hands. They were ready to douse her, to watch her melt and disappear deep into the sand.

Ma'raka pushed through the opening of the tent, one long limb at a time, hovering over the ground, her neck curling up towards the peak. The brave women screamed and threw the pots at her, the liquid coating her skin, falling onto the floor in great clumps. The djinn shrieked, curled over and began convulsing. The children clung so hard to their mothers' arms and backs that they drew blood with their fingernails.

Ma'raka went quiet. And then she cackled. She cackled so loud that the goats tore away from their ropes and some of the children's ears bled. She unfurled herself, larger than they had ever seen her, her skin pulsating with all shades of violet.

They were backed into a corner and Ma'raka, towering over them, said, 'Silly little people. Silly, silly little people. You think you can take on the desert? I am older than any grain of sand you have ground in your teeth. I am stronger than any storm you have weathered. I am wiser than any man you have buried.'

The women scrambled, petrified. One of them spoke up. 'Why, why are you terrorising us? Why won't you leave us? Please leave us!'

The djinn flickered in front of them like a flame and said, 'Fraught little humans. Always asking, never solving.'

'We can give you something,' the woman said, having reluctantly assumed the position of representative. 'We can swap something if you will let us be.'

'Hungry human, now you are talking. Now you are beginning to understand the desert. But unfortunately for you there is nothing here that I want.'

Ma'raka moseyed around the tent, pushing things over, smiling.

Scrambling for a truce, the spokeswoman said, 'You can take a camel. When the men return with them you can take one of the camels … and some goatskin and milk.'

The djinn stopped in her tracks and folded over in a fit of laughter. 'You take me for a fool! You think I don't realise you are trying to reveal me to your men?' Her tone relaxed. 'But, if you really do want me to go away, I guess there is something I could take.'

'What is it? We'll give you anything.'

Ma'raka lingered over them. They contracted as a group, the children's faces pressing hard into the women's chests. She stroked one of the little boys behind his ear. He went white and limp in his wailing mother's arms.

'Please, what will it take for you to leave us?'

The djinn spoke with her back to them. 'My request is a simple one, really; one that will make no difference to you, no immediate change. It is not something you can hear or see or touch.' She turned to face them. 'If you give me the manhood of all the boys in this tent, you will never see me again.'

Confused, the women looked around at one another. 'But they are boys. They have no manhood.'

'Well, then there is nothing to miss.'

Their agreement was unspoken; it was in their eyes.

'Take it,' said the spokeswoman. 'Take it, but do not hurt them.'

Ma'raka swelled. She grinned from the slit in her face and reached out to the closest little boy. Her hand floated over his chest as he writhed then fainted. She did the same to the other boys until they too had wilted over their mothers' knees. Ma'raka pulsated a deeper purple. When she was done, she spun on the spot and vanished.

The women and girls hurried to rouse the little boys by pouring water on their foreheads and they awoke gasping, completely healthy. The little girls told them how Ma'raka had disappeared and would never come back. Everybody began tidying up, anticipating the men's arrival. They all swore to each other that nothing would be relayed to the men.

And it never was. Even when a decade later those boys, whose manhood was usurped by the djinn, didn't grow beards. Even when they didn't quite develop enough gusto to herd the animals or lift the heavy sacks. Even when the confused young men had to be led through the desert.

The women never said a word.

1

Joey had asked for extra chilli in his bánh mì because it numbed his mouth and he liked numbness. He was stoned, sitting on a bench on Waterloo Road watching the cars come and go and wondering how many of them actually had a legitimate destination. Cars were cans on wheels with people in them overtaking each other, colliding with each other. He'd once been in a car accident when his mother sideswiped a taxi on the way to drop him and his brother to school. The damage hadn't been substantial, but his mum had cried. Really cried. And the old Italian taxi driver had told her not to worry, that she should get the boys to school, that his son was a panelbeater and would fix his car.

When he finished eating the roll, Joey stood up, scrunched the paper bag and lobbed it into the tray of a parked ute. The bin was in the other direction from home and he wasn't about to carry the soggy ball around.

When he got home, his mother was on the phone in the living room, squinting her eyes at the old pendant light fixture as she babbled away. There was no prize for guessing that she was scrutinising the dust on it and that she'd ask him to stand on a chair that she'd drag from the dining room (to make the task harder to avoid) and dust it because she was too short to reach.

She swung between English and Arabic with whoever was on the other end of the call, talking about 'eight centimetres' this and 'treatment' that. Joey guessed the topic was what it often was with her and her friends: cancer. He sucked at Arabic. He could understand most of what was being said but his pronunciation was all messed up. Too much throat effort, and the words always sounded recycled coming from him. Maybe it was a genetic thing because his dad was true-blue Aussie.

'Yeah, bowel … no, they only diagnosed him last week, haram, and straight away they started … she was saying her kids are beside themselves … no, apparently not … well, if he gave enough of a fuck about his brother he would go see him and stop involving other people. Mabaarif … yeah, okay, yulla, I've gotta hang the clothes on the line. Bye.'

She turned to him. 'No work today?' she said.

'Nah, chucked a sickie.'

'Why? What's wrong?'

'Nothing. I felt like taking a day off.'

'Right.'

'Why aren't you at work?' he asked.

'Do you listen to anything that goes on in this house? I took the day off to do stuff for Alex's birthday BBQ tonight.'

'Oh. I forgot about it.'

'No surprises there. Did you buy your brother a gift?'
'Nah.'
'Again, no surprises,' she mumbled.

Joey wished she would get the chair already so he could dust the light fixture and move on. He made his way to the fridge, specifically to the chocolate his mum had broken up into bite-sized pieces. She did that when she wanted Joey and Alex to eat stuff. If they let her she'd probably chew the food up and spit it straight into their mouths. Sometimes she peeled mandarins and chopped up apples and put them on a tray in the fridge in full view just so they would be eaten. And she would remind them too, afterwards, that she had done it on purpose and that they were lazy shits. Like she was an absolute mastermind for passive-aggressively chopping up old fruit.

Joey and Alex had once calculated that forty per cent of what their mother said was pure exaggeration. Their grandmother, Tayta Elaine, was the same, which meant it must run in the family. Luckily, they hadn't shown any signs of the curse; in fact, they said the least number of words possible. On nights their mother was out, Joey and Alex could spend hours together without saying a single word. Those were nice nights, rare as they were. Their mother seemed to really enjoy their company, which they found odd. None of Joey's friends' mums would ever hang out with their teenage children, let alone enjoy it.

With his head half in the fridge, Joey heard his mother call out. Her voice echoed through their beige home, the corridor decorated with dorky childhood photos. The worst one was of him dressed as a rat from a primary school performance night. Ms Simpson had insisted that everyone wear red lipstick so that they were visible from the audience. As though the stage lights at Greenacre Public School were state-of-the-art enough to wipe their features clean off.

He ignored his mother's first call and then her voice bounced louder around the white leather sofas, the glass coffee table with wrought-iron legs, the cabinet with giant scented candles on either side of the TV, and the new timber dining table and chairs that had no place among the rest of the curvy early 2000s furniture. He couldn't ignore her call the second time around – he already had two strikes: one for chucking a sickie, the other for forgetting to buy Alex a birthday present.

'What?' he said.

'Will you come with me to the shops? I've gotta get stuff for the BBQ, and you can get Alex a present.'

'Mm.'

'And before we go can you grab a chair and a cloth to wipe the light in here? Tfeh, it's gotten grotty.'

He shoved a handful of chocolate in his mouth.

In the Abu Salim car park, Sudanese quarrelled with Egyptians about their parking prowess. Chubby Lebanese children chomped on sour plums as their mums loaded boxes of tomatoes and gallons of ghee into giant four-wheelers. The Syrian employees dragged the smoke of their cigarettes deep as they unpacked cartons of coffee off a battered truck. Joey was aware his mother had found an in with the gift-buying pretence because she hated to navigate the car park on her own. He couldn't really blame her. Going to Abu Salim meant you had to prepare yourself for a riot. And that wasn't purely due to the byzantine parking lot.

No, inside was equally as raucous. Stock looked like it had been abandoned rather than put out for sale. There was never any clear queue for the checkout, just a conglomeration of tattooed young dads and religious old ladies and sticky school children in a funnel-type situation awaiting the cashiers' frustrated, 'Next.' Oh, and then there were the plastic bags. If the large supermarkets had decided to impose a plastic bag ban, well, Abu Salim saw it as an opportunity for customer satisfaction – like a free gift with purchase. Everything was put into a plastic bag. A single can of chickpeas, a bag of nuts. Once Joey had seen broccoli being double bagged.

By some miracle there was a car spot that nobody was fighting over. Probably because it wasn't an actual parking space but a nook that had nothing obscuring it. There was a council car park directly behind the supermarket that most people avoided for fear of the ibis gang that reaped the discarded manoosh with their scythe-like beaks. These ibis were a product of the area: staunch. If you got too close, they pushed their chests and wings out like guys bridging up before a fight. They had made the car park their slum and punished the plush wives of Greenacre by crapping all over their AMGs and BMWs as they lay back in the salons having their eyebrows fleeked.

Inside the supermarket Joey searched for places to sit while his mum wandered through the aisles. He could lose her for hours in shops. He watched her body change, relax even, in the presence of rows and stacks of products. She squinted at the labels, as though she could read anything without her glasses, widened her eyes, laughed to herself about a slogan on a pack of Jordanian biscuits. She checked the specials, sniffed the capsicums, compared brands, bonded with other shoppers about the price of cucumbers, laughed at them behind their backs. How she ever managed to complete a grocery shop run was beyond him.

She seemed to have forgotten that he was following her from post to post, leaning on shelves, checking his phone, filming her on Snapchat and sending the footage to Alex, who was probably about to get on the bus home from school. Joey missed that feeling – the Friday afternoon bus ride, having a laugh with the boys, planning something stupid.

He sat on a box of dishwashing detergent. Patience was something he'd been trying to practise lately. His mum was weighing two identical bags of pasta as though her intuition was more accurate than the super-precise computers in the factory. A blobby employee with a few hairs combed over his bald scalp tapped Joey on the shoulder and mumbled something in Arabic. It startled him into action; he tugged his shorts up and charged at his mother.

'Ma, what the hell are you doing? You said you were coming for stuff for the BBQ.'

He snatched the bags of pasta from her, dropped one of them among the perfectly arranged items in the trolley and shoved the other in the rice section on the shelf. He worked in the produce department at Woolworths and if he had caught someone doing that with the fruit, he'd lose it, but the lawlessness in Abu Salim permitted the mess.

'Eh, orright, calm down. Yiy, you're such a stress-head,' she said.

'I'm not a stress-head. You're a pest, bro. We've legit been here half an hour and you haven't even been to the butcher and God knows how long you're gonna chat to him before you actually start over-ordering the meat.'

'Joey, I've told you six hundred times, do not call me "bro".'

She slowly reached for a jar of pickles. He could wait it out in the car, listen to music, but she'd struggle with the bags.

'I'm seriously giving you five minutes before I leg it,' he said.

When they pulled into the driveway, Joey beeped twice for Alex to come out and help unload the brimming bags from the car. This was for his stupid birthday after all.

Tayta Elaine popped her head out of the front door. 'We busy, darling. Yulla, bring the stuff down you and your ma.'

'Busy doing what? Tell Alex to come out! There's a million bags in the freakin boot,' he said.

His mum scolded him. 'Can you relax? You haven't even said hello to your grandma and you're already talking to her like that.'

She had nerve to tell him to relax after she dragged him through a two-hour grocery saga and then rushed through the gift-purchasing because she still had 'so much to prepare'. Tayta lingered for a moment, watching them, then turned and went back into the house. Joey slammed the driver's door and moved around to the boot. It took six trips to unload the groceries.

When he peered into the backyard to scold Alex for not helping, he was surprised to see his brother arranging the plastic chairs around a trestle table that had already been set. Tayta was ready to light the BBQ. It didn't look like there would be enough room for everyone at the table by the time Uncle Michael's family and Alex's friends took their spots, but his mother and grandmother almost never sat, running to and from the fridge fetching tomato sauce and toum and slices of lemon for everyone.

He probably wouldn't sit either; he definitely wasn't in the mood to talk to Uncle Michael, who would likely offer him work with one of his stupid office-block cleaning contracts again. As if Joey was ever going to be a cleaner. Uncle Michael was his mother's brother. Joey didn't see him, his wife, Sonia, and their children, Charlie and Chanel, very often and that was a good thing. Even though he and Charlie were the same age, they had grown up in two different worlds: Western Sydney and Inner Western Sydney.

Tayta called out to him, 'Joey, send me the bottle from the shed.'

'Send it? What, via email?'

'Shut up, wleh. Now you want to teach me English?'

He sauntered over to the shed, the yellowing lawn cracking under his fresh all-white Superstars. He picked up the can of petrol and walked it over to his grandmother.

'Here, Tayta.'

'Okay, baby, stand back,' she said.

The warning was unnecessary. He had already started pacing back, aware of what was to come. He'd spent a lot of time trying to understand why Tayta had to light the BBQ this way but, like most neurotic things about his family, it was a mystery. She unscrewed the can, the vapour instantly distorting its surrounds, and lashed ribbons of thin liquid over the shiny new coals. Then, in a well-practised dance, she screwed the lid back on the can, lit a match, covered her eyes with her free arm and threw the match onto the BBQ. She stepped back three times until she bumped into the Colorbond fence.

They all watched from various outposts in the yard as though it were the Sydney New Year's Eve fireworks. The flames whooshed. Too high, too close to the fig tree overhead. One of the coals dropped onto the dry grass. Luckily the whoosh was fleeting, and the flame fell back to something more manageable.

Tayta picked up the rogue coal and flung it back into the BBQ that she was now smirking at, baring her too-white dentures. The gold pendant that hung on her necklace was swinging from all the movement.

There were other ways to light a BBQ. For example, those sweet little easy-light cubes that his friend Emma's family used. There were even gas BBQs – although Tayta would laugh if he were to suggest it. The coal BBQ, and the zany way of lighting it, was part of their history. And it was true that the meat always tasted better.

'Yeah, but what I'm trying to say is that even though I understand where everyone is coming from, the bloke still has a point.'

Uncle Michael was doing his thing at the table again. Picking bits of food out of his teeth as he spoke, turning to his son, Charlie, for validation. Everyone but Joey's mum looked bored as hell. Alex, whose friends had left, was sitting on the stairs leading back into the house, setting up his new iPhone that their mum and Tayta had bought him. Hopefully they came through with a new iPhone to replace Joey's own shattered excuse for a phone on his birthday.

Joey had ended up buying Alex a case and a screen protector to go with the phone. Well, that was when he and his mother had finally progressed from the butcher, after Abu Salim, after the bakery, after the cake shop, servo and then back to Abu Salim for the forgotten mixed nuts. Joey hadn't even bothered suggesting to go without them because his mum would have thought it preposterous.

Sonia was passing her phone around for everybody to see the new puppy. Their third one. Joey barely looked at the screen but he made out a white splotch that looked exactly like the other two and said, 'How cute', to be polite. Sonia's hair was really something today. Teased and curled and glossed into interplanetary oblivion. Surely it could be picked up by satellite. It probably had its own atmosphere.

The only people really invested in the discussion between his uncle and mother were his uncle and mother – which was how any family gathering wound up. Most of the time the siblings disagreed and one of them would storm out in a huff. Usually it was Joey's mum, and she would call for him and Alex to follow her to the car if they weren't the ones hosting. Tayta would uselessly call after his mum in those situations: 'Amal … Amal. Relax … come back.' But his mum would be too determined to remove herself from the grief Uncle Michael brought her.

She'd swear about him and Sonia in the car. Once she called Sonia a 'duck with half a brain', much to the delight of Joey and Alex. Most of the time the insults were warranted. Uncle Michael loved to prod and Tayta would sit there silently as though at some point she relinquished the ability to rein her adult children in.

The conversation was heating up. Joey's mum squinted as she spoke. 'Michael, can you listen to yourself? You think Trump knows what he is doing? He's a puppet, man. He is literally Israel's Cheezel finger puppet. He has no say in anything. He is a celebrity. A scapegoat.'

'Oh, are you an expert in world politics now?'

'Are you?' she was quick to retort.

'No, I'm not saying that I am, but look at the amount of support the guy's got in his country. That's gotta say something for his policies, for what he is about. Wider America wants him.'

'Wider America hasn't encountered anything outside of BBQ ribs, bro. You trust their judgement? Would you be happy if someone like him was running our country?'

Alex looked up from his phone and said, 'Um, hashtag ScoMo.'

'Yeah, exactly – we should really be discussing Australia's shithole politics and George Pell,' she said.

Uncle Michael sat up straight in his chair. 'Okay, well, what do you want to say about Aussie politics then?'

There was a collective sigh from everyone but the debaters.

After Tayta had hiked her leggings up, sprinkled the coals on the BBQ with water, hosed down the concrete and gone home, after his mother had packed the leftovers neatly in the fridge, after Alex had put down his new iPhone, and after Joey had put the extra table and chairs away in the shed and vacuumed the floors of the house – at the insistence of his mother – the three of them wrapped themselves into the giant sofa, heads and feet resting in each other's laps, to watch his mum's favourite show: *The Bachelor.*

In truth it was more like Joey and Alex watching her watch the show. She coached the girls on their dates, tut-tutted at their ill-fitting dresses, gasped at their lewd asides. The bachelor himself was only met with hostility because, she said, 'By nature he is a cheating bastard.' The only times she allowed him a concession was when he undertook some shirtless task. Then she forgot about his treachery and wolf-whistled, palpitating the T-shirt off her chest and fanning herself.

Joey was envious of the bachelor's body. Even though he felt fit and had been working out a fair bit, he lacked the muscle puffiness of the on-screen lothario. Joey worked out with his friend Kyri at the local gym, which was actually an empty office space jam-packed with squeaky equipment. The nicer gym down the road from it had an infrared sauna and loads more free weights, but it was out of Joey's price range. Not Kyri's so much, but since they had promised to get ripped together, Kyri made the sacrifice. Kyri had taken well to lifting heavy and was looking a lot thicker in the past months. They'd put it down to genetics because Kyri's dad was built like a lorry. It made Joey wonder about his own genetics. And steroids.

Tonight's episode was leading up to the finale of the show and the bachelor blindsided the audience by sending home the fan favourite. So stumped was the bachelor by the choice that he cried and walked off the set dramatically as the credits began to flash. Joey's mum threw a cushion at the TV and cussed in Arabic about the bachelor's mother being the daughter of a cow.

'Turn that piece of shit off,' she said as she made her way to the kitchen, texting furiously on her phone.

Joey and Alex were at opposite ends of the sofa, half prodding at their phones and half paying attention to the TV, which had started to play an ad break. The first was of a bleached-blond family shopping for a fridge. The Asian-accented voiceover spruiked the business's forty-year experience in selling appliances. In the end the family opened a fridge door and a blinding light emanated from inside, enveloping them into whitegoods heaven. The second ad depicted another white family. They sat around a beautiful roast lunch under a Queenslander patio. They were happy – together. The third ad showed an Islander family whose car had broken down on a remote road. The flustered dad chased a rogue wheel with one flip-flop on, gut hanging out of his soiled T-shirt. The wheel fell off a cliff. The ad was for roadside assistance. Joey rolled his eyes at the TV.

'Joey?'

'What?'

'Did you know Dad was a mechanic? Tayta told me the other day when we were talking about her car.'

Joey cursed the roadside assistance ad. 'Yeah.'

'Do you remember much about him?'

'Why are you asking about annoying crap, Alex?'

'I'm just wondering. Relax. No-one ever wants to say shit about him.'

'Because there's not much to say.'

Alex asked the same questions every now and again, as though Joey was suddenly going to have more information to provide. He thought about starting to make stuff up just to get Alex off his back.

Their mother called from the kitchen for the empty mugs off the coffee table. They ignored her.

'I was, like, three when he left, yeah?' Alex said.

Joey rolled his eyes. 'Yeah, cos I was six.'

Alex had his bony knees tucked under his chin. He was delicate, like origami. 'And it was because Tayta Elaine and Jiddo Youssef kicked him out, yeah?'

'I think so. Mum has never said.' Joey was still answering from behind his phone.

'You reckon it was drugs?'

'Probably.'

Their mother shuffled into the lounge room with a suss look on her face; she took the mugs to the kitchen, the water still running in the sink.

'Have you ever done drugs? I mean other than weed.'

'Uff, Alex, with the questions tonight!' Joey bounced off the couch and went to his bedroom.

2

When Elaine arrived home, she went straight to the top drawer in the bathroom and popped two tablets of Mylanta out of the packet and into her mouth. Amal's tabouli always had too much burghul in it. She pulled a tuft of her hair closer to her nose. It smelt like smoke and kafta. She stared into the shower for a moment, yawned and walked away.

In the dark of her bedroom, she slipped out of her clothes, folded them over once and placed them on the chair in the corner. She lay on her back in the bed and sighed so hard she felt her body deflate. Then she sat up very quickly and burped, which further deflated her. Good, the Mylanta was working.

She was glad Alex was happy with his new iPhone but she wasn't surprised. Young people devoted their lives to those things. His smile was worth her latest poker machine winnings. And she was glad that Amal and Michael didn't get too heated in their useless debates either. These days she preferred to see them separately, unlike most mothers she knew who loved having all their children around at once.

When she did see her children on their own, she was free to play the different parts they had written for her. Michael expected her to be stupid and agree with all his nasty beliefs. And Amal expected her to approve of all her choices and to always be available but not nosey. Elaine was too old and tired to not play along. She often imagined the look on their faces if they were to see how savvy she was in her daily life or if they knew how she had to exaggerate her grief after their father, Youssef, died. Really, she had felt okay. Still, she missed Youssef – mainly how his straightforward attitude rubbed off on her and silenced their children. Since he'd died, she'd sometimes fallen deep into the valley of nonsense and wasn't quite sure how she'd managed to climb out each time.

Tomorrow, she'd visit the pokies again. It had been three days and three days was good. She'd take fifty, no, seventy dollars, because she'd found that twenty in the pocket of her coat, and she would leave her purse at home. She'd play two-dollar hits on the machine with the lucky cat at Mount Lewis Bowling Club. Maybe she'd even walk there, in the middle of the day, in the sneakers she'd inherited from Amal.

Elaine scoffed. Parents spent their lives pulling their hair out for their children only to be given worn shoes in return. She had barely bought any footwear for herself in the past years. Especially with how fleeting Amal's taste was. Nothing like Elaine's style at her age. Even now, for that matter. Still, Amal wasn't as bad as Michael's wife, Sonia, who looked like she'd fallen through her wardrobe every time she saw her.

As garish and as purple as the sneakers were, they were very comfortable. She'd wear them to the club. Thinking about the club made her less tired. It would be ridiculous to get up and put her clothes back on and go now. But if she couldn't get to sleep, then why not?

She sat up and put her feet on the ground. She tried to stand up. Her knees refused. Then she remembered that her hair stank, and that the club would make it smell worse. Tomorrow wasn't far off; she'd go tomorrow. She nestled back into the bed and pulled the covers over herself.

She woke up panting from a dream she was being buried in sand. It was a dream that had come to her before. She got up, put her bathrobe and slippers on and shuffled down the hallway quietly as if she was trying not to wake anyone.

She peered into the other bedrooms. Amal's was still set up how she left it in her twenties, but Michael's old bedroom had become more like storage; she liked to bulk buy toilet paper and washing powder on sale and there was no space for it all in the laundry because of the big freezer.

The clock on the microwave said it was 4:00 am. She drank one and a half glasses of water, made her way to the couch and switched the television on. Last year, Michael had a device installed for her that picked up hundreds of channels from all over the world. Most of them were useless but a few of the Arabic channels played melodramas that hooked Elaine right in. The actors in the shows looked so perfect they could have been animations. But having your face paralysed for the sake of perfection meant you weren't very good at displaying the necessary emotion for the scene. Perhaps that's what all the dramatic music was trying to make up for.

The show on now was about a historic feud between two families. Elaine had watched the entire series already. This episode was the finale. The lead was about to discover the slumped body of her lover at the altar of an Orthodox church. He had been paid off by her family to leave and never come back but, unable to get over his love for her, he'd returned, been fooled into believing that she was dead, and had chosen to kill himself after theatrically addressing God over two episodes.

The saving grace of the show was the script. Elaine had almost forgotten how poetic Arabic could be, too used to speaking the everyday version of it and English. There was a rhythm and a conviction in proper Arabic that she didn't recognise in English.

The actress was holding her dead lover's head in her hands. She was referring to him as her eyes, her ribs, her soul. She was telling him that she had been dead for much longer than him. That she had only ever been alive when they were together. She called him her moon. She turned to the cross behind the altar and asked God how he expected the ocean to move without the moon.

Elaine sobbed like she was watching it for the first time.

3

THE BACKYARD WAS STILL SOPPING with morning dew when Joey and his mother took a pan of fried eggs, a bag of Lebanese bread, some olives and zaatar out to the patio for breakfast.

Alex had left for the early Saturday shift at Macca's and the hum of neighbourly backyard workings was building up. Joey wiped the chairs with his hand and flicked the water onto the too-long grass off the timber deck. The neighbour's passionfruit vine had been gradually wrapping around the fig tree and was now choking it. That's what an untrimmed world would look like, Joey thought. Plants strangling plants. He had waked and baked.

His mother tore a piece of bread and handed him half. Her lips were less full than a few months ago, which meant any day now she'd come home and they'd be twice their original size again. She held an olive between her fingertips. She had told him once that her ancestors were olive farmers, which made sense. Tayta preserved enough jars every year for the whole of Canterbury-Bankstown.

His mother closed her eyes, chewed and puckered her lips. She turned her head towards the lawn and fired the pip out of her mouth. She slurped from her coffee cup once and lowered it to the table only to bring it back to her mouth. Her acrylic fingernail scratched at food stuck between her teeth. She swore under her breath, gave up on it. She was haloed by the bougainvillea.

'Why didn't you ever date anyone after Dad?' he asked.

'Holy Mary, where did that come from?' Her face flushed. She reached for a glass of water and investigated it like a crystal ball. 'Who said I didn't date anybody after your dad?'

'Mum, get real. You didn't.'

'Why do you discount me, you jahash? I'm a human, you know. I've lived a life.'

'Alright, tell me then.'

'I don't want to.'

It wouldn't take her long to give in, so he just kept quiet. Her face changed as though she remembered something. He threw an olive into her cleavage to snap her out of it. She slapped him on the arm and fished it out.

'I dated a Palestinian guy. His name was Rabih. He was six years younger than me. We met through Rita.'

'Aunty Rita? Mother of Shrek?'

She laughed in her nose. 'Haram, Joey, you kalb. Her son is actually very smart, apparently. Unlike you. Yeah, her and Rabih worked together at this old restaurant that used to be in Dulwich Hill. Rita used to say to me, "Amal, trust me, you need an Arab. Rabih is gorgeous. Look how the Aussie turned out."' She was imitating Rita in a woggier accent than her own. 'But I was never attracted to Arabs. I always found the whole thing a little incestuous. Anyway, at Rita's wedding she of course sat Rabih and me on the same table. The first thing he said to me was so corny – I die when I think of it. He was a proper Arab – like, straight off the boat. He goes, "My God, I want to put you in my whisky and drink you."'

'Why did he say that?' Joey asked.

'As a pick-up line. Because I looked hot.'

'You? Hot?'

'Shut up, wleh. Yes, me, hot. You know, guys used to say I looked like Haifa Wehbe.'

Joey laughed short and exaggeratedly. His mother had been young. She had been young and pretty. She had once been his age. 'You look like you swallowed Haifa more like it.'

'No! I look like I've been a single mother is what I look like, you little shit.'

'Here we go. Alright, continue with the story.' He plopped some bread over the eggs and brought the morsel to his mouth.

'I was wearing this red halter dress. Brown lippie. Hair tied back in a long ponytail. Your tayta thought it was too much but at that point I didn't care what anybody said. Anyway, he actually turned out to be really sweet when he wasn't quoting Arabic poetry and biting his lip at me. He didn't flinch when I told him I had kids. He danced well. At some point during the wedding, he put his hand on my thigh under the table.'

'Alright, Ma. Too much info, yeah?'

'Oh, calm down. My God, you're the one who wanted to know the story.'

'Yeah, but, like, I don't need to know about your thighs being touched.'

She ignored him. 'We hit it off. There was real chemistry. We exchanged numbers and from then we would chat. After a few weeks he asked me out to dinner. Tayta babysat you and Alex.

We met at Auburn Macca's in our cars because he lived in Granville. I got into his and he drove us to Darling Harbour.' Her face puzzled. She glanced away from him towards the end of the backyard. 'I hadn't been there in years and I swear for a moment after dinner when we were walking to a bar, and I'd had a few wines, I forgot all about you guys. And it felt nice to walk with this proud, handsome guy and to laugh and hear music and be around strangers.'

'Gee. Laying it all out, Mum. So, what happened?'

'Nothing. We dated for a few months and …' She sipped from her empty coffee cup.

'Ma?'

'And then I saw your dad somewhere and I broke it off.'

'Where's "somewhere"?'

'Who cares? It was so long ago.' She shook her head and smiled. 'Listen, I've been meaning to tell you and Alex something. I've booked in to get my boobs done.'

Joey wasn't surprised. Most of her friends and workmates at the beauty salon had theirs done and she was always talking about how happy they were with the results.

'Clearly doing your lips and nose wasn't enough. Have you told Tayta?' he asked.

'No. I'm working on it.'

'Do you want to role-play? I'll be Tayta.' He imitated her voice and accent. 'Amal! La shu? After all this time? What will people say?'

His mother narrowed her eyes at him. 'I never thought I would give birth to such an annoying son. Hurry up and eat if you want a lift to work.'

★

Joey liked that his friend Emma didn't come from a complicated family. Her mum baked cakes and her dad spent his free time fishing with her pro-cricket-playing twin brothers. No-one cared that the mugs in their house had chips in them.

Emma never asked the annoying questions that everyone else seemed to ask, like, 'What do you want to do?' She told stories. Mainly about the things she'd read, which she took very seriously. He had wondered if this made her naïve but decided that her naïveté was woven in with her quest for truth. Emma wasn't concerned with becoming an influencer or with the size of her lips. Although one thing she was concerned with was criticising him – the brands he wore, the selfies he posted, the news websites he read.

They'd agreed to meet for a coffee before their midday shift at Woolworths. During the shift they'd only see each other if Emma dropped a customer's tomato at the checkout and needed a replacement. Sometimes she did it on purpose just to annoy him, see him.

The Greek cake shop at the entrance of the shopping centre didn't make the best coffee, but it was that or the chain café relic whose coffee was more like molten lava. Joey flicked through his phone as he waited for Emma to arrive and made a good effort to ignore the grumpy owner's huffs at the fact that he hadn't ordered anything. It was already so close to the start of their shift that it would have to be an express meeting.

Emma's 'hello' came after the kiss she planted on his cheek. When they had first met in the lunchroom a few years ago, he hadn't registered how pretty she was. Maybe it was the awkward getting-to-know-you chatter that obscured it. Once they had, by osmosis, agreed that they enjoyed each other's company, Emma's beauty beamed fully realised and it took a second or two for Joey to get over it every time he saw her. Well, every time he saw her out of their drab uniforms. She had a messy blond bob, hazelnuts for eyes and a nose that made his look like the bow of a ship.

She smiled her Cheshire cat smile at the owner and threw her rainbow tote bag on the floor, gesturing to the man for two cappuccinos. He grinned back at her from behind the counter, blushing the same colour as one of his cakes. Joey placed his phone upside down on the table. Emma glanced at it, raised her eyebrows and fluttered her hand like you do when your body remembers something faster than your brain.

'Did you read that article I sent you?' she asked.

'Which one?'

'The cognitive science one.'

'Oh, nah, I totally forgot.'

'Joey, you're useless.'

'Gimme a rundown.'

'Basically, it talks about how reality isn't really a thing. It's multilevel, and completely objective. Like, what we think is reality is actually our brains' best guess at what everything is doing around us. And because we are so sure our simulation is a decent one, we actually end up living in, like, a collective illusion.'

He felt like he'd been placed on the damaged rack in the back dock whenever Emma spoke about her psychology studies. Surely he'd been born to never have an interest in anything.

Emma continued. 'The scientist gave an awesome example for how it is. I can't remember it perfectly, but it was like, think of our brain, matter, everything, as a computer, and think of our perception of life being a folder on the desktop with only the most used programs or documents in it.'

The coffee machine coughed and stopped humming.

He said, 'Hm, maybe when people do DMT or have like NDEs they are actually venturing out of that folder and using other programs in the life computer?' He finished his remark in an exaggerated American accent.

'Yes, yes, exactly! It's crazy, hey. People go through their whole lives only knowing what they've been fed. Total goldfish.'

The cappuccinos arrived. His had spilt over the edge and pooled in the saucer. Emma's was perfect. They took their first sip in unison.

'Dad has this silly story he always pulls out. He says, in all the time people have been fishing with rods and bait, no-one has ever caught a dolphin.'

'Well, dolphins are as smart as us, hey?'

'Smarter even. Dad says, imagine how many humans would try to swallow a floating kebab.'

'Your dad is a genius.'

'Don't ever tell him that. C'mon, finish your coffee. We're gonna be late.'

'You were the one who rocked up five minutes before our shift!'

Emma made a yapping gesture with her hands.

Although the work may have seemed simple to shoppers (and to his mother, Tayta and everyone else who felt the need to judge his existence) there was a lot more to being a produce assistant than was immediately perceivable.

There was the physical side of things – the lifting, pushing, shuffling, shoving, walking. There was the stock replenishing, the problem-solving and the judging what was good or bad. There was also cleaning. And there was, of course, customer service. That was the part he hated most. The annoying customers with their dumb questions. 'Are there fresher tomatoes out the back?' or 'Where are the Lebanese cucumbers?' He'd always reply under his breath sarcastically with something like, 'I'll show you a Lebanese cucumber, you pest.' His actual responses were mostly polite though, and he would avoid saying anything if he could, by gesturing or pointing or smiling a certain way instead.

At the induction for the role, the manager had left him in a windowless room in the concrete-block innards of the supermarket. The scuffed walls of the room were covered in posters about OH&S with smiling faux employees showing the correct ways to pick up boxes. High on the wall was a television where a welcome video had played. A croissant of a man had welcomed Joey to the team and rambled about the history of the brand, its core values and how everyone played a part. Joey had never actually wanted to play a part and he suspected most people didn't.

The supermarket was host to a motley clientele. The vast majority of them were undeniably Arab and he was glad that he just about passed as white, with his green eyes and brown hair, because it meant they didn't ask him for obscure vegetables in Arabic. It happened often to his co-workers who looked more Arab. There must be something about only knowing the names of vegetables in one of your spoken languages. For example, Joey's mother called all green leafy vegetables the same Arabic word. Much to the dismay of Tayta, who wasted no time correcting her.

Arabs were also the pickiest customers. They spent the longest time seeking out the heaviest lemons, pinching asparagus, knocking on watermelons. They shopped like they expected to be ripped off. Asians closely followed Arabs in their pickiness, but Aussies just bagged whatever tomatoes their hands landed on.

4

THE SEVENTY DOLLARS EVAPORATED IN ten minutes. Elaine had centred her whole day around the trip to the bowls club and now she had nothing else to do. The ATM at the entrance to the club flashed as she passed it on her way out. Cash taken out of one machine and put into another and then never seen again. It was still outlawed, but she imagined that soon enough you'd be able to use your card on the poker machines and never have to see cash again.

Money never really mattered much to her. Except after Youssef died when she let things slip a little – well, a lot – but there was no reason to think about that now.

Amal's sneakers carried her lightly up Wattle Street, past the almost completed St Charbel's aged care centre. She couldn't fathom why a place created for people to spend the end of their lives was designed like an office block. A group of tradesmen were affixing a colossal metal plate with St Charbel's face etched into it onto the grey façade. The hermit from the mountains of Lebanon here in Punchbowl, looking even more solemn than in his usual depictions. Salma from across the road had told Elaine that she'd heard the fees for a room in the centre were set to be astronomical. Elaine had even heard about people selling their homes just to fund a few years of care.

She would sooner swallow a bunch of pills when the time came than squander the home Youssef had built for them and paid off entirely by the year 2000. Youssef had been a hard-working man. Up until his dying days they had lived off his income alone.

Since then, the government had been looking after her by way of the disability pension. She was very grateful for that and, in some way, felt deserving of it. Doctor Chew had helped secure her the pension by writing a letter that exaggerated her anxiety and bad knees, both of which she was feeling as she walked up Mount Lewis towards home.

There was a time when Elaine had worked too. A time when she had understood what it meant to have a job, a manager, a paycheque, a roster: forty-five years ago, at the ice-cream factory on Australia Street in Camperdown, when the area was still a little seedy. She'd often be yelled at by a bum if she walked up to King Street after a shift to pick up the Arabic newspaper for Youssef.

Georgette, her old neighbour in Petersham and a fellow Lebanese export, had secured her the job. Georgette had been in the final weeks of her second pregnancy and had pleaded with Elaine to take the position. She had said it would be worth it and that Elaine may as well do something before she started having children, and that she could even put some of the money aside to buy nice things for herself.

It hadn't taken much to convince her. She had become bored fast, in the small terrace house they had shared with Youssef's brother, with nothing to do but cooking or cleaning. A bit like how she imagined the rest of her day would play out now that her main outing had been cut short. Except these days the boredom was cancelled out by exhaustion. As an eighteen-year-old newlywed, she had needed something to do. Something to get her out and interacting with whatever it was her new life in Australia was supposed to be about. And this is what her life ended up being about. Seventy dollars down the drain and wearing her daughter's sneakers.

Youssef had objected to the prospect of her working because he was jealous of her being around other men. Not that he ever vocalised his jealousy, but she had tested him in the early days by flirting with his brother around the house. Youssef would always be rougher in bed afterwards.

Georgette had promised she would have her husband convince Youssef at the races. She said he would tell him that, except for a few managers, all the employees were women. When Youssef had come home swaying, radiating Marlboros and sweat and Tooheys, and told Elaine she could take the job, she jumped at him and kissed his moustache.

There had been no interview, just an immediate start date. To the factories in Sydney at the time, all migrants were the same. Workhorses. And she hadn't taken it personally. She had known her place. She came from a farming family of thirteen. There was no shame in shovelling shit or battling weeds or spending a day bent over macerating olives. In fact, she had enjoyed the monotony of factory work. She had put labels on buckets, wiped them down and sealed them up. That was it. A few times she'd covered a shift in the shop, scooping ice cream into cones for the customers but, other than that, she went to work and did the exact same thing for two years.

At the top of the hill, she decided to take a rest in the park. She sat at a bench looking back over Wattle Street, over the tightly packed housing estate where the textile factory used to be. In the distance, she could see Sydney's neat skyline toying with the clouds.

Georgette had been right; the money from the ice-cream factory had been a blessing. It had cemented Elaine as a cog in her marriage; a working part that wasn't purely confined to the motor of the house, but that contributed to the fiscal operations too. Some weeks she had worked overtime and brought home more money than Youssef did from the glass factory on South Dowling Street. Those weeks Youssef would retreat into speechlessness. He controlled the finances and she would hand over her pay every Friday but, just like Georgette had instructed, she hid a few dollars in a stocking.

When her little hoard amassed to twenty or thirty dollars, Elaine would go to Fossey's or the boutique on Parramatta Road and buy earrings or a purse. Youssef paid no attention to that sort of thing, so she got away with it mostly by introducing the new items on nights when he was drunk or preoccupied with a long drive to a relative's house.

There had been one time when he'd insisted that he'd never seen the maroon clutch she brought to Easter Sunday mass. He had demanded to know whose it was as they sat in the car outside St George's Cathedral in Redfern. He had twirled it around in his hand, looked inside. She had been calm as she explained that Georgette was given it by her despised mother-in-law and so had offloaded it on to Elaine. Even though she knew Youssef would have been okay with the truth, Elaine had enjoyed the secret.

Now the clutch lived in the lowest drawer of her bedroom cupboard, holding old passports and citizenship documents and marriage certificates.

In that frosty factory in Camperdown, Elaine was introduced to the world. She was also introduced to something – someone – else. Someone she didn't often allow herself to think about but, on the park bench and with not much else to do, she let herself reminisce.

Mr Harvey. What she had felt for him was love that had nothing to do with responsibility. Something she'd never experienced before or felt since. There were times after a shift, her apron stained with strawberry and chocolate and mint ice cream, that she had gone straight upstairs to bed, put her face into a pillow and screamed, her entire body palpitating from a brief interaction with him. A smile to her from the mezzanine. His wide shoulders as he pushed through the back door. His eighteen-carat hair falling over his eyes as he addressed the women about some new process.

She had felt sick for weeks after their first meeting, thoughts of him stifling her constant chatter around the house. Youssef and his brother never really spoke, so the silence had been even louder. When Youssef would ask what was wrong, she would point to her tummy and he'd disappear back behind his newspaper or refocus his gaze on the TV. It had taken a lot of courage to let thoughts of Mr Harvey flood her mind when she was having sex with Youssef.

She stood up and turned around to look at Bankstown before she continued her walk home. It could have been the clouds, but the roads and houses and shopping centre looked like they were drooping.

Mr Harvey had been in love with her too. He'd had a special look for her that he hadn't given the other women. And there was that time in the tearoom. The time he had kissed her. His sea salt lips had touched hers and she had melted into a silly puddle on the linoleum. She had run straight out of the room and back to her position, but she had been so faint she went home early.

There had been a moment when she had thought her life was over. That Youssef would find out about the kiss and send her back to her parents' mud house in the village. But all those years ago on the walk home along Railway Avenue, as the trains screeched by, she had decided that the kiss was so dreamlike that she didn't have to treat it as real.

On Elaine's last day in the factory, when she was inches from giving birth to Amal, Mr Harvey had stayed in his office. He hadn't come downstairs to say goodbye as the others sent her off with flowers and chocolate. Elaine had told them she would be back but, as she waddled to the green Ford where Youssef was waiting for her, she had broken into breathless sobs. She had known she wouldn't return. She had known she was becoming a mother and that her stint at being anything else was over.

At her front door, Elaine kicked Amal's sneakers off her feet and left them how they landed.

5

Joey posed at different angles in the full-length mirror in his mother's room – it was the only one in the house. He wore a new grey tank top, black tapered jeans with cuts across the knees and his grey Nike Air Force 1s. Tanning in the backyard in the week leading up had paid off because his skin popped against the outfit. He took a selfie, flexing his triceps and angling his face to accentuate his jawline, and posted it to Instagram with the caption, *Defqon ready*.

He and his friends had been looking forward to Defqon, a trance music festival, all year. He punctuated his outfit with a spritz of his mother's cologne. It was a men's fragrance by Jean Paul Gaultier and the bottle was shaped like a muscle man's torso. She preferred men's fragrances because apparently women's were too flowery.

He tapped his pockets. Phone, wallet, keys, tobacco pouch, lighter. His heart raced a little. When he entered the lounge room his mum wolf-whistled exaggeratedly.

'Look. At. My. Spunk!' she said.

'Shush.'

'I mean, what is this? Who are you trying to impress?'

'Ma. You better stop.'

He raised his hand to jokingly slap her and she slapped him instead on his arm, her fingers leaving a red imprint.

'Are you serious? Now I'm gonna leave the house with a fucking slap mark on my arm!'

'Shut your mouth, wleh. Don't you ever raise your hand at me.'

'You're so annoying.'

'Who're you trying to impress?'

'You are seriously so annoying and invasive. I'm almost twenty. You think other mums ask their sons these questions?'

'You'd be shocked to know that, yes, I have it on good authority from my friends that they ask their children similar questions. And their sweet angels answer them. But you? No. Mister can only see his reflection. You don't divulge anything to me.'

'Are you gonna give me a lift to Kyri's or what?'

'Yes, I'm gonna give you a lift because I'm a good mother.'

'I don't think good mothers are supposed to be that self-aware.'

Joey made his way past her as she looked up to the ceiling and stretched her palms out in apparent frustration or prayer. She was wearing black athletic tights and a bathrobe and slippers. She called it her uniform.

'Ya Allah, I never understood why you didn't bless me with daughters.'

'You would be living on the street if you'd had daughters and they loved to spend as much as you. You should count your blessings for your two cheap sons.'

'Oh, something crawled out of my arse to judge me and my

spending.' She called out into the hallway, 'Alex, I'm driving Joey. Do you wanna come for the ride?'

A muffled 'no' came from behind Alex's bedroom door.

With a bottle of vodka in one hand and a bottle of lemonade in the other, Joey charged up Kyri's driveway towards the double garage at the back of the yard.

The boys had decided they would have pre-drinks at Kyri's before they made their way to the festival. He knew the house and family well. Mr and Mrs Kyriacos were Cypriot but born in Sydney. They adored Kyri and his little sister and were always welcoming to Joey. Mrs Kyriacos made the best galaktoboureko. And meatballs. And schnitzel. She was just an amazing cook. Maybe even better than his own mother. Which he would never say out loud for fear of being struck by lightning.

He wondered how Mrs Kyriacos managed to do all that amazing cooking and look so impeccable and be so chill. They had money so she was often wearing something from Louis Vuitton or Hermès or Yves Saint Laurent, but you couldn't tell because it wasn't the cookie-cutter crap that the other wogs from the area obsessed over. They probably didn't even stock what she bought in Australia.

Mr Kyriacos was a builder and had designed their latest house with respect to the outdoors. Every room flowed easily to a patio or a courtyard or the pool and cabana. The house belonged in Bondi, not in Greenacre. Mr and Mrs Kyri were high school sweethearts and still doted on each other as though they were teenagers. Joey often referenced their long-term relationship as a functioning one to his mother when she lamented men and women and marriage. 'Yeah, that's because John Kyriacos is one in a freakin million!' she'd say.

Kyri had shoulder-length hair when he came to Birrong Boys, halfway through year nine, from the private Greek school in Bankstown that he said was stifling his creativity. He wanted to be an artist. During lunch breaks he would let out his ponytail until a teacher told him to tie it back up. He looked more Swiss than Cypriot, which he explained was because his grandparents were actually from Thessaloniki. He had been to Greece with his family multiple times and had promised to show Joey around one day.

They had forged their friendship when they were partnered for an English assignment. Instead of getting to work, they'd spent the whole night before the assignment was due taking the piss out of their schoolmates' Instagram profiles, and so made an agreement to plagiarise the whole thing.

They shared an identical sense of humour: a cutting one that didn't afford the subjects of their jokes any concession. They'd test each other, topping their epic comments until even they were surprised at how evil their remarks could get. But they would always come to the conclusion that, 'end of the day it's just for laughs'. Then they'd side-eye each other and burst into laughter because it probably wasn't.

Their friendship really blossomed towards the end of high school when they realised the rest of the guys in the group were gronks. Since then, Joey had joined Kyri's family on holiday, they'd slept in the same bed together, given each other massages, showered together. They had even said, 'I love you, bro', one time when they were drunk, holding each other up and making their way home after a night out. They felt like outcasts all the time but at least they felt that way together.

As he neared the side door of the garage, he heard Kyri firing up one of the sacred pinball machines. Mr Kyriacos had a fascination with the machines and had dedicated half the garage to them. The boys had been strictly ordered to never touch the things. The other half of the garage had a sofa, a TV with an Xbox and a bar fridge. The boys hung out there a fair bit during high school but rarely since then. Mr and Mrs Kyriacos weren't the type to pry so it was always easy to smoke joints and lie around with each other like boys do when they're not being watched.

He paused outside the door. Kyri would only ever defy his father's orders and play the pinball machines if he was trying to impress someone. And then Joey heard Emma's enthusiastic, 'That's so cool.'

She had arrived earlier than him, which was awkward. He felt like he was about to interrupt something special. But Emma was his friend. She and Kyri had only met a few times before, in passing and at another music festival. He pushed open the side door and he could have imagined it, but Emma seemed to pull away from Kyri.

'Sup,' Joey said.

'Youssef!'

He wished he'd never told Emma about the Arabic pronunciation of his name because now she used it at will. He rolled his eyes as she jumped to hug him, dangling from his neck. Joey and Kyri bumped fists and then Kyri took the bottles.

The whirrs and clatter from the pinball machine interrupted the itchy energy.

Joey gestured at the machine. 'Won't he kill you if he finds out?'

'Nah, he's chilled out about them ever since my pappou died. He's gone full soft.'

Emma reached out and touched Kyri's bicep. 'Oh, I didn't know your pappou died. Sorry to hear.'

Why would she know? They weren't friends.

'It's cool. He lived for ages anyway. More importantly, the vodka has arrived.'

Kyri started making the drinks.

'Where's Boxer?' Joey asked Kyri.

'He said he's coming a bit later.'

'And he's got the goods?'

'Apparently.'

Joey walked over to the machine and put his fingers over the buttons lightly.

'You sure your dad won't mind if I play?'

'Yeah, man.'

He'd never played one before. The way you almost straddled the machine with your hands at its sides excited him. He pulled the spring, released it, and the ball shot out into the maze. The machine's theme was outer space. Planets, stars, galaxies, moons. Emma came over and rested her head on his shoulder as she watched. It made the playing cumbersome, having her so close, but he felt owed that moment of contact before a big day of partying and other people. He fired the buttons on the side to save the ball from the abyss. His score was a fraction of the highest, whose player name on the light-up scoreboard was *Zeus*.

Emma then had a quick go and Joey coached her. She would usually tell him she didn't need his help with this kind of thing. It was then he realised she was wearing make-up. It was set to be a weird day.

'My people, drink,' Kyri said as he unloaded the glasses into their hands.

They clinked them and sipped.

'Kyri, are you trying to poison us?' Emma coughed through her words and raised the back of her hand to her mouth.

'Whaddaya mean? This is weak.'

She reached for the lemonade bottle to dilute the drink. The boys shared a confused glance and sipped again. They played more pinball and Xbox and chatted about the DJs they wanted to see at Defqon, who else they knew that was going. Emma knew a whole group from her part of town, Picnic Point, including her brothers, but it was assumed that she would spend most of her time with the boys. She was always teasing her brothers' mates for being too white.

Boxer clearing his throat loudly as he came up the drive quietened them before he burst through the door. 'What's up, crackheads?'

His voice trailed off as his eyes landed on Emma, who seemed unimpressed by the greeting.

Boxer looked like his nickname suggested. Everything about him was thick and square, including his dick, which he often whipped out in front of the boys for a laugh. He fist-bumped Joey and Kyri and kissed Emma on the cheek. The two had only met once before and she had described him to Joey afterwards as someone who hadn't spent enough time out of the area. Nothing more agreeable had ever been said about Boxer.

He was one of the very few guys that Joey and Kyri still connected with from high school. He had access to drugs and was generally funny when they were just kicking back. His brothers were rough, rumoured to be caught up in all kinds of trade. At school, some of the boys doted on Boxer like obedient dogs: went to the canteen for him, covered for him. Joey had once seen Boxer's father bashing him in the Woolies car park, his train-driver shirt straining over his biceps as he laid into him. Joey and his mother had stopped in their tracks, hands heavy with bags of discounted dishwashing liquid. She had yelled out, 'Aybeshoom ahlak!' – how embarrassing for you – her voice echoing in the near-empty lot. Joey had wished she could have acted like they hadn't seen anything, but his mum would never stand for that shit. Boxer's dad had stopped, fist midair. Joey had caught Boxer's eyes, but they were tunnels to nowhere.

The next morning at school he pushed Joey against the wall in the toilets and told him if he ever said anything, he'd set his mum's car alight and tell everyone he was a faggot. And he would have, and his dogs would have believed it.

Boxer made a beeline for the pinball machine, losing the ball within a minute and smacking the side of the machine with his knuckles before turning away. Joey made eye contact with Kyri as he walked a drink over to Boxer and discreetly switched the machine off.

Boxer threw his arms wide and some of the drink sloshed out. 'Shu, are we gonna party today or what?'

'Yeah, man,' Kyri said.

'What about you, Emma? Up for a big one?' Boxer asked.

'I guess so. I have the day off tomorrow so why not?'

Boxer reached into the side-bag that hung across his rig. It was very noticeably fake Gucci. He pulled out three baggies. 'Hectic, cos I got enough to keep us going for a week.'

Kyri clapped. 'Yew.'

Boxer sat between Emma and Joey on the sofa and placed the

baggies in a neat row. 'This one is rack. This one is MD. And this is green, for later.'

It felt like primary school when the teacher reads a page of a picture book to the class and then turns it around for everyone to gawk at the illustrations. Joey needed to poo.

'Emma, you taken stuff before?' Boxer asked as he racked up lines of coke onto the tabletop.

It was a coffee table Kyri had made in year eleven woodwork. Joey had been jealous of its sturdiness. His own table ended up too short and too long, like a sausage dog. Mr Dowd had poked fun at it in front of the whole class. Tayta still used it on the back patio.

'Yeah, once. I took a pill at a friend's house party. I didn't feel much. Just, like, fluffy.'

Joey spoke before anyone else could. He felt especially responsible for Emma, being the bridge between friend groups. 'Maybe just have half a cap later, then, to start off with.'

'Uff. And who are you? Her dad?' Boxer licked the Opal card he had been using to set up the lines.

'Kyri, pass me a note.'

They all took turns snorting decent-sized lines of coke.

'Someone play some fuckin tunes, man. Are we at a funeral or something?' Boxer commanded.

Kyri played an EDM mix on the bluetooth speaker and they bopped around, then lay down on the sofa and spoke over the music for an hour. At one point Boxer had Emma cornered in conversation and Joey could see spit flying from his mouth onto her cheek. He continued watching them as Kyri spoke to him, waiting for Emma to make some sort of rescue gesture, but she didn't.

'Did you hear what I said?' asked Kyri.

'Huh? Nah.'

'I was saying are we gonna do both days of the festival?'

'We'll see how we go today, ay.'

'Aiight.'

Joey went back to watching Emma and Boxer.

Kyri punched his arm playfully. 'Bro, relax. They're just talking.'

One by one they bowed their heads and popped the MDMA capsule into their mouth as the busy train pulled out from Seven Hills station. Emma ended up taking a full one.

At Penrith station they disembarked with the rest of the revellers, who were already wide-eyed, jumping up and down like Indian myna birds; the girls in lycra hot shorts and fluffy socks, their hair glossy and straightened; the guys in tight singlets, crisp sneakers, expensive sunglasses, side-bags swinging at their waists. Joey felt tiny next to the muscle boys who had already taken their tops off.

The shuttle bus from the station to the Regatta Centre was a riot of whistle blowing, music playing from phones and chair dancing. Eventually someone crowd-surfed to the front of the bus, which is when the flustered driver pulled over violently and kicked everyone off, forcing them to walk a few extra hundred metres to the entrance. The crowd were bubbles from a just-opened bottle of Sprite. He was one of those bubbles. He smiled and pulled Emma close to him, kissing her on the cheek. It was a decent cap.

'How are you feeling?' he asked her.

'I'm a bit nervous, but excited.'

'Why nervous?'

'I've got the drugs inside me.'

He hadn't given any thought to how they would smuggle the rest of the drugs into the festival. From what he had experienced the previous year, the organisers had a zero-tolerance policy and there were sniffer dogs and strict bag searches. If they didn't like you, they targeted you, and if they found something you were out. They hadn't taken the drugs in last time; they had bought them inside from an Asian guy in a poncho and tribal tattoos down his legs.

He cursed himself for not having thought it all through. He felt sick to the stomach looking at Emma, at the position he had led her into. Her folks would slaughter him if anything happened to her.

'You don't have to. No pressure, yeah? If you wanna ditch them, we can go over there and you can pull 'em out and we'll go in without anything.'

'Nah, I think I should be okay. Plus, Boxer had a point. There's no way they're not gonna search you three and I'm an unassuming girl. If anyone is gonna get away with it, it's me.'

Boxer and Kyri had seen someone in the ambling crowd who they knew and were chatting to them.

'Are you sure?'

'Yeah, I am. Swear. Forget it.'

'Alright.'

His heart swelled. He kissed her on the cheek again.

Even though the boys were searched, the group had no trouble getting past security and they awkwardly hugged as they channelled through to the main stage area.

'How are you guys feeling?' Kyri asked loudly over the distant bass.

'I'm fucked, ay.'

'Same.'

'Yeah, me too.'

The stage dwarfed the thirty-thousand strong partygoers. It was constructed in the shape of a colossal, open-mouthed cyber dragon flanked by towers of red speakers. The DJ was below the dragon's mouth like a pill waiting to be swallowed. They had arrived late in the afternoon and as the sun set the stage blazed against the sky.

Joey blazed too. He felt a profound rush of energy settle on his shoulders. He was meant to be there, partying with his friends, slave to the music. He didn't know the DJ who was playing, but he didn't care. The sound was euphoria, the dawning of something new, special. He danced. Everybody danced. His stomach, empty, urged him to never eat again. To just dance. The faces of the people around him were koalas and possums and kookaburras from a book he loved as a child. The skin on the arms and torsos of the crowd were in conversation with the light show.

A hakken circle formed near them and dancers went in one by one to show off their skills. Boxer pushed Kyri in. When Kyri started to kick his feet back, the pace of the track picked up and he went off. Kyri was master muzzer. The popping of his knees and ankles and wrists and elbows was innate, inherited. Joey had once tried to hakk in the privacy of the bathroom at home but seeing his reflection in the mirror put an abrupt end to the jaunt. People patted Kyri on the back when he finished, and Boxer yelled out, 'SICK CUNT!' at the sky.

When the fireworks around the dragon began to seduce the crowd, the four of them took their second MDMA cap. Emma had earlier extracted the condom parcel from inside her and put the drugs in her little leather backpack. He didn't need the second one but the thought of coming down was enough to sway him. There was to be no coming down. The only way was up. Up, up, up.

They peaked when the fireworks did. He was overcome entirely by flourishes of ecstasy. In between the flourishes were tiny bursts of panic. He tried to focus on the good vibes but the more he did that, the more conscious he was, which in turn stretched out the panic, leaving space for it to flutter. Emma must have noticed because she asked if he was okay and he nodded, forcing his limbs to dance. He shook his head. There was nothing to panic about. Kyri whispered in his ear to stare into the fireworks. He obeyed and it all felt good again.

Until hours later. Until Joey caught sight of Boxer gyrating on Emma from behind. At first, he thought Emma hadn't noticed, but then she turned around and smiled at Boxer who, taking the gesture as an invitation, wrapped his arms around her torso and kissed her neck. And then they were making out. Kyri hadn't noticed and Joey couldn't bring himself to shed light on it. All he could feel was the ground pulling at him, the drugs draining from his pores.

He faded backwards, still kind of dancing, into the crowd and away from his friends. The wave of lucidity thrashed him as he waded through people towards the portable toilet block. Emma and Boxer making out. His grubby hands crawling all over her body like horny huntsmen. Daffodil Emma and poison-ivy

Boxer. How stupid Joey was for plugging the components into the equation so cooperatively.

The crowd grew taller as he considered his options. Go back, act like nothing happened. Go party closer to the stage, alone. Go home. He couldn't go home so high. Get some water then decide. Where the fuck to get water? A beanpole of a guy stuck his arm out in front of Joey to halt him. He was holding a bottle of water. He had his shirt off and his torso was covered in bronze fur. His eyes were Slavic. They reminded Joey of a spherical ice cube from a cocktail that Kyri had bought at Marquee nightclub once.

The guy yelled into his ear with a splitting Western Sydney twang. 'Hey, dude, you selling anything?'

Joey heard him clearly but stalled with, 'What?'

'You got any caps?'

'Nah, man. Sorry. Can I have a drink?'

'Sure.'

He took the bottle and gulped, hoping it would satiate his thirst and his ache. He handed the bottle back, water dribbling down his front, and yelled, 'Thanks.' As he made to keep walking the guy put his arm back out to slow him while still shuffling his feet to the beat that was belting them from all angles.

'You havin a good night?' the guy asked.

'Yeah, pretty good. I'm super high.'

'I was too but starting to come down.'

The interaction was nudging Joey back into his high. Maybe it was a good place to pitstop. He started shuffling his feet too. The DJ was messing with the crowd. Teasing a beat drop and then reeling it back into the harp-like tune he'd been playing for so long. Surely he had to unleash the drop soon. The energy among the crowd was wound tight.

They came in together, screeched into the night, into the lights, into each other's faces.

The guy came close to Joey's ear again. 'I've lost my mates.'

'Yeah, same here.'

'Fuck, this beat is cracker.'

'It's pretty epic.'

The DJ pulled back the track entirely, exposing the mattress of human sounds momentarily. Everybody went silent except for stray whistles and yelps from revellers imploring the beat to wash over them again. The lights went out for a few seconds. Time had been stretched to the end of its tether, just for him. Just for him to connect with whatever the hell it was that turned all the cogs and pushed all the levers inside him and everyone else.

And then the DJ brought it all back in a merciless deluge. The raging lights around the dragon stage, the revelatory beats, they lifted Joey up and off the ground. His eyes were closed, he was floating, too afraid of what he'd see if he looked, but when he did, he realised he was actually flying above the horde – on the clammy and sturdy shoulders of his new friend. Emma and Boxer didn't exist up there above the constellation of flesh and plastic. Only Joey existed. The DJ in the dragon's mouth was level with him, was playing just for him. The jubilation scurried through his brain, down his back and into his groin, which was packed tight against the guy's nape. Joey's arms were antennas held up to the sky. The electricity from the clouds, the planets, the satellites buzzed against his fingertips. He wanted nothing else than to be cocooned in this sound forever. He shut his eyes.

The guy bent down and placed him gently on the ground.

'I'm Ivan.'

'Joey.'

'You are high as a fucking kite, Joey.'

They laughed and Ivan pulled him in for a hug. Joey's hand ended up on his new friend's sweaty back.

'Thanks for lifting me up,' he said into Ivan's neck. He smelt like a man – whatever that smelt like.

'No worries.'

Where the fuck are ya?

Kyri had sent the text message forty minutes ago. Joey half expected to receive a text from Emma too, but she'd obviously been having too much fun to care about his disappearance.

Coming. You guys in same spot?

Joey waited for a reply for a few minutes by the toilet block but decided to make his way over there anyway. He was going to act normal and say he went to have a rest and bumped into a friend. Emma was allowed to do whatever she wanted. But with Boxer? Joey shook his head.

The group were closer to the fence, probably wobbled from their original spot by the ever-shaking corporeal mass. They appeared slower, like a lagging video. Joey saw smoke rising from Boxer's hand and made the connection. They were smoking a joint, winding down. He turned around to see that the crowd had thinned out. The night was wrapping up.

Kyri took a few steps towards him and asked, 'Where'd you go? I was worried about ya.'

'I'm sweet. Went for a little rest. You good?'

'Yeah, I'm good. We just blazed up a blunt. There's only like half an hour left until the end.'

'Oh, fair.'

Emma approached and put her hand on Joey's bare shoulder. His tank top was hooked into the back pocket of his jeans, where he'd put it after Ivan lifted it over his head as they danced. He didn't mind her hand there. It placed him. And it meant they didn't have to say anything.

Boxer stepped over, offering the joint to him too early so that he walked a few steps with his arm outstretched. Joey took a few hefty drags and it wasn't long before his eyes were slightly hooded over, before arcs of pain in his feet pulsated their way up his legs. Everything looked messy. How does this shit even get cleaned up for the next day of the festival? He had decided he wasn't going to come back for day two. In fact, he had a profound yearning to be alone for some time, in the comfort of his own room, blinds drawn, with a cheese toastie, watching *Bob's Burgers.*

They forced themselves to dance around a bit, but the movements were second hand. For no reason at all, Joey didn't want to be the one to say he was ready to jet. Kyri must have picked up on it and said, 'Should we head?' to which the other three nodded and made their way to the exit. Guys were larking around on each other's backs, pissing out in the open, falling over, jaws clenched. Packs of oily girls jumped around in unison, make-up channelling down their faces, reapplying lip gloss. The security guards herded them all towards the gate like lambs that had been let out to roam freely for a day.

Emma was texting on her phone a few metres behind them. She called out and said, 'Hey guys, my brothers have a spare seat in their Uber so I'm gonna jump in with them.' They turned around to face her and Boxer said they'd wait until she met her brothers like he was suddenly Emma's guardian. She would hate that trivial chivalry crap. Joey wasn't bothered waiting. Solitary confinement was calling.

'Nah, it's okay. They are literally gonna be here any minute. You guys go make that shuttle bus.'

It was agreed. Kyri and Boxer embraced her to say goodbye. Joey's hug was frigid. He couldn't help it.

When they pulled apart Emma asked, 'We good?'

He shrugged and made a face as though he didn't know what she was talking about, 'Guess so.'

She rolled her eyes. Kyri and Boxer were walking away. In the distance Joey saw Emma's brothers gliding over.

Jiddo Youssef would always say, 'After laughing is crying', if there was too much fun being had. It sounded pretty basic in English but the way it was said in Arabic gave the phrase a sort of reverence. He whispered it inelegantly to himself as he caught up with Boxer and Kyri. Something up in the sky must have heard his whisper and wanted to perk him up because Boxer told them he was getting a lift with a guy who lived on his street. Joey and Kyri were left alone to make the gruelling journey home on public transport.

When they were finally on the train Kyri nodded off, resting his head on Joey's shoulder. Joey too closed his eyes; the flare of the dragon stage was seared onto the inside of his eyelids.

6

IT WAS TOO HOT TO be inside so late in the afternoon, and even though Elaine had an air conditioner she felt silly switching it on just for herself. In the front yard, as the sun faded behind the street, she watered the garden slowly. Every time a car drove by or she heard chatter, or a door being shut, she turned and let her eyes linger on Salma's house across the road.

Salma and her grown son had moved in two years ago. From what Elaine could tell there was a father, but he was barely there and Salma rarely mentioned him. They'd had coffee in each other's front yards from time to time and on a few occasions Salma had invited Elaine to join her at Bankstown Sports Club, but Elaine always declined.

Salma's son's purple car was parked in the driveway – a roaring thing that rattled the houses in the middle of the night. There was no way of telling if Salma was home because she parked her car in the garage.

When the garden was drowning, she turned the hose on the flyscreens, the stairs, the porch, the driveway. Eventually she began gathering the leaves on the lawn with the force of the water. The nozzle on the hose had broken months ago, so she was generating pressure by holding her thumb tightly over the spout. She'd been outside for an hour when she admitted defeat, partly because she pictured Youssef on the stairs cursing her for wasting water and partly because her thumb had grown sore. She looped the hose back over the tap.

'Elaine! Walih, come over. The raqwa is on the stove.'

She whipped around with her hand on her heart. Salma was hanging out of her living room window puffing on a cigarette. Her voice was deep, scarred by the bootleg Davidoffs she smoked. Her packets never had photos of rotting feet or dying babies on them. Instead there was just a message in Filipino or Russian, or whatever language was spoken where they'd been smuggled from.

'Walih! You scare me. Yulla, I'll take my pill and come,' Elaine said.

She felt like a child rushing through the house to the bathroom where instead of taking a pill she quickly rinsed her mouth with some toothpaste and swapped her bathrobe for some grey leggings and a sleeveless top. On her way out, she didn't bother shutting the front door because they would be facing her house from Salma's wrought-iron chairs on the lawn.

As she crossed the road, Elaine remembered she hadn't brushed her hair so she patted the sides down quickly. Salma was the type to have a blow wave done to put the bins out.

'Ya ahmi, ya Elaine. Ahla, ahla.' Salma was already pouring the coffee into cups as Elaine trudged up the stencilled driveway.

She put the raqwa down and stood up in her cork wedges so

that they could greet each other. Elaine stretched up from her slippers to kiss her neighbour on the cheeks.

There was a calming breeze flowing down the street as they caught up. Salma spoke about some land she had sold in Campbelltown and how she was planning to buy an apartment for her son with the profit she'd made. Elaine had wondered how Salma afforded the flashy car, the hair, the pokies. All she'd known was that Salma had a part-time pharmacy job. It made more sense now.

After they had finished the second round of coffee, Elaine stood up. They kissed on the cheeks again, said goodbye and she began her walk down the driveway. Salma hadn't mentioned anything about going to the sports club. Elaine turned around as Salma was placing the coffee cups onto a tray, a cigarette squeezed between her lips.

'Salma?'

She didn't hear her.

Elaine turned to face the road and then turned back. 'Salma?'

'Yes, albi?'

'You going to the …' Elaine gestured with her finger in the direction of Bankstown.

'To the sporties?' The whole street heard her.

'Yes.'

'You want to come! I'm leaving in an hour. I'll beep the horn. All this time I've been inviting you, I decided not to ask anymore.'

'Okay, habibti, I'll see you later.' Elaine skipped up the steps to her front door. She would have a shower and blow-dry her hair. Maybe she would wear that top with the gold tiger print on the front, and her black leggings. And her heeled sandals. But then she ran the risk of wearing the exact same thing as Salma.

In the shower, she thought about the three times she had won big on poker machines. The first, in the nineties: three thousand dollars. It was at a pub in Lidcombe in between the ceremony and reception of a cousin's wedding at Westella. The second time was at the leagues club in Revesby. Seven thousand dollars. Lights flashed, music rang. Youssef had come running in from smoking a cigarette. They ate at the bistro and took the cheque home. Most of that money ended up going to Amal and the boys. It was right after Simon, Amal's husband, had gone away. Still, it was one of Elaine's good moments – the jackpot had hit the very poker machine she was playing.

The third time was shortly after Youssef died. She was driving home from Rookwood cemetery after visiting his grave and the grief just fell away as she passed the RSL. She'd swung the car around over the double lines and parked in the side street. She hadn't wanted any relatives to recognise her Corolla out the front of the club and judge her for being there so soon after Youssef's death. That time she had won two thousand. When she had looked around for someone to delight in her luck, she had realised she was the only sad soul in there. That money she had kept in her underwear drawer in a little drawstring bag along with her jewellery. She couldn't think of what it was spent on. Money just slipped away incrementally. A fifty here, a hundred there.

Elaine turned the water pressure up in the shower to drown out the yapping dog next door. She thought of them often – poker machines. They pleased her. It was a stupid feeling that she permitted as a treat. Sometimes she dreamt of the spiralling sequences. Saw the treasure chest popping up three, four, five times, awarding her thousands of free spins. And she would wake with the music ringing in her ears. Of course, she knew that's what they were meant to do: enrapture you, rinse you out, but she also knew she didn't have a problem. Unlike other people she knew, who did nothing else. Like their old acquaintances, Marie and Sam, who had apparently lost their house.

Marie bet big on the poker machines. Elaine had once seen her load six hundred dollars into a machine and play ten-dollar hits. Marie worked at the café in Royal Prince Alfred hospital. She'd given Elaine a coffee on the house when Youssef went in for his final surgery. Convinced that Marie didn't have the authority to do so, Elaine had put five dollars in the tip jar. As she'd taken a seat, she'd seen Marie snatch the note out and stuff it into her apron pocket.

There was word that Marie had been seen collecting bottles and cans from bins in Marrickville. The claims couldn't be taken for gospel because the information had come from the babble bank that people gladly deposited into over coffee and through phones. Gossiping in the community was just part of the everyday. Part of what kept them all entwined far away from the village houses that were so close you knew the contents of your neighbour's fridge. She was glad there wasn't anything people could deposit into the babble bank about her own family.

As she lathered her hair with shampoo she decided she'd wear the tiger print top, black leggings and heels. Salma should know that she owned more than the bathrobe and slippers she was always caught in.

7

A FEW WEEKS HAD PASSED since Defqon and, although Joey and Emma had texted, it lacked their usual energy. They'd only seen each other once briefly at work because Emma had taken time off for uni exams. Joey suggested they catch up because he had decided that he was over the whole Boxer hook-up situation, as long as Emma wasn't thinking of dating Boxer. He had also decided that he was never hanging out with Boxer again.

They met in Punchbowl for charcoal chicken and as they walked down the Boulevarde the men outside the shisha cafés and barbers sized Joey up. They would be trying to draw conclusions about his and Emma's connection, wondering if the dainty girl was his girlfriend. Joey knew it was best to ignore them. He had seen the sizing-up trip-wire being triggered plenty of times. In school, on the road. A weird acknowledgement of camaraderie morphed into one of bravado and ultra-intimidation in a second: car doors flung open, weapons drawn, threats bellowed in streets dotted with fibro homes and wannabe mansions. Epic punch-ons at the train station.

Maybe Emma didn't recognise the undercurrent of the stares. She'd grown up in Picnic Point. She had the nice river, a triple garage with an automatic door. No staring. Not to say there weren't ethnics in Picnic Point, but they were the well-to-do ones. The owners of gyms, property developers. They didn't sit at shisha bars or roll their car windows down so people could put a face to the Mercedes. They taught their children jujitsu and dressed them in linen.

The air conditioning in the chicken shop was set to abattoir. Among the web of plastic furniture was a handbasin and a bin overflowing with paper towel. Emma took a seat and Joey went up to order because it was his treat and he knew what to get.

He asked for a whole chicken with toum, pickles, bread, tabouli, chips and two cans of Solo. The pimpled guy behind the counter poked the order into the screen like he was grossed out by it. He blushed and apologised for taking a while to ring it through. The owner, watching as he polished something with a tea towel, rolled his eyes.

Word was, the owner had started the shop after a falling-out with his sister, with whom he had kicked off the Lebanese charcoal chicken craze at the shop a few doors down. You became privy to that type of gossip after your mum visited the hair salon. Tayta had always said that the world was a village. There was much debate among people from the area on whose chicken was better. Joey preferred the brother's because it was juicier and cheaper. He sometimes saw the sister driving around in her convertible – always with the top down. Her head was so inflated with fillers that he imagined it might pop off her neck and float away as she took a corner one day.

The owner, having given up on allowing his employee to fumble longer, barged forward and took over the order processing. The employee blushed hard.

Emma was rubbing her shoulders as he returned to the table. 'Why is it so goddamn cold in here?'

'Cos Arabs like to take everything one step too far.'

'What do you mean?'

'Like, they just do. They don't understand happy mediums. Everything has to be a grand gesture.'

'Please explain.' Her tone was forceful, cute.

'They like to exaggerate everything. You've tasted Mum's food.'

She sucked air through her teeth. 'It's pretty salty.'

'See? And I guarantee you if I told the owner that it was too cold in here, he would say it was the perfect temperature and that no-one has ever complained.'

'Don't you think that's down to character though? You know nothing about the dude.'

'I know enough.'

'So confident, Joey, just like a true Arab.'

'Hey, I'm half Aussie.'

'Only when it's convenient for you!'

The boy who took the order balanced a giant tray with the food on it. He offloaded the plates onto the table and whispered, 'Enjoy', before shuffling back to the counter, knocking a chair with the dangling tray. Joey and Emma hunched over the plates and lapped up the fumes. They were assaulted by flavour without having ingested anything.

As they ate, Joey corrected Emma's bread to morsel ratio. He spoke to the ceiling as he chewed, 'Poor guy.'

'Who?'

'That little server dude.'

'He did seem a tad frazzled, hey.'

'Yeah, the owner shoved him aside and took over when I was ordering.'

'What an arsehole. You should have said something.'

'Fuck that. Not my problem.'

They savoured the food for a minute before Emma spoke again. 'Speaking of arseholes, why were you acting like one at Defqon?'

Joey had hoped they would never need to speak about it. 'Why do you think I was being an arsehole?'

'Because I made out with Boxer.'

He raised his hands and eyebrows at her in surrender.

'I was so high, Joey, it just felt nice to be … touched.'

'Right.'

'Can you not say that?'

'Say what?'

'"Right." It's a cop-out. You obviously have something to say.'

'Honestly, I was annoyed at the time, but let's enjoy lunch.'

'I am enjoying lunch. This doesn't have to be a thing; we're just having a conversation as we eat.'

'It's … you don't know Boxer like I do. He's … like … he's a scumbag.'

'You think I don't know what he's like? I smelt it on him the very first time we met.'

'Then why hook up with him? You should hear the way he talks about girls. You would lose it. You could have hooked up with … with anyone.'

'I told you, I was high, and I did what my body felt like doing in that moment. I didn't give it much thought.'

'Did you like it?'

'His mouth was dry.'

'Yuk. Do you like him?'

'Hell no.'

'Good. Cos, honestly, I know it's your body your choice blah blah, but I will literally never talk to you again if you even think about dating him.'

Emma threw a pickle at him. 'You're just like him!'

His face drooped as he retrieved the pickle from the floor. 'Don't ever say that.'

'I'm kidding. You're nothing like him. Anyway, why do you still hang out if you have such a problem with him?'

'I don't know. I've been thinking that I need to get the fuck out of Sydney.'

'Tell me about it. I'm so over work and I'm starting to hate uni too. I wish I had taken a year off after school and travelled or something.'

'I wish I had uni so I could hate it.'

'Trust me, you don't. What's on tonight?'

'Gonna hang with Kyri. You studying?'

'Unfortunately. Tell Kyri I said hi.'

After lunch, Joey called Kyri to work out what they would get up to later.

Kyri didn't have good news. 'He's been bugging me to chill. I couldn't say no. I reckon he feels bad or something. Plus you and I are both out of weed.'

'Boxer? Feel bad? Are you whacked?' Joey said.

'Listen, end of the day, Emma wanted it, he wanted it.'

'I honestly don't give a fuck about that anymore. I—'

'Alright, mad then. You're coming. One other thing, I invited Ribz cos he has a car and we need a ride to pick up the weed from Boxer's mate in Livo.'

'Brooo, I'm definitely not coming!'

'Don't be a dickhead, man. Don't leave me with them alone.'

'Kyri, you told me it was us two chilling tonight and then next minute Boxer and Ribz are joining.'

'I know, I know. Listen, we'll go, get the stuff, and then come back and chill. I promise it will be the last time we hang out with them.'

'I swear, you owe me big-time.'

'Ellaaaa. My boy! I'll see ya later.'

Kyri was a strategic bastard. He waited for Joey to arrive at his place before breaking the news that Ribz's car was at the smash repairs and that they would now be taking the train to Liverpool. When Joey tried to leave, Kyri bear-hugged him and kissed him exaggeratedly on the cheek in the driveway. The sensor light flicked on and off in the early evening gloom. Joey shook his head and went back with him into the garage.

After Boxer arrived, the three of them walked over to Birrong train station. In the middle of the Hume Highway, Boxer berated Kyri for having invited Ribz. As though he was any less annoying.

Kyri tried to defend himself. 'Bro, I assumed he had his car and he would drive us. The bloke didn't tell me it was at the panelbeater.'

The outing had gradually become more irritating. Four grown

lads were having to catch the train to Liverpool to score some weed. And a night in on the Xbox was destroyed in the process.

Boxer kept at it. 'Lahsak ayri, and look at us now, catching a train, and with Ribz. Bro, I've told you he's a snitch and a fucking tight-arse and that. I hate tight-arses with a passion. He's a hundred per cent sacked. Anyway, I'll get us a lift from Livo. Fuck getting the train back.'

As much as it pained Joey to have anything in common with Boxer, their thoughts on Ribz were the same. During high school, Ribz had been desperate for their friendship, driving them to and fro, feeding them gossip from other groups. It was his currency, his dues for acceptance, being available and willing. And it was pitiful to watch. Like a rejected puppy, pining for milk.

Ribz was standing with one foot against the wall outside the train station. He wore orange TNs with a red flame gradient on the sides. His Adidas sweatpants were so tight that the outline of his balls was visible. His lean arms were earthworms protruding from a Fila singlet. He pushed off the wall to greet them with a bony hand.

'Sup.'

'Shu.'

'Ay, Ribz.'

'Boxer, long time, man.'

The hollow smacks of their handshakes reverberated off the parked cars on the street.

'What's the plan, boys? We gonna smoke up or what?' At the end of this sentence Ribz folded over himself in laughter, clapping as though he had made a crushing joke, then he turned and skipped towards the stairs.

Boxer made the action of throat slitting at Kyri.

★

'Oi, guess who I saw at the shops yesterday? Miss D'Amico.' Boxer didn't pause between asking and answering his own question. He had his legs sprawled over the seat in front of him.

Ribz leant over the back of the seat and high-fived Boxer. Joey stared at the flurry of feet on the platform as the train pulled out. Those people were so lucky to be catching another train and not travelling with these heads.

'Yeah, I tried to suss her out, but the ganga was avoiding me like I was cancer.' Boxer laughed at himself. 'What I wouldn't do to have those Italian lips around my ayr again. Hands down the best blowie I ever had.' He stretched forward and flexed his forearms.

Miss D'Amico had been their art teacher at school. She was in her early forties, unmarried, lived with her mother – these snippets of her personal life had often been worked into lessons on surrealism and art history. She was also notorious for leaning in real close when overseeing brushwork or linocutting. Apparently, when she had asked Boxer to stay back after class one afternoon, she came on to him and he flopped his dick out onto her desk and 'she went for it'.

After Boxer had told the entire school, some of the boys laced their coughs in her class with 'head-jobber'. They knew the story had filtered through to the staffroom because Mr Mac, the PE teacher that Joey got along with, had asked him about it. Joey had played dumb, not wanting any role in tarnishing Miss D'Amico's career. She was always nice to him, and there was nothing to substantiate Boxer's story from a pile of horseshit, really.

Ribz's bum-bag slid off the bench as the train stopped with a jerk at Sefton. The driver apologised for the sudden brake over the speakers in a thick Indian accent. Kyri impersonated him and

Ribz handed out another high five and then Boxer lifted his arse up near Ribz's face and ripped a fart.

Apart from the four of them, the only other passenger in the lower portion of the carriage was a small Asian girl who didn't look up from her phone, which was hidden in a yellow cartoon character case. And then a girl joined at Sefton and glued herself to a window at the front. She had brown hair tied in a messy bun, almost translucent skin and was wearing grey tracksuit pants with a tight white singlet. She had wired earphones plugged in her ears.

Joey realised he was staring when she turned to him and furrowed her brow. Kyri was searching for something in his jeans pocket. Boxer sniffed hard through his nose, as though summoning courage from the atmosphere, walked over to the girl, and sat opposite her. She just stared back at her reflection as the train plunged into darkness travelling through an underpass, the LED *Chester Hill* reflected over her face.

'S'cuze me,' Boxer said.

She ignored him.

He tapped her on the shoulder. 'S'cuze me. What are you listening to?'

The girl took one of the earphones out and turned to him. 'What?'

'I said, what are you listening to?'

'A podcast.' She smiled and replaced her earphone.

Ribz was watching Boxer, smirking, red-faced. Kyri stole glances from behind his phone. Boxer took another deep sniff, reached over and took out her earphone. The girl did not startle but turned to him slowly. Joey wished Boxer would leave her alone. She wasn't interested and he could see it in her blue eyes.

'What's your name?'

'Lisa.'

'Do you smoke, Lisa?'

'Yeah, but I don't have any.'

'Nah, but like I meant, do you smoke-smoke?'

'Oh. Yeah, sometimes.'

'Alright, cracker.'

Boxer typed a message on his phone. The train stopped at a deserted platform at Chester Hill. Boxer's phone beeped and he smiled as his eyes crossed the screen. The earphone that he'd taken out of Lisa's ear was draped over her freckled shoulder.

'Come join me and my mates for a choof. We're going to pick some up now from my mate in Livo and you can kick back with us, have a smoke.'

'I've gotta babysit my little brother.'

Because she hadn't said yes or no, the boys stared at her until she made eye contact with Joey. Boxer stood up and introduced them all like he had been asked by a teacher to address the class. Kyri reached over and fist-bumped her. Joey waved. Ribz blubbered something and Boxer called him a retard. Ribz drooped in his seat. The train stopped at Villawood.

'What time are you babysitting?' Boxer asked.

'Around ten. Mum works nights.'

'Ooft, it's not even eight yet. There's still yonks. Just come. We'll get lit, chitchat for a bit and my mate will drop you home after. He's comin to meet us. Where do you live?' Boxer drove his hands deep inside the pockets of his shorts as he implored her.

'Cabra.'

Ribz, having recovered from his embarrassment, chimed in, 'Come, man. Wallah it will be fun.' For someone who wasn't Arab, Ribz was always using words like 'wallah' and 'jahash' and 'manoosh'. It was never that surprising at school – most people from the area knew at least a few Arab words and flexed them to fit in – but in the company of the girl Boxer was trying to tune up, Ribz saying 'wallah' made Joey want to hide.

Joey hadn't really seen much of the guys around girls. There was the time they took Ribz to a brothel on Parramatta Road for his eighteenth birthday and he'd had to sit in the waiting room while the workers gave them drinks and joked about their age. They'd chipped in for Ribz's birthday present. He had walked out beaming, telling them he shot so far it landed on his own face. Boxer had also once invited two girls he had met at Macca's to join them clubbing one night. The girls ended up ditching the group after Boxer paid for their entry. There were also the few times Joey invited Emma along to something. Emma would be rolling her eyes into oblivion about this whole pick-up scenario. And yet she'd made out with that box of slime.

'You'll get me back home in time?' Lisa asked.

'Yeah, I swear,' Boxer said.

They stopped at the vending machine on the platform at Liverpool to buy cans of drink. Ribz made awkward karate moves against a pole. Joey was only thinking about the weed. About getting ripped enough to deal with this whole scenario. As he and Lisa fumbled with the vending machine he heard Boxer whisper something that ended with '… old mate' and they all laughed. He knew Boxer was trying to be in control of the situation, as though he had a rival in Joey.

The dealer's house was a few blocks from the station. They walked in two groups, Joey and Kyri trailing the rest.

'What did Boxer say back there when you laughed?' Joey asked.

'Nothing, bro.'

'Did he make a joke about me?'

'No, I wasn't even listening to him. Don't worry about it.'

When they arrived, Boxer collected cash from everyone except Lisa and told them to wait on the front porch. Joey stood on the step above her and saw her send heart emojis to 'Ben' on her phone.

It didn't take long for Boxer to return. He slapped Ribz on the back of the neck and said, 'Let's go', through his grin. They rose from their perches and followed him down a few streets to a small park where they sat on a graffitied table. The one light in the pergola was covered in public scum and spiderwebs. Joey whipped out a pouch of tobacco and tiny scissors he had stolen from his mum from his cargo shorts pocket. Boxer passed him a few buds of weed. Ribz turned on his phone torch to assist in the joint-rolling but Boxer told him to turn it off before someone called the cops, so Ribz walked over to the bubbler and busied himself pressing the button on and off.

The park was surrounded by a row of old red-brick houses broken up sporadically by new beige builds. Joey imagined the uniform street before the double garages and giant façades of the new houses were erected. He lit two joints, dragged them and passed them either side of him to Lisa and Kyri. Finally, something to make the night worth it.

They went back and forth in that formation until both joints were out, but Joey had definitely smoked the most. During that time Ribz told the story about how his cousin had worked for a guy who had a weed operation going from a house in Strathfield.

He was supposed to check the watering levels and change the bulbs on the lamps, but one day he rocked up and found the house burning down. Apparently, the cousin watched from behind a hedge across the road as cops eventually carried out half-burnt marijuana plants and loaded them onto a truck.

Joey had only been half listening, having heard and doubted the story before, and he was still trying to imagine the old version of the street. He tried to zone them all out: Ribz's groper lips as he yapped, Kyri's nervous pigeon feet, Boxer's fat head, the smell of Lisa's deodorant. But it was all too pervasive. He needed to get more baked.

Boxer pulled out a small packet of powder from his pocket and waved it, 'Anyone wanna try this? It's K. My mate gave it to me for free. Here, Lisa, you have some.'

Lisa was calm in her reply. 'I'll have a bump if you guys do.'

Ribz gave Boxer a key, which he dipped into the bag and then held towards Lisa's nostril. After she snorted, he did the same for Joey but it was double Lisa's amount resting on the end of the key. It looked comical, like snow gathered off a driveway in an American Christmas film. Joey snorted and Ribz readied himself for a dose, but Boxer pressed the baggie shut and put it in his pocket before anyone else could have any.

Kyri looked relieved.

'Have any of you even had K before?' Lisa asked with wide eyes.

The four boys shook their heads. A heaviness filled Joey's gut. He rolled another joint and smoked it on his own until all he could hear were crickets and all he could smell was grass and dog shit. But then he was really high. Too high. And the ludicrous pantomime began.

Lisa played the damsel in not-so-much distress; Boxer, the hairy oaf; Ribz, the jester; and Kyri, the extra. Joey watched them goofily. He was convinced his eyes had grown to double their size and come closer together. There was no autonomy in the limbs of the players. Something larger than them, and out of sight, was suddenly in charge. Their faces contorted. The park – the whole street – was two-dimensional.

The oaf was wooing the damsel by petting her hair and she didn't seem uncomfortable, or even aware, but a moment later his arm was around her shoulder and she was being walked awkwardly towards a car that had pulled up and whose stereo was blasting a high-energy beat that made Joey's insides bounce. The car was breathing. It had gills on the side that were sucking in oxygen. Maybe it would transform at any moment into an electric eel and swallow them whole, one by one.

Joey's outward parts were entirely useless. He needed a guide, someone to take his hand. The oaf eased the damsel into the car and instructed the hopping jester to open car doors, clear seats of hoodies and protein shakers.

The extra stood by Joey, perplexed. 'Bro, this is suss as fuck. What's going on?' he whispered in Joey's ear.

But Joey's mouth had switched to a gaping black hole that engulfed his whole head, so he couldn't talk.

The oaf gestured at them violently to come to the car. The jester and the damsel sat with their seatbelts fastened like children who had been reprimanded by a parent at wits' end.

A figure appeared in the window of the house across the road.

'Get in,' the oaf mouthed through the window of the front passenger seat.

Had they wanted to object, they could not be heard, for the

music fleeing from the open doors of the car blanketed everything around them, rattling the loose parts of the car, interrupting logic. The extra helped Joey into the back seat, his skin tingling where his and the damsel's bare arms met. They looked at each other but it was more of a collapse than a look.

Then he noticed the driver, Haz, who in the play was the bull, for his nose and arms and legs were those of a bull. His arched neck, the crown of his head facing the steering wheel and his starving eyes fixed on the windscreen were a bull's. His jaw, chewing gum like he had a vendetta against it, was a bull's.

Joey had met him at the oaf's eighteenth birthday. From what Joey had gathered, he was not someone to be messed with. The bull's immediate family had more people behind bars than not. The other time Joey had seen the bull was at the barber. Joey had tried to say hello that time but the bull had looked right through him. The bull had also started smoking inside the little shop and when the barber asked him to put the cigarette out, he dropped it on the shop floor and spat on it to extinguish the ember.

The bull revved the engine hard and, before the extra had even shut the door, he thrust the car forward, desperate to stake his matador. He drifted the car ferociously around corners and along roads with shops called Tong Dee Noodle and JJ's Dry Cleaning. The oaf and the bull chewed important words at each other. Joey realised he was a stagehand in the pantomime and laughed hotly but wasn't sure it was out loud.

The car whirled its way up a concrete coil until it had reached the rooftop of an empty car park. The players clambered out of the car, their shoulders packed in anticipation. The damsel needed some help getting out, her eyes completely removed from their sockets. Maybe her eyes had been left on the grimy table under the pergola. The boot was popped open and that is where she sat. The music from the car stopped and in its place grew the sound of air and lights interspersed with grumbles from the actors, directions, confusion. Joey's legs made to leave but they were clouds. He was as far as the ramp before the bull pulled him back by the collar, his face in contortions of rage.

Joey couldn't leave the car park. That tug on his collar offered a moment of complete lucidity in the haze that signalled how delicately folded into the scenario he was. Just like the damsel at the rear of the car. He was propped into the semicircle of bodies around her. The jester stared at the ground, and the oaf watched the bull, who was lighting a cigarette.

The bull spoke. 'Who wants a BJ? Boxer, go.'

The oaf fell forward towards the damsel. She put her arm out but it dropped. He caught her hand and placed it on his crotch. His other hand was weaselling its way up her singlet. The damsel laughed from somewhere far away. Joey closed his eyes. The jester stared. The bull fiddled with the car stereo.

The oaf attempted to set a scene he might stomach. 'We're just having a little fun, yeah?' His brow glistened with sweat.

There was a sickly ease about the air, as though mother nature had turned her back. The oaf helped the damsel onto her knees. The jester rubbed his crotch. Joey walked away, smoked another spliff and held the smoke in his lungs in the hope it would float him further away. He ambled towards the ramp once more, but the bull pulled him back again with such ease that Joey felt like paper.

The oaf finished. He heard the oaf finish. He hoped it was over and they could go home but when he turned he saw the jester with his pants around his knees, one hand bunching up the front of his singlet moving towards the damsel. The weak moon reflected off his hairless arse. Joey turned back towards Bankstown, held on to a pillar.

The jester's laughter meant he was done. Again, Joey turned, thinking it was time to pack up, but he saw the bull blow cigarette smoke through his nostrils, reach through the driver door and play a bass-heavy track.

Joey considered the ending of the play from the wings, staring out at the lights that kept whirling into one big mess. He assumed that, being part of the production, he should have been privy to its suggestions, its outcomes, its politics, that maybe he should have been briefed on his part, but nothing had been explained. Instead, he came to his own conclusion: the damsel would be hurt, changed. The bull, the oaf and the jester would be momentarily satiated. The extra … where the fuck was the extra?

Panic shot through Joey and then he was pushed out of the wings by a quiet hand, as though he had missed his cue to enter stage left. He followed the length of the hand, arm, neck until he recognised the bull's clenched jaw. Joey's shoulder, limp from the push, collapsed over his chest. His left leg folded. Someone – something – laughed. He stared at the ground, comforted by the constellation of hardened chewing gum. It reminded him of the school playground. Having been shoved twice more he found himself inches away from the damsel in her underwear. She reached for his jeans and fumbled with the fly. He screamed at the other players, the sleepy sprawling audience outside the car park. He screamed into their cars and their homes and their churches and community halls. But the sound did not escape his puffy lungs. His limp dick was in the palm of the damsel's cold hand. She wore a gold ring with two merging hearts. His arms, like his dick, were dead. The bull propped Joey up from behind and shoved him in the small of his back once more to jumpstart him but, instead, the reverberation of the hit sent a plop of vomit out of Joey's mouth and onto his dick in the damsel's hand. And he continued retching and recoiling, until he was on the other side of the car park wiping himself, gasping for breath as though he had been underwater the whole time and had only just come up.

Having been jolted back to life by the retching, he screamed, and this time he was heard. The players were suddenly themselves again. Haz kicked Joey, the thud landing on his thigh. Lisa told them to 'stop it'. Stop what? Hitting him? Boxer stroked her hair, told her everything was 'okay'. She reminded them she needed to go home to babysit her brother. Joey looked around for Kyri. He had vanished. And then he stood up to leave, standing as tall as he could, but Haz told him through clenched teeth, millimetres away from his face, to get in the car and wait for them to finish.

Haz turned and lifted the front of his T-shirt over his head, so that it clasped around his shoulders, and began unbuttoning his jeans. Joey stared into the eyes of the tiger tattoo that covered Haz's back and shuffled towards the car. He sat in the back seat where Ribz had already taken post and was staring out of the window. Boxer was in the front passenger seat.

'Where's Kyri?' Joey asked.

They ignored him.

Joey turned and saw, from the corner of his eye, Haz and Lisa heading away from the boot to a darker corner of the car park.

After around five minutes, Haz reappeared at the window. He had taken his T-shirt off and was wiping his shredded torso and his pubes with it. He said, 'Shu, boys', and cackled at himself as he swung into the driver seat, shirtless.

Haz's eyes stabbed at Joey in the rear-view mirror. 'How fucking cooked were you, you dope?'

Lisa sat in the back seat, sandwiching Joey against Ribz.

'Where's Kyri?' Joey asked, and he was ignored again.

Haz tore the car through the streets to Bankstown station and stopped in a bus zone.

Boxer turned towards the back seat and said, 'Lisa, it was good to meet ya. See, told ya we'd get you back on time.'

She left the car without shutting the door and walked straight-backed to the entrance of the train station.

Joey acted on impulse and hopped out of the car too. 'Boys, I'm gonna get out here.'

'Get in, you gronk. I'll drive you home,' Haz said.

Joey shut the door. 'Nah, all good.'

'Oi, come around here for a sec. I wanna tell you something.'

Joey walked over to Haz's window.

Haz handed him a twenty of weed that Boxer had pulled out of his pocket. 'Take it. Don't fucking make a big deal out of tonight. So what, we copped head jobs. You're a messy fucker – you and that faggy friend of yours who dipped.'

Haz's conversational tone contradicted the wildfire in his eyes. He spat out of the window and it landed near Joey's feet. Boxer was staring out the passenger window. Joey was backing away when he heard Haz ask Boxer, 'What kind of fucking dropkicks do you hang out with, bro?' The car revved and zoomed off.

Inside the train station Joey scanned the platforms for Lisa. He hadn't heard any trains arrive, but he could not see her. He walked into the women's toilet. One of the cubicles was shut. He peered underneath and recognised Lisa's sneakers.

He said something incomprehensible, paused and tried again.

'Hey, it's Joey, from before. Sorry for spewing on you.'

His voice sang out louder than he wanted. She didn't answer. He entered the cubicle adjacent to the one she was in, shut the door and sat on the toilet seat cover.

'I … I thought they were gonna drive you home. Are you still gonna babysit your brother?'

He heard her shuffle through her handbag.

'Yeah, heading there now.'

Joey spoke to his feet. 'Hey, um, I didn't know what was gonna happen tonight, hey. I was completely munted.'

'Yeah, same. Do you really think that was K?'

'I don't fucking know. But it didn't feel good.'

She flushed the toilet and unlocked the cubicle door. Joey jumped for his door and they met face to face. For a second he felt like kissing her, but he went over to the handbasin and plunged his head underneath the tap. He inhaled the water, let it roll over his eyeballs. Lisa waited for him after washing her hands. They walked out to the platform and sat on the ground away from the few other people waiting for the train.

'Are those guys your mates?'

'Not really. See them once in a blue moon.'

'Do you have a girlfriend?'

'Nah.'

'Boyfriend?'

'Nah. Do you have a boyfriend?'

'Nope.'

The train arrived. Lisa stood up. Joey stayed crossed-legged on the concrete.

She kicked his shoe. 'See ya.'

Joey whispered, 'Sorry', as the train doors closed.

8

There were never any car spots in Petersham. Every time Elaine came to visit Georgette, which was only once or twice a year, the area was busier, classier. Con's corner store had long since become a café where fluffy dogs on leashes outnumbered the actual people waiting for coffee. The chemist, butcher and fruit market on Palace Street had been turned into palaces for pretty families. And the cars. There were just so many of them.

Georgette still lived in the same terrace house on Brighton Street. In the late eighties, when everyone else bought houses with driveways in the west, Elaine and Youssef included, Georgette and her husband had decided to stay put. They had both still been working in factories in the inner west and had preferred a shorter commute over space. What a smart decision that had been. Georgette's house would easily be worth two and a half million now.

She finally found a car park a few doors from the old terrace she'd lived in. So much of Elaine was buried in the streets of

Petersham, but it was another life entirely. Another version of her. Their old place was ten houses up from Georgette's and across from the park where they had first met. It had been the week after Elaine arrived in Sydney. Tired and frustrated of being confined to the skinny house, she'd told Youssef she was crossing the road for some air. Georgette was in the park, pushing her son on the swing while she sang 'Frère Jacques'. The sight and sound of another village girl had twisted the knife of homesickness deep into Elaine's side. They'd known each other so well from the get-go without having to say much at all.

The façade of Georgette's terrace had been renovated awkwardly in the nineties. The original Victorian features were shaved off, the archway windows bricked up into squares and replaced with aluminium frames. The old heritage tiles were covered with two-tone brown ones. And the wrought-iron balcony railing was swapped out for beige jail cell bars. The house was at odds with the rest of the terraces on the street that had been returned to their original condition much too deliberately. Elaine respected the way Georgette's featureless old house stood among its pretentious mates.

The front yard was littered with toys and bikes that she had to step over, holding her handbag tightly for balance, to reach the front door. Georgette was too good to her five children and spent most of her time looking after her grandchildren. She had so many that Elaine had lost count, but there were adults and infants. The two oldest grandchildren lived with Georgette full-time because their father was a junkie and their mother had died from an overdose when they were babies. Georgette's brothers had introduced their nephew to the stuff.

Elaine could hear children shouting and thumping as she knocked three times.

Georgette swung the door open. A child was holding on to her leg and another was wailing behind her. They hugged and Elaine had to stop herself from crying. Every time she whiffed Georgette's shampoo and the nutty smell of her house, she was transported back in time.

'Elaine, habibti, why has it been so long?'

They pulled away from each other. 'Wallah ya, Georgette, the days are racing. Before you know it we'll be in the ground.'

Elaine pinched the children's cheeks as she followed Georgette towards the kitchen at the back. The cornices in the hallway had been smoothed out. And the floorboards had been covered in gigantic beige tiles. On one wall was a colossal photo in a gilded frame of Georgette's late husband. It was from the seventies; he had big thick hair like Elvis with a handlebar moustache, and his chest was popping out of a tight shirt with boats on it. It was exactly how he'd looked when Elaine had met him all that time ago. He had died a while back from a heart attack on a job site. He was a very kind man and he had helped her and Youssef a lot in the early days, lending them money and driving them around before they bought a car.

Georgette's grandson and a girl were at the table in the middle of the kitchen, sleepy-eyed and eating toast. He was the modern version of his grandfather in the hallway. And of his father, too, as much as Elaine could remember: bulging muscles in a white singlet and a perfectly groomed beard.

He sprang up from his chair to greet Elaine. 'Hi, Aunty, long time no see!'

'Hi, habibi. Promise last time I see you, you were half this size. Ism el salib.'

They kissed on the cheeks and he pulled Elaine in for a hug.

She revelled in the embrace, wished her own grandchildren were as generous. Georgette stood beaming at the exchange from the kitchen sink.

'Aunty, this is my girlfriend.'

The girl stood up and extended her hand. Her hair was a nest, but she was striking. She had an English accent. 'Pleased to meet you.'

'And you too, darling.'

'Aunty Elaine is my tayta's oldest friend. She used to live on Brighton Street too.'

He sounded nothing like Joey and Alex. They chatted some more while Georgette made coffee and then Elaine followed her out to the back porch where they sat on the same outdoor table and chairs that had been there for as long as she could remember.

Her body hung loosely in Georgette's presence, and her tongue reverted entirely to Arabic too. 'He's such a good boy. You've done a good job, Georgette.'

'I'm very lucky. Very lucky. Him and his sister are smart, respectful. Nothing like their father.'

'How is he?'

'Same. Same as always. He lived with us for two months recently but then I realised he was stealing from me again. And the kids, they weren't happy. When he's around, he ruins their happiness. So I kicked him out. He's living in a granny flat in Dulwich Hill.'

'Look after the kids and yourself. Hopefully he will get better one day.'

'We can hope, but I know that he won't. It didn't happen with my brothers and it won't happen with him. I've just learnt to live with it. I realise now that if he's sick it doesn't mean we have to be sick too.'

'That's a good way to see it.'

'Anyway, how are you, habibti? How are the kids and the grandkids?'

'They're the same. Healthy, happy – as far as I know.'

'And what about you?'

It had been so long since someone had genuinely asked how she was. She thought to be honest and say she could be better, but why burden her friend who she didn't see often? 'I'm fine.'

They spent the morning reminiscing and catching up on gossip in between Georgette soothing and feeding her younger grandchildren. When Elaine suggested that the children be left in day care when their parents were at work, Georgette admitted she wouldn't know what to do with her time. Elaine had never looked after her grandchildren so selflessly. When they were young, she grew tired of them as soon as they nagged.

There was a sluggishness to Georgette's movements that Elaine was seeing for the first time. Her friend was old. When Georgette said she was making warak enab for dinner, Elaine insisted on staying longer to help her stuff and roll the vine leaves. Georgette was so pleased that she played Sabah on the stereo and, as the little ones napped, the two of them sat at the kitchen table and rolled the warak enab together as though the past forty-five years hadn't happened.

Even though she had lost most of her pension payment the other night with Salma at the sporties, Elaine couldn't resist stopping over at the Wests Leagues club on her way home from Georgette's. It was hard to recall but she was sure she had good luck there once.

She was two days off from the next payment, so if she could make something out of the twenty she had left it would be helpful. The car was coughing through its last drops of petrol because she had only been filling the tank up with five or ten dollars at a time. If she lost the twenty, she'd be stuck at home for two days, too afraid to drive and break down somewhere and be forced to come clean. Seeing Georgette had filled her own tank with hope. It had also filled it with sadness that she believed the bright lights of the machines would help filter out.

She sat at the Cleopatra-themed one-cent machine and bet five cents per spin on ten lines. Betting so low was pointless but it was the only way to make the credit stretch. After ten minutes she was up nine dollars. She decided to play until it was back down to her original twenty at least.

When the credit was at ten dollars her hands shook. There was no point backing out now. It was all or nothing. She gained a six-dollar win and decided to bet it. Red of spades. The win was doubled. Red of spades again. Quadrupled. That meant if she took the payout now, she'd leave with thirty-four dollars. Fourteen dollars up. Then she could fill the car with fifteen dollars of petrol and have plenty for milk and whatever she was going to cook for dinner the next day. Probably mujadara. Her finger hovered over the collect button. She'd worked it out, that was it. She had done what she came to do at the club. All that was left was to press the button and cash out the ticket.

She hit black of diamonds and shut her eyes. The winning sound rang out. Her credit was now at fifty-eight dollars. She touched her pendant and didn't hesitate to slap the collect button.

★

In between sips of whisky, she massaged her wrists in front of the TV. The lights were off, and the TV reflected blue scenes onto her face and nightie. Something told her to look through the sliding door and she was mortified to see a man standing right up against the glass pane, his figure shrouded by night. Her heart fumbled – this was how she would die. At least it had ended with whisky. The figure waved at her and she realised it was Joey. She rushed to the door, making the sign of the cross so fast it ended up being a circle. She slid the door open with two hands.

'Ism el salib, Joey. What's wrong, albi?' she said as she kissed his cheeks and ushered him in.

'Nothing, Tayta. I was walking past and thought I'd check if you were awake.'

'Okay, but why stand like this? You scare me. I thought something wrong.'

'Sorry, I didn't mean to. You looked comfortable I was gonna leave you alone.'

'Leave me alone? What kind of talk is this?' She kissed him again on his neck.

'What did you get up to tonight, Tayta?'

'I go to visit Georgette and I end up staying for hours helping her with rolling warak enab. She have army of mouths to feed, that lady. I was too tired to go in first place, but I have to.'

'Why did you have to?'

'Wejbet, albi. She came here last two times.'

'What's wejbet again?'

'Like, ah, you respect me, buy me a gift; I respect you, buy you a gift. Like contract.'

'A contract forcing you to respect each other?'

She rolled her eyes at him. 'Yes, exactly. How was your night? You go out?'

'Yeah, kinda. Just for a drive with the boys.'

'Boys from school?'

'Yeah.'

She made a sound to show her disapproval.

They migrated from the sliding door to the kitchen. She poured some milk into an old saucepan to make hot chocolate, opening cupboard doors and peering into jars to make out the contents. Eventually she found the cocoa and whisked it into the milk. When the boys were young and would sleep over, she always made hot chocolate before ushering them to bed. And it was never long before they'd cross the hallway and get into bed with her.

'Your mama come over for coffee today.'

'Yeah?'

'She talk about you.'

'Yeah.'

'Everything okay with you and her?'

'Everything seems okay to me.'

'Your mama worries a lot. She worries a lot for you. About the future. After finishing school, you know …'

Elaine set a mug down in front of him and poured the hot chocolate into it while watching him.

'Do we have to have this conversation?'

'Baby, don't be upset with me. I want you to be happy and your mum to be happy. She's had tough time.'

'Tayta, I get it. But what am I meant to do? It's not my fault her life didn't turn out the way she expected. And I'm nineteen, for God's sake. I don't think any nineteen-year-old knows what they want to do. I've got a job.'

'Yes, but part-time in a supermarket. Is this a future?' She saw the dangerous territory unfold before her.

'For now, yeah!'

Elaine waved her hands in the air. 'Okay, okay, okay. Forget it. Forget I say anything.'

They moved to the lounge and drank their hot chocolate. The new Turkish soap she'd been watching was still playing. She got Joey up to speed: the rich man had put a hit out on his daughter's fiancé who was a thief, but the hitman accidentally killed the wrong person, who turned out to be the rich man's illegitimate son. Elaine could see Joey wasn't looking at the TV as the on-screen father cried maniacally. She followed his line of sight. He was staring at a photo frame on the side table. The picture was of Elaine, Youssef and a young Amal and Michael at the Three Sisters in Katoomba in the eighties.

'Joey, you sleep here tonight? Yulla, I'll make the bed. Message Mama.'

She stood up and made her way to Amal's old bedroom. The light she switched on throbbed into the dark hallway. She began changing the floral fitted sheet and pillowcase on the old single bed. She heard Joey follow and turned to find him watching from the doorway.

'Don't worry about changing it,' he said.

'No, habibi. It's okay, I haven't changed in a while. Probably dusty. Here.' She handed him a pillow to strip.

The walls of Amal's old room still had framed posters of nineties popstars.

'Why have you never taken Mum's old stuff down?' Joey asked.

'I don't know. Remind me of simple time.'

Elaine turned away from the bed and sat on it with the pillow in her lap. It pained her that her grandsons grew up without their father.

She patted the mattress. 'Come, sit.'

Joey sat beside her. He smelt like cigarettes and sweat, maybe vomit.

'Don't smoke, habibi.'

'The boys were smoking in the car.'

Something about the late-night encounter encouraged her to go a little deeper with him. Maybe if he knew more about his past he would make better decisions about his future. 'What you know about your dad?'

She felt Joey tense up.

'Not much, really. Just what I've heard from you guys. Mum never talks about him.'

'Your mum is too hard sometimes. Like remehn.'

'What's remehn?'

'The fruit in the back, next to the fig.'

'Pomegranate?'

'Yes.' She paused. 'I remember first time your father came over for BBQ. I thought, he's handsome and blond. Skinny. Like you. Same hair, but lighter. And your eyes exact same. I thought, what he want with Amal? She is dark and hairy, pretty, but lazy. All day walking around the house with the Walkman in her ears eating sweets.'

'She does that now, but with her phone instead.'

She laughed and slapped his thigh. 'Your Jiddo Youssef finally agree to have Simon, your dad, over after weeks and weeks of your mama saying she's in love. And then when he came, we can't shut your dad and Jiddo up about football and cars.'

Her grandson's body went limp beside her.

'After six months they say to us: Mum, Dad, we ready to get married.'

They were quiet for a moment. Both with their gaze fixed on the same floor tile, as though reflected on it was the scene she described.

'Your mum, she … she shine bright and then …'

'And what?'

'And then life happens. Ach, maybe I tell you another time. I'm tired.'

She kissed Joey on the cheek and made her way to her bedroom. There was too much to be covered about the past before they could even talk about the future. And maybe it was too late in the night for all of that. Maybe it was just too late to ever bring that up.

9

Joey watched his grandmother hobble out of his mum's old bedroom. If she had bad dreams tonight it would be his fault. He switched off the light, stripped out of his clothes and climbed into the bed. He started jerking off. The feeling of Lisa's arm against his. The Turkish actress's lips. The tattoo on Haz's back, his biceps as he wiped himself with his T-shirt. He came.

He hummed a tune in his head to nudge himself into sleep. It was one his mother had taught him as a child. He didn't even know if it was a real song. Just as he was about to drift off, his mind's eye was plastered with snapshots of the night: Lisa on the train. The pergola. Lisa at the boot of the car. His spew. Her sneakers under the toilet cubicle. Tayta in her chair. The family photograph. And then something he hadn't actually seen that night. Something that was described to him by his grandmother only a moment ago. An image of his young father shaking hands with Jiddo Youssef.

He sat up quickly. Surely there wasn't anything interesting to know about his father. Why had Tayta brought him up so randomly? And the conversation that she had with his mum about his own future. Why were they so concerned about him? Why had Haz called him a 'messy fucker'? Was he missing something every time he looked in the mirror? He should never have let Kyri persuade him to go. And Kyri had disappeared. Kyri had forced him to hang out with those gronks and then he had disappeared. Was it all part of a plan? Boxer capturing Lisa. The K – if that's what it was. Haz and his car. Only him and Lisa had taken the K. No-one else.

Joey reached for his phone on the side table and called Kyri. It was eleven. He'd be up. Joey needed answers. The call went straight to voicemail. He sent Kyri a text: *Call me*. But it was undeliverable because he'd probably switched his phone off. He thought about going over to Kyri's place, knocking on his bedroom window, but Tayta would hear him leaving. She would make a big deal out of it.

Joey's breath was shortening as though the drugs from earlier were having a wicked revival. Why on earth had he come to his grandmother's house? He opened Instagram on his phone and searched *Lisa*. Maybe they had a common friend. Everyone in the west was connected through somebody. A flurry of brunettes named Lisa smiled, pouted, posed back at him. It was too common a name. It would be impossible. What was there to say to her, anyway? Their train station interaction had been awkward enough. She had taken the whole thing in her stride. As though she had seen it all before.

The hot chocolate rose in Joey's throat. He was a puking fucking fool. That's all he would ever be. A puking mess. He looked at his reflection in the mirrored wardrobe at the foot of the bed. In the dark, illuminated by the unforgiving light of his phone, he looked gaunt, weak, like Edvard Munch's *The Scream*. It was the only painting he remembered from art class because it reminded him of what it felt like to be high. He was cursed. He had to be. His incapacity had to come from somewhere.

In Instagram, again, he typed *Simon Boyle*. There were at least fifty nondescript results. Any of them could be his father. He cleared the search and typed *Ivan*. There he was, the very first result, the dude from the festival. They shared four followers. No-one substantial. There were only five posts on his profile. Two were of a motorbike, one was a portrait of an old woman with the caption 'RIP Baba', one was the sun setting in Santorini, and the most recent was a close-up selfie, with the Defqon stage in the background, captioned *Yeeewww*. Joey noticed his breathing was returning to normal. He hit follow, tapped the message button, typed *Heyyy* then backspaced a *y* and hit send. He started humming his mother's sleeping tune again, and this time it worked.

Tayta's lolly-bag perfume woke Joey up in the morning before her knock at the door.

She peered into the room, made-up and smiley. 'I am going to shops to pick up couple things and I come back and drive you home. I make you manoosh and fried eggplant on the bench.'

Fried eggplant was his favourite. 'Thanks, Tayta. What time is it?'

'Eleven.'

'Fuck, already?'

'No need for fuck, Joey.'

'Sorry.'

'Bye, baby.'

She shut the door and clopped down the tiled hallway. Joey reached for his phone. Nothing from Kyri and his battery was about to die. He checked Instagram. Ivan had replied at two in the morning.

Ayyyy look who it is.

He had also followed Joey back and liked a bunch of his posts, including a shirtless gym selfie.

Joey put the pillow over his head. Last night had happened. Last night had happened and he was starving and now that his tayta's perfume had dissipated he could smell the zaatar and the eggplant. He put his shorts on and made his way to the kitchen bench. There was enough food for three, but he scoffed it all down with a can of Pepsi. He tried calling Kyri and again it went to voicemail. He clicked into Ivan's message window and typed, *How's it going, man?*

On the coffee table in the lounge room, apart from the doily and the porcelain horse that had been there as long as he could remember, Joey caught sight of an old VHS tape in a blank white case. Tayta had left it sitting upright, like a book on display in a shop. He popped the case open. The label on the tape had been peeled off, leaving a fluffy rectangle of residue behind. Joey slid the tape into the player.

A warped image flashed up on the screen accompanied by a corny R'n'B love song. Joey couldn't see much except for smoke and lights. Then, at a bizarre camera angle, appeared a slow-dancing couple. A bride and groom. He was about to hit eject when the video cut to a close-up of the couple's faces. Joey's heartbeat quickened; the profile of the bride punched him in the guts. It was his mother. Younger, pre nose job, pre lips. The waltzing couple were his parents. This was their wedding video.

He hit the rewind button and after a minute the tape played from the beginning. The opening shot was of a blue sky with the words *The Wedding of Simon and Amal* superimposed in Comic Sans font. The shot lasted too long and faded clumsily to a clip of the outside of his grandparents' house, the one he was in now. There was a rosebush, and the brick fence wasn't hodgepodge because it hadn't been reversed into by Tayta yet.

Another fade into his grandparents' bedroom, where his spritely mother stood in front of a mirror in her boob-tube wedding dress, her bridesmaid, Aunty Rita, stared straight into the camera while fluffing the bride's dress. The soundtrack was Prince's 'The Most Beautiful Girl in the World'. He knew the song because it was on one of the two albums his mum played on repeat in her car. The other was Mariah Carey.

He felt simultaneously gobsmacked by her prettiness and responsible for its demise. His mother had become too involved in him and Alex and it had slowly eroded all that was dazzling about her. He wished she'd back off a little and stop worrying. It might do her some good.

The music transitioned to Arabic and the scene cut to a troupe dancing and clapping around his bopping mother in the backyard. There was Tayta, less crumpled and in a smart beige suit; Jiddo Youssef, undead; his much leaner uncle Michael; and various other faces that were as recognisable as they were not.

The music was turned down and the ensemble froze while Tayta recited an old village poem to her daughter. After each line was delivered, she paused for the congregation's reprisal, which was a loud and drawn out 'eh'. When the final line was delivered, everybody cupped their hands over their mouths and ululated. The hairs on Joey's arms stood up. His on-screen mother dabbed at her eyes with a tissue. From his poor effort at translation, he gathered that Tayta was warding off the evil eye and wishing her daughter plentiful days with her soon-to-be husband.

Watching it was too visceral, invasive. Joey knew that all the hope and vitality turned out to be a giant knot of failure. He hit the fast-forward button and the video raced to his other grandparents' house. And there the ghost of his father stood, flanked by his demure parents. They clinked champagne glasses and smiled and attached corsages on one another's lapels. The videographer must have been ethnic because the song that played over the scene was too deliberately white – soft rock.

Joey tried to conjure some kind of feeling for the unknown family on the screen whose genetics he borrowed from, but there was nothing. These people were strangers. He paused the video to analyse his father. He'd seen him in photo albums on rare occasions, but the video animated him, projected him out of two dimensions. Tayta was right; he did share his father's eyes and brows and hair, and Alex was in there too – his chin and smile and lankiness. It shouldn't have come as a surprise, because that's the way procreation works, but it was jarring to echo a man you only knew for the first six years of your life. His grandparents looked awkward in a sweet way. Like they had never expected to be filmed. He was related to these people. Direct descendant of these Aussies on the screen.

Joey pressed the fast-forward button again and through the squiggles he made out his father parking a motorbike outside the church and then his mother also getting ready to leave. He hit play and mouthed, 'Oh my God', into the still lounge room. She was being taken to church in a horse-drawn carriage. It was the most jarring thing Joey had ever seen: white horses and white carriage projected against the backdrop of the humdrum houses and souped-up cars of Punchbowl. Alex had to see this video.

His parents cried through their baby-faced smiles when they met at the altar. They seemed enraptured, spellbound by each other. And yet it all ended up so corrupted. He fast-forwarded through the church service until the newlyweds were being announced into the Adel's Palace reception hall by an emcee. The lights dimmed, the smoke machines were set to savage, the Lebanese drum was being belted, then the doors flung open and the newlyweds swanned in holding hands, dancing, beaming for their guests, who clapped to the beat of the drum.

Joey hit the fast-forward button to the speeches. His father stood up. 'Youssef and Elaine, you have welcomed my parents and me into your family so willingly and lovingly. Thank you for being wonderful, hospitable people. And Michael, ahkbelak, bro.'

Joey had not imagined his father to be well-spoken and charming. He pulled away from the TV, having been frozen right in front of it the whole time. His parents had only been a few years older than he was now. They were robust. He was a flake. And his father was able to recite an Arabic term impressively.

The speech went on with more obligatory thanks until his dad raised a scotch glass and said, 'Now, can you all raise your glasses, please? To the absolutely smashing Mrs Boyle.'

The guests whooped and clapped and clinked their cutlery against their glasses. He had a commanding voice, and there was something endearing about his accent that rippled between Aussie and wog and all-round suburban.

'You have changed my life in so many ways. For one, my hands have never been this clean and soft.'

The guests laughed raucously. His mother placed her hand over her eyes and laughed too. His father was funny. Joey had a feeling like when you're close to finishing a video game and you lose your last life.

His father went on. 'Babe, you are my sun and my moon. Without you, I'd be in total darkness.'

Then he looked away from his bride and let out a speedy breath like men do to spur themselves out of emotion. His mother was crying. Joey let out a speedy breath.

'I am so grateful to the universe that we found each other, and I can't wait to live our lives together and start a famil—'

Joey bounced forward and ejected the tape. Longing was a putrid thing. Humans were so obsessed with snapshotting their cutesy histories, and for what? Life always ended up a pigsty.

10

Elaine could have sworn the wall of milk at the supermarket grew on a weekly basis. Soon enough there would be potato milk and kangaroo milk.

She looked around at the other shoppers. Midmorning on a weekday the crowd was measly. Young mothers pushing prams the size of cars, tradesmen loading up on energy drinks and chocolate bars. When Elaine first arrived in Australia in the seventies, people made a ten-cent bottle of milk last. That was when milk was delivered. After that service ended, she would swap an empty bottle for a fresh one at Con's corner store. Now, though, she had to contend with the wall of milk. Sometimes she punished the supermarket by covering the bottle in her trolley with a cardigan and putting on her best old-lady smile for the checkout person as they scanned the other items. But she wouldn't do that today. Joey's impromptu visit last night made her want everything to be good. And for things to be good she had to be good. She wasn't going to go to the pokies – not today, tomorrow, or the rest of the week even.

She chose a one-litre bottle of skim milk, put it in the trolley and pushed on through the aisle.

Anyone who drank milk should be forced to milk a cow at least once in their life. Of course, she had done so as a child, in the village, but it had mainly been goats. That village was so far away to her now. In distance and in fondness. It had taken three days by plane and four stopovers to get her to Sydney in 1972. Youssef had gone ahead of her to find a home and a job. She'd only been back to the village once, when her mother died. The people she grew up with, her relatives, siblings, had all seemed like characters from an old tale she learnt as a child.

Elaine was seventeen when her father informed her she'd be meeting her husband. She hadn't been shocked or sentimental at the news because that was the way of the village and she had only ever existed in its wounds and gullies and song. Three of her sisters had already been married off: one to a cousin, one to an old farmer from a neighbouring village, and Aida, the pearl of the family, to the priest's son – a pilot. The families were by no means a match, but the most educated and striking man in the village had to have the girl whose beauty was talked about all the way to Tripoli.

The thing people hadn't known about Aida was that she was a nuisance. Jaded by her own reflection and hand. She would force Elaine to brush her hair for her. And on the very rare occasions Elaine was given a sweet, Aida would wait until no-one was looking to snatch it.

Aida had been taken all the way to Beirut by the pilot's mother to have a wedding dress made. The veil was thick, heavier than the dress, which Elaine had rubbed her grubby hands all over when the women were busy shaving Aida's legs.

Elaine sniffed the bars of soap in the toiletries aisle, remembering the way the women had crowded around Aida as she dressed on the morning of her wedding. She had worn the heavy veil stoically, her golden locks peeping out as she swished around the relatives who were singing songs about girls leaving their parents' homes to become women. Their mother had asked a cousin for some lipstick for the bride, which had come as a complete shock to everyone. Elaine's mother had not been the type to indulge in extravagances, toughened into the shape of a man by a life of farming and war and humility. She had used a little of the lipstick as blush on the bride's cheeks too. The brightest red Elaine had seen.

When the family and relatives had gathered around Aida and ferried her down the dusty hill, through the windy village to its centre-point church, the people had stopped their ploughing in fields, paused their bickering in kitchens, halted their coffee-sipping on rooftops to line the streets and catch a glimpse of the pearl.

Vanish Oxi Action was on sale – thirty per cent off. Elaine put a tub in her trolley and pushed on before remembering how much money she had and coming to a stop. She waved at a tiny employee who came over.

'How long this one on sale?' Elaine asked.

'You mean, when does the sale end? Next Wednesday.'

Good. Elaine could come back after her next payment and still make the saving. She handed the employee the tub and kept going past the procession of toilet paper.

No-one had lined the streets to see Elaine on her own wedding day. Her dress had been an itchy hand-me-down from a neighbour. It was so ugly that when she saw it on the morning of her nuptials she ran from the house, sliding on the gravel, up the hill and through the huge maroon gates of the cemetery. She'd weaved through the crypts and out the back gate arriving at her aunts' home sweating, sobbing, her hair a falcon's nest. Her aunts had greeted her at the door as though expecting her, ushering her in to the smell of fried eggs and yogurt.

The women were her father's two sisters. Elaine had loved them more than she'd loved her own parents. They had been brutal, oftentimes spiteful, but only because they had spent their lives being treated like the dregs of the village – because they didn't have husbands. One of them had been married, but, after failing to fall pregnant, had been returned with a sack of belongings to her parents' doorstep. The other had not at all been interested in men and had managed to scare any suitors away.

As she had crumbled and bawled in her aunts' arms, it had dawned on Elaine that the dress was only a trigger. She was being forced to marry a stranger thirteen years her senior who was ripping her away from the only world she knew.

She had pleaded with her aunts to save her, but they had told her to wash her face in the barrel before her father came to fetch her. Then they had sat her on the daybed on the verandah and convinced her that marrying Youssef and moving to Australia was the best thing she could do to escape the village. They told her she would have children who would love her and look after her, unlike them, and that she had the spirit of her grandmother in her – the grandmother who, they reminded her, once hypnotised a snake using the pendant that hung on her necklace. The story went that the snake had been coiled up in her newborn's crib, was poised to attack, and her grandmother had lured it away. Apparently she had been able to communicate with djinns, too.

Elaine pushed the trolley at a snail's pace with one hand past ice cream and frozen pizzas and fish fingers.

The aunts had gestured to each other while Elaine composed herself, and the smaller one had disappeared into the storage room, reappearing after a moment with a cedar jewellery box. They had opened it together, one hand each, and, from a mess of gold, untangled a dazzling necklace that had momentarily bewitched Elaine out of her panic. It was made of gold chains that twisted around each other like a grapevine. Dangling from it was a frilled pendant depicting Mariam Our Saviour.

When it unfurled into full view, Elaine recognised it from the last memory she had of her grandmother – lying in a coffin with her grey plaits draped over her shoulders, the pendant resting on her chest. The aunts told Elaine that they had gone into the crypt and fetched the necklace the night their mother had been slotted in there because if they hadn't some other poor soul would have. They flanked Elaine and lowered the necklace over her head.

Her aunts were milk and honey and dirt and plums and chickens. They were the village, its past and its bosom. They had tucked the necklace inside her dress so that it wasn't visible. A moment later, her father had come to drag her to her wedding. Elaine had hugged her aunts and kissed their necks, their hair, the sweat on their foreheads. At the doorstep, she had turned around for one last glimpse of them and they had winked at her in unison.

When she had arrived at the altar and her father had handed her over to Youssef, Elaine had been convinced she was suffocating. She'd thought about jumping out of the high window – the village was so fickle that if she broke her legs no-one would want to marry her. And then she'd thought of the secret buried under the ugly wedding dress. She'd felt its warmth, the warmth of her aunts. As the priest swung his thurible and chanted, she'd vowed to accept her fate and be whatever and wherever it was that she had to be.

The checkouts were empty. Elaine went to the express section and unloaded the milk onto the counter. She pressed the pendant into her chest. Hopefully Joey had watched the video by now. She just wanted things to be good.

11

After messaging briefly back and forth, Joey and Ivan organised to hang out at Ivan's place. Ivan even offered to pick Joey up from Canley Vale station because the trains didn't go as far as Greenfield Park. Joey had asked to borrow his mum's car, but she'd started rattling off all of her appointments – the doctor, the hair salon, a coffee date, a wedding, a funeral, a bungee jump. He'd walked off before she even finished the list.

He'd been planning to open a savings account to buy a car, but you had to have funds to open the account. He teased himself often on Carsales and Gumtree, searching for half-decent Audis and Volkswagens that people from the eastern suburbs were trying to offload. He didn't bother checking local ads because the cars were more than likely thrashed.

He opened the selfie camera on his phone to see what he looked like as the train approached Canley Vale station. After he'd come home from Tayta's he had made Alex shave his hair off. Alex had tried to convince him not to, but Joey had needed a change. Without hair, he looked more Lebanese.

It had taken him ages to decide what to wear. Ivan said they would go to his place for a bit and afterwards he wanted to take his dirt bike out to Eastern Creek, which almost caused Joey to flake on the whole thing. First time hanging out and the guy wanted to do adventure sports. Surely Ivan wasn't expecting Joey to ride the bike. He'd just watch Ivan do his thing and then they could get some dinner or something. In the end he'd decided to wear black Nike shorts and a plain white tee.

Canley Vale exploded in front of him like it didn't exist before he stepped off the train and because he was early he walked around the shopping district. A lot of the signs for the high school coaching businesses and family doctors had faded to a watermark, like the sun had a personal vendetta against them.

It didn't seem as though the Canley Vale folk needed signs, anyway. There was a conviction in the way they walked and chose their vegetables from the teeming shops. Many of the shopfronts and little arcades hadn't yet been renovated like around Greenacre. But Greenacre was arrogant. Greenacre was trying too hard to play catch-up with other parts of Sydney. Even people's car choices had jumped the gun. Most of the beat-up fibro houses in Greenacre had top-of-the-line Range Rovers and Mercedes four-wheelers parked on their front lawns. Sometimes the cars looked bigger than the actual houses.

There were queues outside the bubble-tea windows and the customers were walking away with the things in little bags instead of drinking them straight away. He felt the urge to fix his cracked phone screen at one of the many repairers but realised it was just the energy of the place spurring him on.

From their messaging, and from what Joey made out via Instagram, Ivan was twenty-one, an only child to Serbian immigrants. He lived in a granny flat at the back of his parents' place, was studying health science at Western Sydney Uni. He'd been on a big trip to Europe that year. Experiences that made Joey look like an absolute sad case in comparison. He put it down to the two-year age difference.

At their meeting spot, Ivan had to yell out 'Yo!' over the house track blaring out of his Ford Ranger before Joey realised it was his lift. The ute had gigantic black rims to match its shiny midnight exterior. He had expected Ivan to drive something a lot less flash because he hadn't mentioned having a job. The interior of the car was immaculate and smelt new. Ivan wore a white tank top and when he reached his arm over to fist-bump, Joey caught the smell of his body odour. Ivan seemed taller, his mouth wider, than when they had met at the festival, but it also could have been because the steering wheel was in between his knees and he was grinning in a goofy way.

'You look different when you're not so munted.' Ivan smiled at his own remark.

'Really? Different how?'

'Nah, like, your jaw isn't bouncing around like a goose.'

They laughed.

'And you shaved your head?' Ivan reached over and rubbed his head.

'Yeah, man, got bored the other day so I made my little brother shave it off.'

'Suits ya.'

'Thanks. Thanks for picking me up, ay.'

'All good, any excuse to drive this, t-b-h.'

'It's pretty decent. You had it for a while?'

'Nah, literally few months. Mum and Dad got it for my twenty-first. Perks of being an only child and shit.'

'What a flex. I'd be lucky to get a Happy Meal from my mum.'

Ivan laughed genuinely. 'What about your dad?'

'Don't have one.'

'Ah, sorry to hear. How long ago?'

Joey wasn't bothered to tell this story yet. 'When I was a kid.'

'Shit, man. That sucks.'

'It's alright. I'm used to it.'

'You're not full Lebo, are ya?'

'Nah, half. Dad is – was – Aussie.'

'Yeah, I could tell there was more to ya.'

'More to me? Is Leb not enough?'

'Nah, Aussie isn't.'

They laughed and looked out of their respective windows. Ivan drove well and naturally, and after ten minutes he pulled into a short cul-de-sac and then a wide driveway. The kerbsides in Ivan's neighbourhood curled into the road like they do in young suburbs. The house was a light-brick double-storey with an archway garage. The front yard was half-lawn and half-concrete patchwork that was covered in various-sized statues.

'Don't mind them,' Ivan said, pointing to the lot.

'Yeah, I was gonna say, they're pretty epic.'

'They're my dad's. Fuck knows where he picked them up from back in the day, but they've been here forever.'

There were renaissance women, Greek gods, cherubs, a lamb, frogs, and even some sort of chariot with a gnome in it.

Joey shut the car door and walked over to it. 'I have to take a pic of this.'

'Go for gold.'

The roller door flung up and a tubby old man with a white moustache stood gripping the handle as though he was hanging from it. He looked surprised to see Joey and not just his son.

'Ivan. Hello.'

'Dad, this is Joey.'

'Hello, Joey. Ivo, take the car on the street. I'm gonna wash driveway.'

The concrete was spotless but for a few leaves. Joey's tayta was the same.

'Alright, I'll move it later,' Ivan said as he walked towards the side gate. Joey followed slowly, trying not to disrespect the old man by walking away too soon.

'Ivo, please. I'm gonna wash now.'

'Far out, Dad. Alright, I'll move it soon.'

They passed the gate and Joey looked back to see Ivan's father shaking his head.

Joey whispered close to Ivan's ear as they walked down the side of the house, 'Ivo, move the car for Papa', and Ivan laughed. When they passed underneath the kitchen window Joey heard a foreign radio station and dishes being cleaned in a sink.

The granny flat was on the other side of a well-kept kidney-bean pool in a vast backyard that was home to even more statues. Inside it smelt like Ivan and popcorn and socks and was sparsely furnished but comfortable. A space Joey would have killed for. Ivan switched the TV on, pulled two beers from a small fridge and handed one to Joey. They sat on the couch and took their first sip in unison.

'So, you only part-time at Woolies?' Ivan asked.

'Yeah, more like casual.'

'You happy doin that?'

'Fuck no, but no clue what else to do.'

'You wanna study?'

'Maybe, but yeah, no idea still. I was thinking about computers, coding and shit.'

'That's where it's at, man. Coding is taking over.'

'Yeah. But I worry I'll get bored as and quit, and if I do that my mum will lose it.'

'You don't paint a good picture of your mum.'

Joey laughed awkwardly. 'She's alright. I'm just sick of being at home. Wish I could move out. So over the area.'

'Yeah? I love living here.'

'You can't talk. You've got your own place pretty much.'

'Yeah, but even so I reckon I'd still stay around here. I can't stand anything outside the West. They're all wankers. Where would you live, anyway?' Ivan asked.

'Like, Newtown or something.'

'What, with all the cool cats and art kids?'

'Nah, it's not just like that.'

'I'm fuckin with ya. It's alright. That's the furthest I'd go, but. Everything is so dank around there, man. Out here there's fresh air, space, parking spots for fuck's sake. Went to Enmore last weekend for gelato, legit had to circle for half an hour before I found a park. And then we had to line up outside the shop.'

'Were you on a date?'

'Kind of. Not really.'

Ivan went into the toilet to piss and from the couch it sounded to Joey like a fire hydrant was blasting into the toilet. His own piss was never that raucous. When Ivan returned, he went to a cupboard in the kitchenette and fished out a packet of mixed lollies.

'Take off your shoes. Should we hang here, watch a movie for a bit?' Ivan asked.

'Yeah, set. Did you still wanna take your bike out?'

'Yeah, we can go later. The track is indoors so it's open at night. Did you have plans later or anything?'

'Nah, nothing.'

'Mad. Well, I'll drop you off at home after, anyway.'

Without Joey's input, Ivan played the latest season of *Black Mirror*. Half the lollies had disappeared into his gob before he said sorry and threw the pack at Joey's chest, and although he didn't usually eat lollies, Joey was glad for something to do. They were side by side, bodies slumped deep into the couch. Both of their T-shirts had gathered so that an identical sliver of their abdomen was exposed.

Ivan gestured at Joey's and said, 'You're pretty hairy for being half Aussie.'

'You can't talk.'

'Yeah, you should see my thighs.' Ivan stood up and pulled his shorts down to his knees. His thighs were covered in chestnut hair. There was a piss stain on his white briefs.

Joey stood up and pulled his shorts down. 'Yeah, I'm not as hairy as you.'

'Do you trim your pubes?'

'A bit.'

'I have to, man, otherwise it's a jungle.' Ivan lowered his underwear enough so that the top of his dick was showing. His pubes were trimmed neatly.

Joey followed suit. 'I'm lucky cos mine are pretty fair. Don't have to do much trimming.'

In a moment their shorts were pulled back up and they sat to continue watching the show.

There was a contraption in the tray of the ute that the dirt bike sat into and Ivan used a wide plank of wood to roll the bike up into it. Joey helped strap it in even though he had never used the straps before and he worried, on the short drive to Oporto, that the bike would somersault out of the tray and wreak havoc. When the ute was parked and Ivan had started walking towards the restaurant doors, Joey quickly tugged on the strap to reassure himself.

They ate like pigs. Joey overestimated his hunger and couldn't finish his second burger, but Ivan gladly demolished it for him.

The energy at the motocross dome left Joey feeling puny. The structure was a colossal inflatable tent that encased a bunch of dirt. Like a greenhouse on the surface of Mars. The riders zig-zagged and careered all over the place, hungry motorised rats searching for food. The sound was deafening, and Ivan's bike was the loudest.

Apart from him and Ivan, everyone in there was pretty bogan. He joined a spectator group of girlfriends and mums and dads who side-eyed him as though he wasn't meant to be there. He tried hard to be interested in Ivan's moves on the track but it all just became one thing. He wished he could be on the back of the bike with Ivan, feeling the dirt push back on the tyres, the jumps, the skids.

After half an hour of messing around, Ivan rode up to the barrier and took his helmet off. The sweat on his face took Joey straight back to Defqon and the moment they met. He held on to the barrier tighter.

'Alright, I'm done. I'll meet ya at the car,' Ivan said.

They loaded the bike back on the tray and Ivan stripped out of the protective gear. Joey must have looked cold as he waited near the car and smoked a cigarette because Ivan threw a Champion jumper at him and said to put it on. It was too long for him, but he was glad to be wearing it. It smelt like Ivan's couch and mud.

They didn't speak much on the drive to Joey's place, but the house tunes were good.

Ivan parked the car and switched the ignition off. Joey had expected to hop out while the engine was still running.

'Alright, Mr Joey. It was good to hang out with ya,' Ivan said.

'Yeah, man. Thanks for the ride home.'

'All good, all good. Maybe next time I'll get you on the bike. You'll love it.'

'Yeah, maybe.'

They stared out of the windscreen silently for a moment and then Ivan laughed in his nose, put his hand around the back of Joey's neck and massaged it. Joey melted into the seat. Slowly, by some symbiosis of the pressure of Ivan's hand and a magnetic force inside his soul, his head travelled towards Ivan's. They lingered for a moment, smiling goofily nose to nose. And then they kissed, and his whole universe folded up real tight for a second before it burst into absolute and unequivocal harmony.

12

'Ma, since when do you have a membership here?' Amal asked as she and Elaine stood side by side signing into the kiosks at Bankstown Sports Club. Alex was already up the stairs staring at something on the ceiling.

'I got one while ago.'

The three of them had decided to have pizza at the fake piazza at the back of the club. Joey was out with a friend. Elaine hoped it was his nice friend Emma from work.

Alex called out to them. 'Can you hurry up? I'm starving.'

When they were at the top of the stairs, Elaine looked over at the poker machine section to her left. 'You go get us a table and I meet you. I need to go toilet.'

They would likely have to wait for a table because the car park was full. When Amal and Alex were out of sight, she slipped into the pokies section.

There wasn't enough time to be fussy about which machine

to play so she fed fifty dollars into the nearest one, which was themed with a dragon and Chinese symbols. She decided to play all lines at five-dollar hits just in case there wasn't a queue at the restaurant, which meant she would have ten hits before her credit ran out. If, within five taps, she doubled the fifty, she was collecting the ticket and paying for dinner.

There were no wins on the first three. The fourth gained her ten dollars, which she gambled on black of spades and lost. She cursed, looked into the dragon's eyes, touched the pendant on her necklace and pressed the button. One dragon head. Two dragon head. Three dragon head. Four dragon head. Five dragon head. The machine sang out. The dragons came alive, swishing all over the screen. The feature had dropped in an almost perfect line. She gasped, looking around, and two women a little older than her gave her a thumbs-up. She hadn't had this kind of luck in a while. It would take a few minutes for the free spins to play out. Amal would surely come looking for her, but she had no choice.

Fifteen spins later, Elaine hit the collect button. The payout was $653.80. She stuffed the ticket into her bag and skipped towards the piazza. Halfway through dinner she'd say she needed to go to the toilet again and cash the ticket in.

Luckily there was a queue to be seated. Amal and Alex were both on their phones and barely looked up when she joined them. Maybe it hadn't been that long.

'Hello, we come to dinner to be on the phone?' she said.

'Tayta, we're waiting for a table.'

'I know, but doesn't mean we can't talk.'

They put their phones away.

'How's school, habibi?'

'It's alright. I got full marks for my English multi-modal assessment.'

Elaine pinched his cheek. 'Bravo, baby!'

Amal gushed, 'He's gonna be our little university graduate.'

'Maybe,' Alex said sheepishly.

'Yeah, well at least we'll have one in the family,' Amal said.

'Mum, uni isn't the be all and end all, you know?'

'Yes, I do know, thank you for reminding me. I didn't go to uni and I'm just fine, but Joey is actually smart and he could have gone to uni instead of doing whatever he's doing now.'

Elaine interjected. 'Hey, leave this conversation tonight. We come here to eat pizza.'

It didn't take long before they were seated beside a big family who were about to eat a cake that had *Happy 70th Pop* written on it. There were at least twenty of them. Balloons, party hats. The man who appeared to be Pop had two small children in his lap. One of them was lunging for the cake.

Elaine looked at Alex. An angel behind a giant pizza menu. He had his grandmother's grey eyes. Not hers, but his other grandmother, Sue's. Sue was the most graceful human being Elaine had ever come across. After their first meeting, she had worried about how backwards Sue and her husband, Tom, must have thought them to be. But Simon's parents weren't at all judgemental, as she came to know over the years.

When it all fell apart with Amal and Simon, his parents had tried hard to be part of the boys' lives, but Amal had been so bitter that she had shut them out. Eventually they gave up, and Sue had called one last time to tell Elaine that they were moving to the Gold Coast. She would never say it, but Elaine had come to believe that much of the aftermath had been an overreaction on Amal's part. Especially changing the boys' surnames.

Sue and Tom, like the sweet family celebrating the seventieth birthday in the fake piazza, were unjaded people. They weren't drowning in longing and obligation, escaping poverty. Australians like Sue and Tom had, from generation to generation, shed their guilt. They had more time and space to breathe, because this place was taken for them by their ancestors a long time ago. Maybe that's what it meant to be privileged. Alex was always going on about it but the whole thing confused Elaine. Maybe Elaine hadn't stopped Amal from overreacting all those years ago as a kind of punishment for the lovely Sue and Tom and all that came with being them. But at what cost? Now she could see how her grandsons had missed out on having a whole family. Now she could see the loss in it all. Maybe if they had grown up with their Australian grandparents in the picture, Joey and Alex would have absorbed some of that privilege and done something good with it.

Elaine considered her own ancestry. What could be shed from her side of the family to give her grandsons more space to breathe?

The sound of the family singing 'Happy Birthday' snapped Elaine out of her thoughts. She opened her handbag and read over the amount on the payout ticket.

'Tayta, what pizza do you want?' Alex asked.

'Any pizza you want, habibi. Get everything you want tonight. I'm paying.'

While Amal and Alex decided what to order, Elaine looked around. Above them were balconies with Italian football jerseys and flags hanging on a line. There were fake plants in fake windows, and the cobblestones on the ground were stencilled on. The walls were all terracotta, sun-drenched pink gyprock.

There was a lamppost that was probably made from plastic. Wine barrels for tables. The designers had committed to the fantasy, but there was no escaping the giant glass-ceiling structure that shielded the diners from the night.

Ever since Elaine had watched *Roman Holiday*, she'd dreamt of going to Italy. This was the closest she would get.

'Ma, did you hear me?' Amal asked.

'Sorry, no.'

'I asked if you want a drink. We have to order them from the bar.'

She thought for a moment. 'Get me scotch.'

'Shit, Tayta is getting lit,' Alex joked.

Amal laughed as she walked away. One of the members of the big family was standing and addressing the rest of the table. They broke into raucous laughter.

Elaine took Alex's hand and kissed it. 'I can't believe how beautiful and big you are now.'

He squinted at her. 'And I can't believe how beautiful and big you are too, Tayta.'

She laughed. 'Shut up, wleh.'

'You okay tonight?' he asked.

'Yeah, baby. I'm okay. Why you ask?'

'You seem distant. Like you're thinking about something.'

'I'm thinking. I'm always thinking.'

'About what?'

'I'm thinking now about this,' she gestured at the balconies.

'It's pretty weird. I hope I get to see the real thing one day.'

'Of course you will see. You will travel the world, albi.'

'Where in the world have you been, Tayta?'

'Me? I been in the village, and I been in Sydney. That's it.'

'Did you ever want to travel?'

She didn't want to burden him. 'No, I'm happy here. I'm happy with my family.'

'But we're all grown up now. You should do what you want.'

'You expect old lady like me to go Italy by myself?'

'I didn't say Italy, but you could go to, like, Tasmania or something. Plus, you're not old.'

'Why I'm gonna go Tasmania? It's probably same as Sydney.'

'I'm going to take you with me somewhere one day, Tayta.'

She kissed his hand again.

Amal returned with the drinks and Elaine had to stop herself from downing the scotch in one go.

'Mum, you went to Europe when you were younger,' Alex said.

'I did. Me and Rita. We spent a month on buses and trains, and back then there weren't smartphones or anything, so we literally had a paper map. Far out. Memories, man.'

Alex looked around. 'Was Italy like this?'

'You know what, it seriously wasn't that far off. Except the people. And it's the people that make the place, really.'

'Are the Italians in Italy like the ones here?'

'Nah, not quite. They're less self-aware of what makes them Italian over there. Like here, the Italians – and not just the Italians, the Greeks, the Lebs – they're too aware of what makes them wog, so they kind of try too hard to perform it. Overseas, they just are it. It's hard to explain.'

Elaine interjected. 'Yes, but it's because when everyone come to Australia back in the day, they leave their culture behind. Here, it's like blank stage. If you don't perform, like you say, then it go away and you end up being same as everybody.'

'Yeah, that's kinda true, Ma, but sometimes it's all a bit forced, you know? Like that Italian jersey right next to the Italian flag up there.'

'You want them to put Australian flag?'

'Not really.'

'Amal, when we first come here, everything – the government, the people, the law – try to make us be like them. Imagine Australia if everyone stop their own culture. Maybe now, yes, stupid people give us bad name, but back then, we have to be Lebanese, Greek, Chinese.'

'I know what you mean,' Alex said.

'You, Alex, Joey, you very lucky that you have two culture.'

'I don't know how you and Jiddo did it back then, Tayta. Came all the way here not knowing English or anything about the place.'

'How I did it? I have no choice is how I did it.'

The pizza was heavenly. It soothed the weird feelings inside of Elaine as it went down.

The big family were packing themselves up to leave, and the man whose birthday it was walked over to their table carrying a hefty piece of cake on a napkin.

'Hello, I was wondering if you'd like this last slice. I promise it's good. My daughter made it and she's a pastry chef,' he said.

Amal replied for them. 'That's so nice of you, thanks. I'm sure Alex would love that. Is it your birthday?'

Elaine stared into the man's kind eyes.

'It is.'

'Happy birthday,' Amal said, and Elaine followed suit.

He thanked them and walked back to his family, who were huddled together smiling at him. Elaine couldn't see a wife among them.

She stood up. 'I'm going to toilet.'

The cashier for the payout was on the other side of the club. By the time she returned to the restaurant to pay, she was panting.

13

Joey was on his third piece of peanut-butter toast when two emblazoned police cars swept into the driveway. A paddy wagon and a Chrysler. At the sight of them through the lounge room window, his soul bolted out the back of the house.

There were three knocks at the door. Each one quaked his innards. Humans were just messes of meat, so easily reverberated. He wanted nothing more than for the boom of those knocks to vaporise him. He wanted to stand there until they turned away, hopped back into the cars and drove off, but he did what he had been conditioned to do by habit, by his mother, by something so terribly obedient inside him. He opened the door to four police officers, two in uniform and two in suits. The female officer wore heavy make-up, fake eyelashes, eyebrows bolstered by ink. She looked like she could reveal a tiny dress underneath her uniform, ready to go clubbing. The familiarity of her style cushioned Joey for a second.

The officer with the most badges on his chest asked if he was Joseph Harb, and when he replied, 'Yes', the officer told him to step out onto the porch. That is where he was arrested. Where he was told that he didn't have to say anything and that anything he said could be used as evidence. The moment, the spotlight cast on him for his neighbours to see. It all floored him. There was something so prestigious and provincial about him in his tracksuit pants and Ivan's jumper, Adidas slides, crumbs on his face from the toast, being directed, morphed, losing responsibility for his everyday, to these four well-made authoritarians. But they were people too. Who ate peanut-butter toast and slept and wanked and fucked up.

Joey had put himself in this position, to be handled by these people who were transformed by fabric and weapons. He had done what he had done and maybe whatever happened to him from here on in was viable. A sort of calm came over him. Maybe he would try to die as soon as he had the opportunity. No, that would make it worse for his mum, Alex, Tayta. He would exercise his right to not say anything. He would wait until he was at the police station. He would call his mum; she would know a lawyer or a relative of a lawyer.

The female officer shut the front door as he was led towards the cars. He was being shut out of his own home. The Greenacre folk, with their heightened ability to sense drama, were already out watching. The young dad from a few doors down filmed with his phone. The nonna from next door squinted from her verandah, and a black Jeep came to a stop in the middle of the road to watch as Joey was folded into the back seat of the police car. At least they didn't use the paddy wagon.

★

They were in a cold interview room like the ones on TV.

The officer asked, 'What's your full name?'

'Joseph Harb.'

'Have you ever gone by any other names, Joseph?'

'I was born Joseph Boyle.'

The coming together of two grandfathers. Joseph after Youssef, and Boyle from the grandfather he couldn't remember.

'And how old are you?'

'Nineteen.'

'Joseph, do you know why you are here?'

'The other officer said something about sexual assault.'

'Sexual assault. That's correct. Do you know a girl named Lisa Morris?'

'No.'

'Lisa is the young woman you and your friends attacked in Bankstown. Does that ring a bell?'

'I didn't attack.'

'Uh-huh. I wouldn't say much more until your lawyer arrives.'

The officer left the room for a while. In that time, Joey, in all his numbness, thought about how his body wasn't attached to anything. He could get up and walk out of this small room and keep walking until he died. That is, if he was ever allowed out of small rooms again.

Another officer came in and, as the door opened, Joey heard his mother from down the hall. Her deep exhalation laced with prayer. He pictured how hard she was holding Alex's arm.

The officer swabbed the inside of Joey's mouth and recorded his fingerprints on a device plugged into a laptop. He was left alone again. The prayers bashed into his head like moths into a light bulb. His mum had tried to believe in God once, but his earliest memory was of her standing on a chair in the lounge room taking down the crucifix that hung next to their baby photos. It was never seen again.

There was a knock on the door and a man in a well-tailored navy suit and baby-blue tie entered. He had grey hair on his temples, tanned skin, friendly eyes like his tie.

He shook Joey's hand and introduced himself as Marco Mamone. 'I'm a friend of your mother's. And I'm your lawyer. What have you said to the officer so far?'

His mother had never mentioned Marco before. 'Just my name and why I'm here.'

'Okay, good. Now, first things first, I'm going to come straight out and ask you for the truth. You have to understand, Joseph, as your lawyer I will take your word as the truth, even if you are lying, and that's what I will use to fight for you. Do you understand what I'm saying? That's my job. I can only go off what you say, and the evidence put forward against you. Do you understand?'

'I think so.'

'Bravo. So, did you sexually assault the complainant?'

'What? No! I mean, I was there, but—'

'Okay, enough. That's all I'm asking for now. Listen, Joey, the allegations put against you are very serious. If convicted, you could be looking at prison time.'

Joey flopped. His soul shrunk to a flicker. He thought it might extinguish at any moment, but then Marco's hand was on his shoulder.

'I've seen the police report filed by Lisa. She does not name you specifically as an assailant. In fact, she explicitly states that you and another male did not harm her, but the crown has charged you with aggravated sexual touching based on what she has told them. Either way, the fact that you did not intervene when the others were carrying out the rape does not look good for you.'

'But was it rape?'

'From how it has been described, yes.'

Joey thought about the other boys. Were they at Bankstown Police Station too? How many of them were already in a prison cell? Their lives, their futures – what were they now? He thought of Lisa. They had drugged her. They had lied to her on the train and messed her the fuck up. He needed to spew.

'Joey, I know you are scared but you need to listen to me. I can probably get you bail but you need to let me help you. Even if it means that what you will say could harm your friends' cases.'

What friends? They were not his friends. Kyri, yes, even though he hadn't called Joey back – it had been three days now – but the others could hang for all he cared.

Marco looked at his shiny watch. 'The sergeant will be back in a minute to formally charge you and they will move you to a holding cell. You will most likely be here at least until tomorrow, provided I can get you bail and your mum can organise the assurance.'

The assurance – his mum had been saving for her boob job and now she was going to spend that money, and probably more, on getting him out of jail. He'd never be able to face her again. The door opened and the sergeant returned with paperwork and another officer. They sat around the table and Marco exchanged pleasantries with the newcomer. Joey was charged. Aggravated sexual touching. The words drilled through his ears and met in the middle of his head in an eruption of absolute emptiness. He marvelled that everything inside of him could be switched off with a few words.

He couldn't feel the handcuffs around his wrists as he was led to the cell. He didn't even hear the door shut behind him. He stood in the one spot, thoughtless, for what seemed like hours. Then he lay on the metal plate that was supposed to be a bed and drifted into a horizontal state of teeth-chattering, leg-quivering, decadent anxiety.

14

On the Turkish soap, the rich man's illegitimate son was preparing to take his father to court and claim a share in the shipping business, which he was completely unaware was a front for human trafficking. The phone rang. Elaine's eyes shot over to the clock. It was 10:06 pm. Her body prepared itself for grief. No-one calling this late had good news. She had to shake her legs out of their stupor to walk to the phone on the kitchen bench.

'Hello?'

'Mum, it's me.' Amal was sobbing.

'What happened?'

'It's Joey. He's been arrested.'

'Why?'

'He was with his mates, and they did … they did something bad to a girl.'

'Not Joey! How?'

'I don't know the details.'

'Okay, I'm coming.'

'There's no point now. Come over in the morning.'

She was damp with sweat underneath her nightie. She shouted, 'Why you not call me earlier? What I'm supposed to do now, Amal? Allah y mowetni!'

'God, taking you isn't going to solve anything, Mum. Sorry, I shouldn't have called so late. I just don't know what the fuck to do.'

'Where's Alex?'

'He's here.'

'Come here, come stay here.'

'Ma, I'll see you tomorrow.'

'Amal? Amal?'

She put the phone down and peered at the golden puddle on the floor. She had pissed herself. She placed her hand over her mouth and screamed. Some of the screaming was only sound but some was curses, hexes, profanities at herself and how her life turned out.

She undressed, mopped the puddle up with her nightie and plopped the sopping thing into the laundry sink. She scalded herself in the shower, leaning against the wall to stay upright. If Joey had really done something to this girl, if word got out, it would be enough to put her in the grave. Her tummy twisted. She retched, but nothing came up. She promised the devil her life right then and there if this all turned out to be a big mistake. But it wouldn't be a mistake, because Joey was a fool.

She put the water pressure up to dilute the nasty thought about her own flesh and blood. It didn't work. He was lazy and Amal had indulged him too much. He smoked. She was sure he took drugs. He worked in a supermarket. He'd flunked the HSC. Sins of the father. She cursed his father. And then she cursed her father and the men who came before him and all the men to come after him.

She realised she was red hot, partly from the shower and partly because a rage had started to fill her. She stepped out of the shower and dried herself. The only other time she had felt a similar rage was when she was halfway through menopause and had heaved the cabinet with the nice plates across the tiled floor. She had asked Youssef to move it for months so that she could dust behind it. Some of the plates and a bottle of arak had smashed, and she had left the debris as a trophy for Youssef to see.

She wanted to act on her rage in a similar way now, but she didn't know how. She could break the ugly vase in the formal lounge that Michael and Sonia had given her one Mother's Day, or strangle the yapping terrier from next door, even though it had been quiet all day.

She took a deep breath, popped two aspirins from the top drawer of the vanity into her mouth and swallowed them dry. She lay on her bed naked, her hair soaking the pillow. She shut her eyes and let the images play. First, she saw skinny Joey behind bars, crying, then Amal, haggard, reaching out for Simon. And then her blasted mind showed her something she hadn't seen since it had happened. An uncle, a bristly chin, kisses on her tummy, kisses on her little thigh, kisses on her—

She jumped out of bed, put on her robe and charged into the kitchen.

She set about making sambousik. She did that when things had gone bad. And conveniently it meant she ended up with food that she could ferry to her children's houses.

She rolled out the dough with the rolling pin she'd bought from a charity shop in the eighties. The one she'd stormed after Amal and Michael with when they drove her up the wall as children. They'd cowered away from her fury like lambs from the slaughter. She'd have sooner hit herself with it, and they had realised that by the time they were in school. Amal had laughed and sauntered away to her bedroom when Elaine lunged for the kitchen drawer, hot from one of her teenage comebacks. In the end, the rolling pin had become a flag Elaine waved for a minute of peace.

She sprinkled flour on the grey benchtop. The one Youssef had installed with his bare hands all those years ago. The one Amal had perched on after school to tell her she wasn't cut out for study, too practical to sit down and read. She'd fed her daughter dollops of kibbeh in between kneading the mince and burghul with her fists.

She pushed her anger into the dough as she cut circular portions with the rim of a scotch glass. The surviving one from an old set of six. She could have used any glass, but she had developed the belief that the sambousik wouldn't turn out right if the dough wasn't cut with that same scotch glass.

She stopped, rinsed the cup, glugged whisky into it and sculled. Her Joey. When he was a child he'd hidden from big men and loud noises, holding her hand or clenching Amal's skirt for fear of getting lost.

She moved back to the round pieces of dough. She spooned the filling into the middle of one, flipped it over and rolled the edges shut. When she died, she wanted to be buried holding the rolling pin across her chest like a warrior with his sword.

The microwave clock ticked over to 12:00 am. Elaine had

made four trays of sambousik. Two of them would need to go in the freezer in the laundry.

During the hour or so of sleep Elaine managed, she dreamt of an angelic baby girl crawling around the backyard. Baby girls in dreams were a good omen, a prize. At least, that's what her grandmother used to say.

She thought to call Amal first thing in the morning but decided she would go straight to her house. She didn't bother brushing her hair or teeth, just splashed some water on her face, put on the same dress she had worn the previous day and backed her old Corolla out of the driveway. It was barely 7:00 am. She should have let the engine warm up but there was a haste in her bones that was out of control.

Amal was in the driveway about to hop in her car when Elaine roughly parked on the road. They hugged and Amal cried into Elaine's shoulder. Alex appeared in his shorts on the front porch, rubbing at his eyes.

When Amal pulled away from her, Elaine asked, 'Does anyone else know?'

'What are you talking about, Mum?'

'Anyone find out or just us?'

'You think that's what I'm fucking worried about right now?' Amal went to open her car door.

'Kiffou Joey?' Elaine said.

'He's a wreck. I didn't see him, but the lawyer said he's a wreck.'

'Amal, is it … is it …?'

'Is it rape?'

Elaine winced at the word.

'Yes, Ma. It is. But apparently Joey didn't do any of it. It was the other boys. He was just there.'

'I tell him these boys are no good. I tell him!'

'I've gotta go. I'm meeting the lawyer at the police station. Joey should be getting out on bail. Stay here with Alex. He's not going to school today.'

Elaine watched her daughter reverse the car out and drive down the street. She tried to remember her aunts' saying about life being a maze with no end but she couldn't place the words the right way. Alex came and put his arm around her shoulders.

'Don't worry, Tayta. I think it will be okay.'

She rested her head on his porcelain chest for a moment and savoured his smell.

Inside, she busied herself cleaning Amal's oven to a state it probably hadn't been since it was installed. Alex, sitting at the bar eating a bowl of Coco Pops, said, 'You know she's gonna hate that you've done that.'

'Your mum hate everything I do.'

She couldn't stop thinking about the girl as she scrubbed everything in the kitchen. Where did she live? What did she look like? What kind of family did she come from? And yet it felt completely invasive and futile to wonder these things. She made her way to the laundry where there were at least two baskets of washing to be done. Amal had a front-loader, which was treachery in Elaine's eyes. She doubled the dose of detergent, slammed the door shut with her foot and switched it on.

15

Marco came into the cell in the morning to explain that the police had agreed to release Joey on bail. His next court date was in three weeks. He had to surrender his passport and was placed on an 8:00 pm curfew at his mother's home.

Marco delivered his homily swiftly and with a considered amount of jargon. He had a finesse that eased Joey. He was dressed well again in another tailored suit, hair swept to the side, and he smelt like the ocean, which had never seemed further away. Marco could have been delivering a death sentence and Joey still would have felt at ease. Well, at ease was a stretch. It was like he was observing his situation, privy to it in a benign way.

Joey followed Marco out of the cell through the entrails of the police complex and into the small room where his mother was waiting. His knees buckled as he approached her, and his head ended up in her lap. She had half risen to catch him, but the weight of his body sat her back down. He wept and drew deep breaths that sounded like he was drowning. Probably because he was drowning. She held him tight and kissed his head, her tears dampening his hair, his saliva soaking her leggings. She smelt like their kitchen.

Marco left the room clumsily.

'I'm … I'm so sorry,' Joey said,

He thought she was about to say something but she cleared her throat instead.

'Ma, say something. I'm sorry.'

Marco re-entered the room. 'We're going to have to go. There's a shitstorm of media out there. One of the boys just went out the front and his father smashed a journo's camera, so we'll have to go out the back. I'll bring the car around and drive Joey home so we can make a quick getaway. Amal, you follow us in your car. Officer Vin will lead you out.'

The officer appeared and handed Joey a sandwich bag with his phone in it. Joey floated behind him, his mother in tow, until a door was pushed open and it was daylight and the magpies sang as if he hadn't just spent the night in a jail cell. Marco pulled up in a black Audi and Joey got in.

'Here, wear this.' Marco passed him a hat.

Joey pulled it on tight and put his head between his knees as the car began to move. 'Is it that bad out there?' He didn't recognise his own voice.

'Just don't put your head up.'

The roar of the car's engine wasn't enough to stifle the camera clicks, the incoherent journalist mumbles, the scrambling as the car emerged at the front of the building. He didn't look up the whole way home.

Tayta's car was parked out the front of their house.

'Get a good night's sleep and I'll be in touch tomorrow,' Marco said.

Joey wished Marco would keep driving all the way to the beach and into the ocean. He hadn't given any thought to how Tayta would react, how he would explain himself to her. He was glad Jiddo Youssef was dead. Joey had visited her that night. He had slept over. She had been open and sincere. And right before that he had been in the car park where it all happened.

His mother pulled in to the driveway and got out to talk to Marco. He thought about waiting until she was done to walk in with her, a cushion for the shame, but decided to rip it off like a bandaid.

Tayta and Alex were sitting in the lounge room. The TV was switched off. Alex glanced up from his phone, didn't say anything, and Tayta had her arms crossed, staring at the floor. Joey paused for a second not knowing where to go or what to say and then she looked up at him very slowly. Her eyes were red. She stood and extended her hand to him. Confused, Joey placed his hand in hers limply and she shook it hard.

'Mabrouk ya, Mr Joey. Congratulations. You out on bail? Good boy, good boy.' Her voice was light, singsong. 'What, the cat take your tongue? You don't have nothing to say?'

Joey tried to pull his hand away, but her grip was enthusiastic. 'What do you want me to—'

'What I want you to say?'

With her free hand she whacked Joey across the face. The boom echoed through his empty head. She stayed there frozen in time with her arm still poised.

Joey stumbled towards his room, blistering with embarrassment. He had never seen Tayta smack anything.

★

Their faces were on the morning news. Joey's was a tagged photo from his Instagram, baby-faced in school uniform and a dry-fit cap. He had his arm around Kyri who was cropped out of the photo. He was grimacing, eyes wide and tongue wedged between his top lip and teeth. He looked deranged because it was supposed to be a funny photo. It was taken on their last day of school, outside KFC.

He watched the TV until his head was lead, until his thoughts were a series of thuds. His mum was in the shower. Alex was out. Joey called Emma but there was no answer. He left the house and started jogging.

He ended up out the front of Kyri's house. From the street he could hear Kyri's mother yelling and his father trying to calm her down. He walked up the side passage to Kyri's bedroom window. Kyri was in a ball at the side of his bed. Joey tapped the window and Kyri helped him through. They sat on the bed and stared at the ceiling.

Kyri started chanting quietly. 'What the fuck have we done? What the fuck have we done?'

The walls of Joey's stomach came together.

Kyri went on. 'I can't go to jail, Joey. I can't.'

'Get up. Let's go,' Joey said.

'Where?'

'I don't know. Let's just go.'

'We can't get stoned. The lawyers said not to do dodgy shit.'

'I know. Don't worry, we won't get stoned. Let's just go somewhere. Do you wanna listen to your mum crying?'

They went back through the window and down the side of the house. Joey's phone rang, a landline number starting in 07. He switched his phone off. They smoked cigarettes as they walked to Parry Park. He stared into the cars that passed, sure that the people in them were looking at him.

They sat on the steps outside the community hall. He had been there years ago for the pre-wedding party of a cousin whose name he couldn't recall. She had been wrapped in tulle and was marrying a Bible boy who probably thought he couldn't do any better. To Joey and Kyri's left was the giant Australian National Sports Club that looked like a new-age mosque.

'I didn't touch her, man. I'm the only one that didn't touch her,' Kyri said.

'It doesn't matter. We were there.'

'Surely they'll understand, but. We were only on the sidelines. We didn't actually do anything. I even legged it before anything really went down'

'I don't know, bro. The lawyers will know what to do. Why the fuck did you leave me there that night?'

'What did you expect me to do, Joey? You were off your fucking face. Did you want me to carry you? I had to get out of there. I didn't want to be a part of that shit.'

'And you think I did?'

'Well, why didn't you leave, then?'

'You think I didn't try?' Joey raised his voice. 'That fucking animal kept pulling me back.'

Kyri whispered, 'Did you do anything with her?'

'No. But I didn't stop anything, either.'

They sat in silence for a minute and then Kyri turned his head right away from Joey and asked, 'Was she fighting against them? I know it doesn't matter. But was she?'

Joey went cold. 'No.'

'Did she tell them to fuck off? Did she scream, shout, hit them?'

'No.' Joey took a deep breath. 'But she was high. She was outnumbered by a bunch of blokes she didn't know. She saw Haz hitting me. Imagine what she would have been thinking.'

Kyri sobbed into his hands. 'I don't know what to do. I can't believe this shit. My parents are losing it. I thought … I thought we'd get out of here or something, you know? I thought we were bigger than this shithole.'

Joey held Kyri tight around his shoulders.

16

Here Elaine was, the day after Joey's release, curtains drawn, lights off, heart palpitating, watching images of her grandson – his friends, footage of a car park in Bankstown, hooded young men entering police stations, leaving police stations – being broadcast on TV. There was her surname, a word that meant 'war' in Arabic, being blasted into homes across the country.

In truth, she had imagined such a moment to be a lot more debilitating and traumatic, but something about the reportage made it surreal enough that the rapists being described sounded like actors and not her very real grandson and his friends. To anyone who didn't know the full story, she was the grandmother of a monster.

The 6:00 pm news presenter described the group as Middle Eastern, but Elaine knew that only Joey and one of the others had Middle Eastern ancestry. Besides, they were all born in Sydney like Joey was.

Elaine pictured years of lying low until it blew over – having groceries delivered, not leaving the house. Instead of calming her, the thought made an insatiable fury erupt in her chest. Men, always senseless men doing things without any concern for the repercussions. Always men deciding what way to go. Like their dicks were compasses. She cursed all the dicks in the world, bid them fall off their hosts. So often she felt manlier than any of the men in her family and she didn't have a dick. She hoped the boys were tried by female judges and juries who would not give them any concessions. But one of those boys was her grandson. Her thoughtless grandson.

She switched the television off, cast herself into quiet and darkness. There had to be something she could do to control the situation – make it play out fittingly. A promise she could make to some deity, a spell she could conjure. If only she could speak to the djinn, like her grandmother. At that thought her mobile phone buzzed against the coffee table, casting a wicked glow into the room and startling her.

It was Amal. 'Ma, you're not watching the TV, are you?'

'The TV? Kess ekht el TV. Yes, I'm watching TV, Amal.' She was yelling.

'Okay, calm down a bit.'

'Calm down! You think I can calm down? The fucking country know everything!'

'We can't do anything about it. I'm coming over.'

Amal's complacency triggered her. 'No, no, Amal. Mabadi anyone here. I don't want see anyone. I want to lie in the bed and not wake up to see morning.' She hung up and swore loudly.

There were things that had happened to Elaine that nobody needed to know. For instance, she had never told her children about the miscarriage she'd had in between their births. A dark little thing. It had come out of her into the toilet at the emergency room in Canterbury Hospital. Elaine knew from the minute she had laid eyes on it, bobbing in the water, that she never wanted to think about it again.

No, there was nothing good lurking in the dark alleys of the family. None of it needed to be out in the open, and neither did Joey's ordeal. That kind of stuff led people to think of you differently, treat you differently. As a child, if Elaine had seen something she wasn't meant to, like the hiding spot for money, her mum would swipe her index finger across pursed lips. The action used to render Elaine entirely wordless. She wished she could stand before every living soul and swipe a finger across her lips.

The house phone rang, followed by her mobile. She ignored them both. The relatives must have seen the news too. It would be them calling, disguising their hunger for insider information in words of concern.

Two weeks passed by with Elaine ignoring more calls, checking messages occasionally, and barely leaving the house – except the time she went to the VIP lounge in Campsie in the middle of the night to relieve some stress. One of the voice messages she had listened to on WhatsApp was from a cousin complaining that she wasn't answering her phone. Their other cousin had died. He gave her the details of the funeral.

There really wasn't much Elaine could do to avoid going. They had all come to Youssef's and she had to reciprocate the gesture. The obligation to wejbet was part of her DNA. She could feel its pull as she waited by the front door for Amal and Michael to pick her up. They weren't as bound to the community as she was, but it was important to her that, while she was alive, they respected tradition and came to funerals. Plus, Elaine had convinced Amal that if she didn't go, she would be suggesting to the community that she was ashamed, and if she was ashamed, the relatives would immediately assume her son was guilty. They had to let their tails out from in between their legs at some point.

Luckily the story had only been in the news on the day after Joey's arrest, and she hoped that her relatives had moved on to the next scandal. She also hoped that the three of them could pay their respects quickly and leave.

Michael beeped the horn of his new BMW and Elaine hustled out of the house. She didn't want to give her children any reason to be cross with her since they had so teeteringly agreed to go to the funeral in the first place.

When Michael found out about Joey's arrest, he had called Elaine and blasted her ear off about how he always knew his nephew was a low-life and how it was all Amal's fault for the way she raised her boys. As though Elaine hadn't already been dealing with enough, she'd had to hear that too. She had tried to reason with Michael and persuade him to support his sister, and she had tried to convince him that Joey wasn't capable of such a thing, but Michael wouldn't listen. In the end he'd agreed to send Amal a text message just to make Elaine happy. And when Amal received that text message, she had called Elaine, crying, bruised by her brother's insensitivity.

Amal moved to the back seat so Elaine could sit in the front. The tension was thick. She was surprised that the two had even agreed to ride in the same car.

She reached over the console and kissed her son on the cheek. 'Mabrouk for the car, habibi.'

All new cars looked the same to her.

The silence in the car persisted until they were halfway down the M5. She couldn't handle it anymore. 'Any news from the lawyer, Amal?'

'No.'

Michael tapped his fingers on the steering wheel and said, 'How did you find this lawyer?'

'Why?'

'Just curious.'

'Is that what you're curious about in this whole thing, Michael?'

'What are you on about?'

'Nothing.'

'Say what you wanna say, Amal.'

'Oh, just drive. I'm not bothered for this shit.'

'Bothered for what? For making our family look like absolute trash?'

Amal raised her voice. 'Fuck, how long have you been holding on to that one for? Have your piece, go. Tell me what you think of me and my sons. You think you can make me feel worse than I already fucking feel?'

Elaine was compelled to interject. 'Khalas!'

Amal wasn't finished. 'And if you're so interested to know how I found the lawyer, we met on a date! We're dating.'

If Elaine's family were a cake, it would be a big, tall cake that the baker dropped right after adding the final touches. She searched in her heart for a response to her daughter's admission, but nothing came out.

Amal sobbed and blew her nose.

Michael laughed sarcastically. 'Wise move.'

'You know what, Michael? Fuck you. Pull over. I'm getting out of the car.'

They were still in the tunnel so Elaine didn't even bother panicking at the request. 'Maybe Michael is saying, for Joey, it's not a good time for him to know about this.'

'Yeah, well, that's why I don't want you guys to say anything. And Michael, not even to Sonia.'

'Don't tell me what I can and can't tell my wife.'

Amal mumbled something under her breath and Michael floored the car. Elaine cursed her cousin for dying amid this whole dilemma.

The service was underway when the three of them arrived at the church and they slipped into the black puddle of mourners. Elaine took a veil from the basket and put it over her head to really remain inconspicuous. Amal did the same. There were no speeches, only prayer from the priest and half a homily. At Youssef's funeral the four grandchildren had all said something, and Elaine had made sure that there were three priests and a bishop present. Not that she and Youssef had ever been that faithful, but it was a trend among the community to pay more than one priest to conduct the service. If you didn't, people talked.

As soon as the priest farewelled the congregation, Elaine and her children went straight to the car to avoid any interactions outside the church. The real test, however, was the openness of Rookwood Cemetery. Any of the relatives could come up to them there, and they couldn't avoid going because that's where the family of the deceased lined up for people to pay their respects.

There was more silence on the drive to Rookwood. When they parked the car Elaine said, 'We go see Dad after.' She knew

Amal and Michael never came to visit their father's grave. She hadn't been in months either.

There were far fewer people at the burial, but she spotted the two women who would likely bring up Joey's fiasco, gasbagging behind their hands. Elaine and her children stood quite some distance off under a tree so that it looked like they were just there to shade themselves from the sun.

The coffin went in the ground and the sand was sprinkled. As soon as the deceased's family stood in line for the onslaught of respect, she charged over the graves with Amal and Michael in tow and said, 'Allah y yerhamo', with her hand on her heart. The whole thing took less than a minute. She had shown her face and that's all that mattered.

The flamboyant crypts of the Lebanese and Greeks and Russians began materialising in the distance as they walked away from the burial and towards Youssef's grave. Some people, like the cousin who'd just died, had to be buried in the Catholic section, as the spaces in the Orthodox section were filling up and becoming more and more expensive. Luckily, Elaine and Youssef had bought a double plot, so her final resting place was already claimed. She tried not to think about it because knowing where your flesh would eventually rot was bizarre.

She stopped, exhausted, and spun around on the spot, dizzied by the graves and by how predictable life was. You were born, you were married, there were happy times, shameful ones, and after all of that you died. Where would her children and grandchildren end up when all the space was taken and bodies were layered three, four, five on top of each other? Was the earth deep enough to contain all the people still to come? She shuddered at the thought.

On their way to Youssef's spot, they passed gigantic monuments to young men and women who had succumbed to tumours, motorbike accidents, suicide. Elaine knew their stories from encountering the families, back when she used to visit the grave often. There was the yiayia in the row over from Youssef whose granddaughter left a fresh Snickers bar every time she visited. Apparently the yiayia had become obsessed with the snack after her dementia set in. There was no Snickers on her grave today, just dust.

When they arrived at Youssef's modest tombstone Elaine was ashamed to see a pile of leaves and a meat pie wrapper at its base. She dropped to her knees and stuffed the leaves and the wrapper into a plastic bag she had in her handbag. Amal and Michael stood beside her, their arms around one another's shoulders. Nothing like a dead father to bring the family together. She finished stuffing the leaves in the bag and then licked her finger to create adhesive for the minute bits of dirt on the granite. She wept while she worked.

'He was a good man, your Youssef. A good man.'

The line, in Arabic, sliced through the air like a spear. Elaine whipped around to see the two gabbling relatives from earlier approaching.

She stood up. 'Yes, he was.'

She was as cold as her husband's bones beneath her. The ladies ambled over and, after they had all greeted each other, one of them gestured towards the plastic bag and said, 'I don't blame you for not coming for a while with all that your family has been going through.'

Maybe Elaine could smash their heads against the tombstone, spend the rest of her days in prison and fall for a woman in there who would protect her.

The crones turned to Amal and delivered their lines one after the other without pause.

'Terrible, just terrible what they are saying in the news. No-one knows what to believe.'

'Who knows what goes on in the minds of young men when they are trying to outdo each other?'

It took everything in her, but Elaine was determined not to say anything. She would let them finish and move on. Michael and Amal on the other hand were red-faced and ready to burst. They lacked the composure that the village had hardwired in her. Australia, Sydney, Greenacre: it allowed them to be rageful. She didn't mind it so much, but she wished that today they would not talk back to the relatives. It was futile. There wasn't anything in the world that could combat their negativity.

The lanky relative went on. 'Anyway, maybe it's a good thing Youssef isn't around to see his namesake being rubbished.'

Michael replied, 'It's never a good thing to not have your father around', and in doing so he set them up for their next critique. She saw it coming.

'No, that's right, it isn't? And maybe Joseph wouldn't have ended up in this mess if his father …' The woman gestured limply towards Amal, who stormed away.

'Oh, I hope we haven't upset her. Well, it was nice seeing you, habibti. We really do wish all the best for your family in court.'

Elaine's feet bore into the ground. She wished she could prematurely crawl into the final resting place beneath her.

17

Joey spent three weeks in his bedroom smoking cigarettes out of the window, only emerging to use the toilet and microwave. His boss at work had sent a text when the story was in the news to say it might be best if he didn't come in for the foreseeable future. Joey had just straight-up typed a resignation email and sent it through.

Kyri was only replying to Joey's texts matter-of-factly. Initially Emma wouldn't answer any of Joey's calls or texts but more recently when he tried to call the number was unavailable. When he'd dialled from Alex's phone the call had gone through, which meant she had blocked his number. There was so much to feel sick about, but Emma hating him was a real infection. She was supposed to be his lifebuoy in a lake of tedium. He wondered what Ivan would be thinking of him. He checked to see that he was still following him back on Instagram and he was. Joey had deleted all his content and changed his profile name on the day of his release. He sent Ivan a message, *Hey man.*

When the day came for the hearing at Bankstown Court House, to decide if he would be tried by a judge only instead of a regular jury, Marco all but guaranteed it would be approved. The public were too aware of the case since it had been covered widely in the media. Kyri had had the same hearing only a week prior and was granted a judge-only trial.

Joey had no concept of the judicial system apart from what he had seen on TV, and most of the time that wasn't even set in Australia. He just agreed with what Marco suggested because he trusted him, which was stupid. Trusting people had landed him where he was now. But he found it easy to admit to himself that he had no hand in how his life would play out anymore. The thought sometimes comforted him, but mostly it just added to the turmoil he'd felt since his arrest.

Inside the courtroom, the bob-haircut stenographer chatted idly with the presiding police officer about *My Kitchen Rules* as everyone waited for the magistrate to enter. Marco was sitting to Joey's left, shaking his leg and licking his thumb to flick through notes, and on the bench directly behind him were Joey's mother, Alex and Tayta. He avoided turning around to look at them but could hear their rustling through handbags for chewing gum and their patting of clothes and their biting of nails.

In his line of sight there were TVs, cameras, speakers, microphones, cabling and computers. It smelt like paper and coffee and hair gel. Just as he thought to ask Marco if they would be waiting much longer, the public entrance clicked open loudly. Everybody twisted to see a bearded man with thick arms forcing the door shut against the pressure of its self-closing mechanism.

Alex flicked back around to face Joey and was trying keenly to say something with his eyes. Joey looked again at the man striding down the aisle and the hairs on his arms stood up like an army. It was Simon Boyle. His father.

Before he had time to process anything, the magistrate entered and everybody stood up and sat back down and everything was underway.

The most awkward thing about Joey's father bursting their bubble was the circumstance of his resurrection. He had finally come back for them, but it was because his son was a criminal. Joey and Alex stole glances at each another in the café – their whole family at the table.

His mother recapped the court proceedings. She had drunk too much coffee. 'It's a good thing. A good thing – being tried by the judge only, you know. Because God knows what racists they could put in the jury. They'd never let you off. Especially with all the media stuff about you guys being Middle Eastern.'

His father shifted in his seat. It struck Joey that the man was handsome, and the thought reminded him to look around the café to make sure nobody had recognised him.

His mother went on, because she didn't know how to talk about anything else. 'Like the magistrate said, it wouldn't be fair because the case had so much publicity, too much open prejudice around it all. Marco is pretty hopeful that he will be acquitted.'

Joey was a subject.

'How did you find the lawyer?' His father's voice was croaky.

She chewed her lip. 'It was a recommendation.'

Alex ignored everything, scrolling through his phone. 'Can we go?'

Joey realised the barista was looking at him, or through him.

'Yeah, c'mon boys. Simon, where are you staying?'

'Oh, I haven't booked anything yet, actually.'

'Come to ours. You can have Alex's room.'

Joey and Alex glared at her. Was she on drugs? How was she suddenly inviting the ex-husband she hadn't seen in thirteen years to stay at their place? Surely he wouldn't take up the offer.

'Ah, yeah, I guess. If that's alright with you guys.'

Joey made a sound.

His mother kicked him under the table and said, 'Of course it is. Yulla, let's go.'

It was impossible to reconcile that Alex, him and the two hopeless adults who had given birth to them were going to be under the same roof. Joey wasn't going to leave his bedroom.

Joey woke up panting from a dream in which his mouth was full of sand. The sunlight flooding through the window meant it had to be the later part of the morning. He peered over the side of the bed to see Alex on the blow-up mattress tapping on his phone.

'What time is it?'

'Ten thirty.'

It was Saturday, which meant their mother had left for her shift at the beauty salon already. Which meant their father was somewhere around their house, willy-nilly.

'Where is he? Have you been out yet?' Joey asked.

'I think in the kitchen. No, and I'm busting to go to the toilet, but I don't wanna go out on my own. It's awks. What are we meant to talk about?'

'Piss in that water bottle. I'm happy to stay in here until Mum gets back.'

Alex stifled his laugh in the pillow. 'Joey, we can't.'

'Fuck my life. I'm gonna kill Mum.'

'What if we told Tayta to come over?'

'Honestly can't be arsed for her, either.'

'Well then, we should get out of the house, take him somewhere, make it less awks.'

'Alex, are you forgetting that my face is all over the fucking news?'

'I mean, it's not anymore.'

'I'm not going out.'

The night before, they hadn't really had to interact. It was just a take-out dinner in the lounge room. Tayta had come over too and was oddly courteous to the point of flirting with her ex-son-in-law. She had spoken about how Jiddo Youssef had withered away and Joey's father had gazed at his interwoven hands pensively. Their mother had spoken about the house, which their stranger-father had lived in too, and the repairs it needed. And then there had been a catch-up on how the Australian grandparents were doing (which was well). Then they had gone to sleep, Joey in his bed, his father in Alex's, and Alex on the floor in Joey's room. But of course Joey had hardly slept. He was too wound up by the rage that his father's return had brought on.

His father was staying two nights and said that he would come back for the trial in three months. He was living in Surfers Paradise. He had set himself up as a mobile mechanic and was enjoying beach life.

Joey hadn't been to Surfers but had heard from the guys in the year above him at school about the terrible time they had at schoolies. Apparently they were followed around by cops and shop assistants and felt like they were only allowed into the clubs because there were no obvious reasons to reject them. They'd expected to pull heaps of girls but very few had shown interest so they spent most of their time in the hotel room getting high and ordering Uber Eats. And then some private school kid from the eastern suburbs who was staying in a room a few doors down fell off the balcony and died and the hotel became a crime scene. They couldn't escape fast enough.

Even though he could pass as Aussie, Joey had no desire to go to the Gold Coast, even less now that he knew his father lived there.

'I think he's coming,' Alex said as he raised the doona up over his torso. They stared at each other and then at the door. There was a knock and the door opened and there was their father in a T-shirt and shorts, saying, 'I'm about to cook breakfast. You boys getting up?' as though he had done so a million times before.

It was less awkward once they had washed their faces and sat at the dining table. They watched while he fried eggs in butter (their mum only ever fried them in olive oil) and cooked bacon. He must have gone out for the bacon, but he had no car, which meant he'd gone to the corner store that no-one ever bought groceries from. He moved around the kitchen with ease, knew what cupboard the pans and plates were in. Here he was, this man that had jizzed Joey into existence, trotting through the house, sleeping in Alex's bed, shedding his ginger pubes in the bathroom, cooking them breakfast.

He was thicker than in the wedding video, had the kind of physique Joey wished he could have. His clothes were daggy, probably from Lowes. Alex gestured with his eyes towards the man's feet. His flip-flops looked like they were made for hiking. The only word to describe them was *ugly*. Most of the talk revolved around Alex and what subjects he was taking at school, what his friends were like, his job at Macca's. Then there was a lot of talk about Netflix shows (in which they had very similar tastes).

Joey began cleaning up as soon as they finished eating, hoping that his father might have somewhere to be, some old friends to catch up with, and that would be the end of it, but instead his father sat back in the dining chair, spread his legs. 'And what about you, Joey?'

He threw the cutlery into the sink. 'What about me?'

'You were working … before?'

'Yeah.'

'What were you doing?'

'Woolies produce section.'

'Bit of a fruity boy, then?'

The joke was deplorable. 'What?'

'Nothing. So, I was thinking we could go do something, get out of the house. A hike or something in the Royal National Park.'

Alex looked at Joey for a reply.

'I don't really feel like going out,' Joey said.

'Come on, it's a nice day for it.'

Joey was suddenly egged on by something to be honest, cutting. 'Mate, thanks for coming and all but, like, you don't have to do this. We're all good. Plus, how do you expect to get to the national park? Hitchhiking?' It was easy to say, washing the dishes, staring out of the window into the backyard.

His father walked out the back and lit a cigarette.

Alex whispered to Joey, 'Don't have to be a dick. He's trying.'

'Trying? For what? I'm not about to sit around a campfire and sing "Waltzing Matilda".'

'I know, but like, we literally just have to get through this one day with him.'

'So what do you expect me to do?'

'I don't know. Act normal.'

'Alex, seriously, you need to shut the fuck up.'

'You shut up. Stop acting like you own everybody.'

Joey looked out the window and saw his father turn towards the house, then back to the garden. Alex took the empty milk bottle out to the bins then walked over to him. They stood side by side chatting and pointing around the neighbourhood. He scrubbed hard at the burnt butter on the pan, cursing the cook.

He spent the rest of the afternoon in his bedroom. His father and Alex were watching a movie in the lounge room. When he heard his mother arrive, he waited for the greeting murmur between the three to die down before he emerged and followed her into the kitchen where she was unloading groceries.

He was on the war path. 'Are you sick in the head or something? Why the fuck did you tell him to stay here? Do you know how awkward it's been?'

'God, you gave me a fright, Joey. And hello to you too.' She lowered her voice to a whisper. 'Why are you in your room? Why don't you go sit with them?'

'What is going on here? Am I in a fucking alternate universe? Are we ignoring the fact that you kept this guy a secret this whole time and he's suddenly back? And that I might be going to jail?'

'Joey, please, I can't do this right now.'

He yelled, 'Do what right now?'

The film in the lounge room paused for a moment before resuming.

'I'm going to a friend's place for dinner tonight. I'm gonna put this roast on for you three and I'm going,' she said.

'What? You're leaving us with him again? You orchestrated this shit, didn't you? This was all planned. Just say it.'

She turned to him with wet eyes and flushed cheeks. 'Joey, please. Please.'

He stormed out of the kitchen and slammed the door to his bedroom.

The film stopped again and there was chatter in the kitchen. A minute later there was a knock at the door and in walked his father. Joey scoffed and stood up to leave but his dad shut the door and stood against it.

'I'm going to need you to get away from the door, please,' Joey said.

'I just want to talk. I know this is complicated, and I know you're scared and in trouble. Trust me, I know the feeling.'

'What would you know about being in trouble? It's in your convict genes, is it?' Joey's words came out hysterical, singsong.

'Joey—'

'Don't call me Joey. I'm Joseph to you, understand?' They were standing face to face and a blob of Joey's spit landed on his father's shoulder.

'I've been where you are right now, mate.'

'What are you on about?' Joey asked.

'I got into a brawl when I was your age. In a kebab shop in the Cross. We got arrested.'

Joey clapped slowly. 'Damn, you're a heavy motherfucker, aren't you?' The sarcasm poured from his mouth, plopped on the floor.

'You have a very bad attitude, you know that?'

'Thanks. I get it from Mum.'

Joey looked out the window at the backyard that Jiddo Youssef used to take care of. It had become a dust bowl. He could hear his mother busying herself in the kitchen exaggeratedly. Drawers slamming, cutlery tinkling.

'Can you get the fuck away from the door?' he asked again.

'I told you, I just want to talk. Why don't you sit down on the bed?'

For a second, Joey was overcome by the desire to obey him, which had more to do with the man's heftiness than the fact that he had any sort of authority over him, and then without any thought, he grabbed his father's arm and tried to pull him away. His father didn't budge. He tried again with more force and the door rattled against the pressure of their staunch bodies. After a second of tussling, his dad hit him across the face with the palm of his hand. Joey punched him back in the chest and in a moment they were on the air mattress that Alex hadn't put away, brawling and tangled in the two-metre phone-charger cord.

His mum burst into the room, yelling at them to stop. Alex stood behind her, cupping his hand over his mouth. His father got up and stood against the wall. Joey pushed past his family, barefoot, shirtless and proud and ran for the front door. His dad bounded after him, knocking into things.

They made it to the reserve at the end of the street before Joey turned and yelled at him to fuck off and then his body shut down in one convulsive sweep and he dropped to his knees and cried thick tears into the dry grass. His shoulders heaved to the rhythm of his panting, the crying onslaught following its own trajectory. His father dropped to his own knees in front of Joey and wrapped his arms around him. Lorikeets squawked overhead, his father sat back and lit a cigarette. It rested between his fingers so lightly that it could have slipped away without him realising.

'I was arrested another time too. That's why I had to leave. I was in jail most of your life.'

His words entered Joey intravenously. They swam around inside of him, soothing sores in his nervous system, palpitating fright in his chest, ageing him.

In the middle of the park, sitting cross-legged across from him, his father said, 'I crippled somebody.'

The gravity of his father's words carried them back home, grubby with sweat and anticipation. His mum and Alex stood in the front yard with their phones to their ears. They dropped them to their sides in unison when they saw them approaching.

His mum stormed into the house, but Alex stomped over to them. 'What is wrong with you two? You think she needs this crap?'

His dad reached out and put his hand on Alex's shoulder and Joey continued to the front door.

'Mum!'

'You have the hide to yell out my name—'

'Stop talking and sit down right here.'

Joey pointed to the sofa nearest the front door. He expected her to resist, to tell him to shut his mouth, but she must have read his face. His father and Alex entered the room and needed no direction. They sat across from his mum. His dad put his arm around Alex's shoulders. Joey expected Alex to flinch, but he didn't.

He pointed at his father. 'Tell Alex what you just told me.'

'Joey, why don't we chill for the rest of the day and maybe talk tomorrow before my flight? Everyone is a little exhau—'

'Maybe talk about it tomorrow? Maybe talk about it tomorrow? You think you have an option, do you? You think you can just come here and fucking call the shots. And you' – Joey spun around to his mother, his accusatory finger poised in the air – 'you better be prepared to talk too. Today is the day you both come clean to us. No more bullshit. You think we've gone through our whole lives believing your crap?' He looked at his father. 'Start talking.'

'Amal, I …'

She stared at her lap.

His father pulled his arm away from Alex and put his head in his hands before taking a deep breath and looking up. 'I don't know how to start.'

Joey spoke up. 'Okay, I'll help. Why did you and Mum break up?'

'Well, it's tied to what I told you earlier.'

'So start with that.'

His father turned to Alex. 'When you were around three years old, Alex, I … I got into an incident that resulted in a man becoming quadriplegic … because of something … stupid I did.'

'I think you are misunderstanding what is happening here. You and Mum are going to give details, do you hear? No talk of incidents. Details.' Joey looked at his mother. Why wasn't she saying anything? His father started again.

'When you boys were kids, I went out with my mates. I

hadn't been out with them in a long time because your mum and I had been busy with you two and with work. I drank more than I should have. Way more. And I drove at the end of the night with my mates in the car. There had been a storm so there were puddles everywhere. There was a cyclist. I drove into him and … and I broke him. Broke him to the point that he can only move his mouth and eyes. I went to jail for a long time.'

Alex flinched. Joey sat down next to his mother who still hadn't moved. The knot of their family was coming undone.

Alex piped up. 'So it was an accident.'

'Well, in a way, yes. I had no intention of harming him, but …'

His father's unease stank. It wrapped itself tight around them and Joey welcomed it, basked in it.

'We had been having a lot of fun. We were very loose. Drunk. And when boys are drunk and around each other in that way, you know, you lose sense of … of good measure.'

A knife twisted in Joey's back.

'There was a puddle of water in the gutter. I thought it would be funny to veer into it and splash the cyclist, to make the guys laugh.'

Alex wrapped his arms tight around his chest.

'I swerved too hard and hit him.'

A balloon of silence had been expanding against the walls of the house in the past years. As his father finished admitting to his crime, the balloon finally burst, but it made no sound.

The sun was setting, and its light, fed through the slits of the venetian blinds, cast gashes over his mother's arm, his father's leg, the coffee table. So much of what was unfurling in their lounge room was storytelling. The thought comforted Joey, reminded him of how much he loved story time in primary school. A man used to come to tell them Dreamtime stories. Stories that had made Joey feel tiny. And that's how he felt now.

His father went on. 'Being inside is hell. It's not something I was prepared for. Your mum came to visit me in the beginning. She brought you boys once, with my mum too, but I told her I didn't want you to see me there. I got mixed up with a group of guys. Basically, if I hadn't I would have ended up dead. They cared about me, but they also led me into some dodgy shit.'

Alex's face was resting on his fist. He mumbled, 'Like what?'

For the first time since they had convened to thaw it all out, his mum spoke and looked directly at Joey. 'Like drugs.'

'What are you looking at me for?' Joey's attempt at defence sounded meek. They all knew why she was looking at him.

Alex asked, 'Dealing or using?'

'At first, they got me using. Being high was the only time I wasn't counting the hours until my release. Until I got to see you again.'

The sentimentality was passing straight through Joey. 'What was your sentence?'

'I was given seven years for the cyclist and, because of the dealing, another three years on top of that.'

'So you've been out three years?' Alex asked.

'Around that, yeah.'

'And in that time, you didn't want to try and see us?'

'It's complicated.'

'How?'

Their father looked out of the window. 'I tried, but maybe that's something your mum wants to explain.'

She cleared her throat and breathed out slowly. 'I could tell your dad was on shit by the third visit. I thought he would get over it, that maybe it was a one-off type thing cos he had just gone in. But then … the last time I went to see him he was trying to get me to bring shit in and, you know … be part of the process.'

Joey thought of Emma, the festival, Kyri, Ivan. It hadn't even been that extraordinary an experience, but he wanted to go back to that. His parents had been young. They had made bad decisions, done stupid things too.

'That's when I told him it was all over. I sent him the odd photo of you guys over the years, and he sent letters that I never read to you. And since his release, yes, he has messaged me to say he wants to see you but I … I was working up to it.'

Alex kept asking questions. 'So, you didn't even give him a chance to get clean and come back?'

Joey was filling in the gaps in his head without the need for detail.

His father chimed in. 'There was no point. I was in pretty deep and your mum could see that.'

Alex was angry. 'And you just gave up?'

'It's not that I gave up. I … I was lost,' he said.

'That whole time? That whole fucking time you were lost? You had me, you had Joey, you had mum out here to help you find your way, and you were lost? That's all you're going to call it? And now you decide to come back when Joey is about to get lost too?'

Joey's anxiety whirled. His mother had tears falling down her cheeks. The conversation was doing nothing good for any of them. Words out of mouths and into ears.

His father went on. 'I tried. I promise, I tried. And I failed every time. And that's something I have to live with—'

Alex cut in. 'It's something we've had to live with.'

'Yeah. Yeah, it is. But I've been clean for a year now. I wanted to be clean for a while before I came back into your lives.'

Joey laughed. 'I think it might be a bit late for that.'

His father looked at the floor and then shut his eyes.

Where were they all supposed to go from here?

18

Elaine pushed a twenty-dollar note into the poker machine. The twenty lasted ten minutes. She'd thought to only play the twenty, maybe have a free coke at the bar and head off, but it had been a while since she'd won anything, and she had a good feeling. She peeled a fifty-dollar note from her purse and fed it to the machine. She lost ten, made twenty. So, she was ten dollars up. She would play to forty. That way she would have only lost thirty all night if the machine hadn't paid out by closing time.

She had a hunch and doubled the bet. She was at forty within a minute. Then thirty and then ten. There was no point pulling ten out of the machine. She lowered the bet to ten-cent hits. When she was at around four dollars, the feature hit. The graphic was a silly coin that flipped and glimmered on three lines. Fifteen free spins right after she had lowered the bet to this pathetic amount. She cursed the composer of the poker machine music as it rang. She didn't bother waiting for the winnings to rack up. All that drama for a five-dollar gain. She hit the play button and let the free spins roll. The feature was entirely fruitless. One or two dollars gained in the last few spins that she bet on black of spades and lost. Both times it was red diamond. 'Kess ekht el red diamonds,' she whispered.

She played the remaining few dollars in the machine and on the last hit kept her fingers on the button, staring at the flashing *Insert credit* graphic, the blood draining out of her. She reached into her purse. There was ten dollars left. She was keeping it for half a kilo of ground coffee because she had used the dregs that morning. The next pension payment wouldn't come until Thursday. That was two days away. She had enough food in the fridge to last until then, but she was definitely out of coffee. She would not last two days without coffee. If the ten dollars got to thirty, she would take it out immediately.

She walked to a machine on the other side of the cluster, where there was only one other person, a Chinese man she had spoken to before. He smiled at her, but she wasn't in the mood to be courteous. She sat at the machine that she always thought of as quite welcoming. Its theme was the Australian outback, and the feature character was a smiling kangaroo wearing one of those hats with corks hanging off the brim. She squinted at the kangaroo, beckoned his good fortune with a prayer.

The credit vaporised in a minute. Her chest tightened. Her face sagged into her neck. She would go without coffee until Thursday. 'Fucken ugly kangaroo.'

Hopefully Salma would wave her over for a coffee tomorrow morning and then she could have one at Amal's the following day, even though she had been trying to avoid going there.

She couldn't believe that Amal had been in touch with him and not mentioned anything. All the time and hurt and effort

Elaine had invested in their relationship and Amal didn't have the decency to say that she had reached out to Simon. And what was the point, anyway? He was hardly going to be able to become the boys' father out of the blue. They didn't remember him. Even though she wanted her grandchildren to know more about their father, she wasn't quite prepared for his real-life existence. It was just too late. It was obvious that Amal was only prepared to reintroduce Simon to his sons now that she had the comfort of the lawyer boyfriend. Humans were leaves in the wind.

Elaine's mobile rang. She plopped her handbag on the seat she had just been sitting on and fished the phone out. It was Amal. Every time her daughter's name had flashed on her mobile since the arrest, Elaine had been overcome with anxiety. It was late. Amal never called this late.

Elaine answered. 'What happened?'

'Ma, are you going to answer the phone like that every time I call now?'

'Everything okay?'

'Yeah. Where are you? What's that music in the background?'

Fucking stupid phone-call anxiety. She wouldn't get away with it. The sounds were too recognisable.

Amal continued. 'Are you at the club?'

'Yes, I come with Salma last minute. We leaving now.'

'Okay. How often have you been going?'

'Never. I come once or twice with Salma, that's it.'

'Are you sure? Cos if it's like when Dad died, you can tell me—'

Elaine was electric. Charged by the machines surrounding her. 'Amal, khalas. If I'm going, I know what I'm doing. Why you call?'

'I was just going to tell you that the boys know everything. About Simon, and me, and all that shit.'

'Everything?'

'Yeah.'

'Ya allah, why? What good is it for them?'

'It kind of just happened. Joey lost his shit and he wouldn't stop until we told him everything.'

'Okay. Anyway, I talk to you tomorrow.'

'Alright. Mum?'

'Yeah?'

'You can talk to me if there's anything wrong, you know?'

'I don't know what you saying. Bye!'

Elaine threw her phone into her bag and went to the smoking area. A guy covered in tattoos stood near the door. She asked him for a cigarette and he obliged, smirking as though he were amused by the request. She dragged on it like the tar was keeping her alive. By the time she finished smoking, she was venomous. She needed a drink.

At the bar, she ordered a double scotch and coke that she grabbed as soon as it was placed in front of her. When the young bartender asked for sixteen dollars, she put on her sweet-old-lady act, apologised and said she'd be back in a minute with her husband's card. She downed the drink as she walked to the club's other bar near the restaurant. The bartender there was even younger, and she repeated the act, but only ordered a single this time. The club quickly became a soup of lights and faces.

She walked to the exit. Her senseless daughter patronising her like that, as though her own life weren't a mess. Elaine knew what she was doing. She was in control, wasn't relying on anyone. If she cut it close from payment to payment, that was her prerogative. She didn't go hungry; her bills were paid.

The bills. That's how Amal had found out last time. Stupid

Elaine, letting them pile up in the letterbox instead of stashing them away somewhere. But she hadn't wanted them in the house, and she hadn't been game enough to just bin the blasted things. Amal and her sticky beak. Thank God she had agreed not to tell Michael. Elaine wouldn't have been able to deal with his judgement.

A tall man bumped into her on the stairs leading to the car park. He apologised, and Elaine glared back at him. Maybe she would sell the house, move in to a small unit and have a huge chunk of money in the bank. But she'd probably lose her pension if she had money in the bank. And her children would expect a share in the profits. She'd gladly squander it all before they could get their hands on it. She dropped into the driver's seat clumsily. It didn't matter that she was too drunk to drive because she was so close to home.

It had rained. The roads and buildings sparkled before Elaine's windshield as though they'd been strung with fairy lights. She cursed the clouds. She could never see the lines on the road when it rained at night. Wary of her state, and the state of all that was glistening, she decided to brake hard at the amber light on Wattle Street instead of going through it. Her foot slipped. She hit the accelerator momentarily, and the car launched itself. She braked and the car skidded and swerved, coming to a stop almost on the other side of the road. Elaine hadn't breathed through the whole thing. Her hands were shaking. She pulled over to calm herself for a moment.

A young woman in lycra was approaching the car. 'Are you okay?'

Elaine put the window down.

'Yes, yes, I'm okay. Thank you.'

The girl bent over, looking underneath the car, and said, 'Your tyres are completely bald. You might want to get them checked out.'

'Yes, thank you, love. Thank you.'

Elaine couldn't remember the last time they had been changed. She couldn't even remember the last time the car had been serviced. She was entirely sober now.

When Elaine stepped out of the car in her driveway, she glanced over at Salma's place. Even with her bad eyesight she could see the ember of a cigarette bobbing under the carport. Salma waved her over, the bangles around her wrists clinking in the night. Elaine was too tired to even make an excuse. She shuffled across the road like a zombie and sat down across from her neighbour. Salma looked just as tired. Without asking, Salma lit a cigarette for Elaine, using the end of her own, and handed it over.

Elaine took a thick drag and slouched into the chair. 'You know what, Salma?'

'Tell me, habibti.'

'Sometimes I don't know if I'm coming or going.'

Salma let out a short sigh. 'You're telling me.'

'Everything okay?'

'Okay and not okay.'

'You want to talk about it?'

Salma stubbed her cigarette out in the ashtray. 'As of today I'm officially a divorcee.'

Elaine felt compelled to say something funny. 'Mabrouk.'

They laughed.

And then Elaine asked, 'What happened?'

'What happened happened years ago. He has another woman. I still let him stay here every now and then to keep things going, but a few months back, his other one said it's me or her, and ...'

Elaine put her hand on Salma's knee because she couldn't think of what to say.

'How's your son taking it?' Elaine asked.

'He's fine. It's not his father. His father left me too.'

It was hard to imagine why men would leave such a sturdy and open and handsome woman.

Elaine squinted at the moon. 'Maybe when men leave – for another woman, for jail, for a hole in the ground – maybe we are actually better off.'

'I don't doubt that for a second,' Salma said.

Sitting underneath Salma's carport, across from her house, the street damp from the rain, Elaine felt the most at ease she had in weeks.

Salma cleared her throat. 'Elaine, I heard what happened with your grandson. I didn't really want to mention anything because I'm sure you've had enough, but if you ever want to talk, you know where to find me.'

Elaine held back tears. 'Thank you, habibti.'

'And I have a short tongue, so don't ever worry that I'm going to go around and spread your story. I'm not like the others.'

'I could tell that from the moment we met.'

'Were you at the club tonight?'

Usually Elaine would lie. 'I was.'

'Any luck?'

'Luck is avoiding me lately.'

'Maybe we're better off without luck too.'

19

The desperation to talk to Emma boiled over the day after Joey's father left. He put his running shoes and a hoodie on and jogged to Woolies. If Emma was working, she would be finishing her shift at 7:00 pm. She always parked her car in the same spot at the back, the passenger side real close to the wire fence that separated the shopping centre from the neighbouring empty lot.

He checked the time on his phone and the jog became a run. Past the pizza shop where jumpy children waited for their order with tired parents. Past the brotherhood boxing gym where a group of guys were chilling outside. Past a deserted gelato shop with a bored girl behind the counter scrolling on her phone. Past a house that he remembered had goats in its backyard when he was a child. He ran and sweated and coughed until he stopped, bent over with his hands on his knees, panting in the back dock of the supermarket. He peered around the corner and saw his old manager smoking outside the door that fed into the staff area of the store. He held back and waited, listened. The loud click of the door sounded, and he heard Emma's voice. 'Night, Peter.'

'Laters, Emma. Hold the door for me.'

Joey ghosted her as she searched for her car key in her bag. 'Em.'

She spun around. Her look was punishing, saw into him. 'What?'

'I've been trying to contact you.'

She held her bag close to her chest, one hand frozen inside, her hair unkempt at the sides, the car park lights reflecting against her skin. Her shoulders slumped. 'Well, obviously I'm uncontactable.'

'Em …' Joey stepped closer. 'Em, I …'

He tried to put his arms around her, but she punched him in the gut, the chest, his arm. She hit him with her bag too. He stood there and took it until she stopped and all they could hear was the sound of distant car doors being shut and an aeroplane and the vibration of the concrete all around them.

Emma drove them a short distance and parked the car in an industrial area of Chullora that bustled with trucks during the day and was hauntingly empty at night. He had no idea what to say or where to start but knew she probably did. He had to be home by 8:00 pm.

She spoke to the night outside the window, her breath fogging the glass momentarily. 'Did you do it?'

'Do what exactly?'

'Touch her. Did you fucking touch her, Joey?'

'In a way, yes. But I was forced.'

'Don't say that. Don't use the word forced as though you were the victim.'

'Em, I had no idea what they were going to do. What happened was … was absolutely fucked. I'm not denying that I had a part to play, but—'

'You're a hypocrite, Joey. And a farce. You probably haven't heard it from anyone, but you are. You wax lyrical about being better than those boys, like they're beneath you, but it's all smoke and mirrors. You're just like them. Just like every other fucking arsehole with a dick.'

How detrimental would it be to this sliver of reconciliation if he was to bring up the fact that she had hooked up with Boxer?

'Don't you have anything to say?' Emma asked.

'Actually, nah. I'm out of fucking words. And it seems like you've made your mind up.'

In a way it was calming to know that Emma hated him and believed he was a rat.

'Don't you at least want to try to say you didn't rape the poor girl?'

It was revolting to hear those words come from her mouth. He pulled the door handle and had one foot out of the car before she told him to stop. He did, but he left the door ajar. The gutter was piled with cigarette butts and there was a flayed-open bag of McDonald's, its contents gazing up at what few stars were visible in a sky poisoned by the guzzling city.

'You say "rape the poor girl". Who said she was a poor girl? Who said … who said it was rape?'

Emma fiddled with the keys dangling from the ignition still.

Joey pressed on. 'You think I'm the demon that the media played me out to be? You think my part was on par with what's being sprayed all over the shop? I'm not saying that I wasn't fucking complicit, but I didn't rape her, no. I didn't.'

For the first time in a long time he didn't stem his tears. His voice cracked. He focused on the airbag sign on the dashboard as he spoke. 'I'm in this constant spiral. Trying to validate my innocence and then seeing that as absolutely trivial compared to what Lisa had to go through. I … I wish I could talk to her, or something. I want to know where she's at. I want to know why she didn't implicate Kyri and me as much in the report. I mean, Kyri left, he didn't even touch her, but we were there, we didn't stop it.'

'Why didn't you stop it?' Emma was almost whispering.

'I can't say it. I can't. If I say it then I'll believe it. I'll be just like them.'

'What do you mean?'

He took a deep breath. 'Em, there was no struggle – and before you think it, I'm not trying to say that for it to be rape she had to be fighting – because I'm not. But in the moment, I didn't know it, or it didn't occur to me enough. And … and I was scared.'

Emma reached out her hand towards him, but then placed it on the handbrake.

'I was scared of Boxer. And Haz,' Joey said.

They sat in silence for a few minutes, the revelation of his fear quietening everything in the world.

'They're the only guys I know. And they're backwards as fuck and I've spent so long sucked into their void because of where I was born, grew up, went to school.'

Emma spoke slowly. 'Joey, you're a good person. She probably saw that in you and didn't want you to get in trouble.'

His tears started up again. 'But I'm not. I'm not a good person. I'm a fool. I'm a weakling who couldn't stop it. And my lawyer says I have a good chance of getting off scot-free.'

He hadn't expected to pour this much out.

'I don't know what to say,' she mumbled.

'No-one does.'

'How are your mum and Alex?'

'Good. Confused. Mum avoids me. Alex has gone really quiet. And my dad's back, so that's made it all the more confusing.'

'Shit.'

'Turns out he's a criminal too.'

'What?'

'He ran over a cyclist, like, fifteen years ago when he was drink driving. He was in jail for a long time. He's been out a few years. Mum used to see him when he first went in but apparently he ended up on drugs and she broke it off.'

'Shit. That's brutal.'

'Yep.'

'What's he like now?'

'Clean – off the drugs. Basic.'

He could tell Emma was itching to say something. 'Joey, Mum and Dad don't want me to see you anymore.'

He was cut. More cut than when she blocked his number. 'And you're an obedient little girl all of a sudden?'

'Well, I still live with them. I need to kinda respect what they say.'

'You're not a child, Em. You're almost twenty, for fuck's sake.'

'Yeah. So are you, and look where you are.'

So, Emma had thought he was a complete flop this whole time. They had barely made eye contact since getting in the car but now he was really craning his neck away from her as he said, 'Your parents are just like everybody else.'

'Maybe they are.'

'And you know what, Emma? You're just like everybody else too.'

Emma laughed and started the car. 'When are you going to drop this me-against-the-world bullshit, Joey? Look around you.' She gestured with her arms. 'You're a dime a fucking dozen.'

He slammed the door on his way out. Emma made a too-fast U-turn, mounted the kerb and sped away.

20

Elaine had more or less broken even that week. Well, broken even if she didn't include the two gold rings she'd sold to the jeweller to get the car serviced and the tyres changed. They were daggy rings that she hadn't worn in decades anyway. There'd been enough left over to pay the bills too, which she had just done at the post office in Mount Lewis. Now she was sitting in the car waiting for the rain to calm down. She travelled down the Hume Highway in her mind's eye, hovering over the spots she could go.

To avoid being seen by anyone she knew, she had taken to visiting the smaller VIP gaming areas in pubs and bars. In the last week she had been as far west as Casula and as close to the city as Enmore, where a woman with a shaved head had complimented her on her pendant. Elaine had hastily tucked it inside her black blouse. There was also a moment, at a pub in Liverpool, where she had glimpsed the profile of a man who looked like Youssef's cousin. She had hit the collect button swiftly, taken the ticket and ducked out to her car through the door that she always made a point of sitting close to. Other than that, everyone else who frequented the gaming rooms paid her no attention and she reciprocated the gesture.

When the rain stopped, she drove to Ashfield RSL. It was a little further than she wanted to go but it was spacious inside, and the barman was always smiley with her.

Elaine chose a spot where she could see the television screens. Most of them were playing the races, watched intently by a few seedy men. One of the screens played a panel show whose hosts looked tacky, with winged eyeliner and furious hair. The look struck Elaine as quite woggy, at odds with the hosts' Australian names and skin. She'd never really paid much attention to those shows because she couldn't relate to the people or any of their discussions. She guessed that no woman in Australia could, no matter where they came from, so it didn't make her feel left out or like a philistine. The women were clowns whose lines were probably written by men anyway.

She tapped the play button on the machine as she watched the TV. The camera only ever rested for a split second on one of the panellists before it jolted to the next. It was hypnotic, plus she didn't need to watch the poker machine screen because she could tell what was happening from the sounds. The machine she had chosen was Arabian themed. A purple genie swished around the screen. A golden lamp, jewels, a camel. Elaine spoke to the pretty genie, barely opening her lips. 'Come on, stupid. Give me something.'

The panel show had gone to an ad break. The men around the TVs dispersed. Elaine had an odd sensation that time had folded around her. She could have been there for ten minutes or ten hours. There was no sound, and then the feature on the machine peaked. She had been playing two-dollar hits on all twenty-five lines. The payout was going to be decent. She sipped her water and hit the play button to let the free games roll.

Just as the last game spun, Elaine felt a presence over her shoulder. She turned to find one of the men who had been watching the TVs now standing behind her with his hands in the pockets of his suede jacket. He was clean-shaven, handsome for someone their age. She sipped her water again, tried to delay hitting the button that would add the two-hundred-odd dollars she had won to her credit amount. She checked her phone for any missed calls, ate a Mintie that had been in her bag for God knows how long. When she looked over her shoulder again, the man was smiling at her. He stepped closer and she was enveloped in a cloud of cologne.

His voice was robust, Balkan. 'Good win.'

'Thanks.'

'Where your husband?'

Elaine was in the mood to be charming. 'Rookwood.'

'Ah, sorry.'

'Where is your wife?'

He laughed in his nose. 'I hope far away from here.'

'It was good marriage, then?'

'Beautiful. She take the house, the money, the kids. Perfecto.'

Elaine offered him a Mintie that she fished from another forgotten corner of her handbag. He took it and dropped it into his jacket pocket without saying thanks. He looked out the window, assessing the clouds for a moment, and said, 'I've never seen you in this club before.'

'I haven't seen you here before too.'

The man shrugged, rocked back and forth a little like a rejected schoolboy. The gesture put her off. She turned back to the machine and hit the collect button and the man moved away. The women on the panel were yapping, and another young woman who looked out of place and was very obviously wearing a wig had joined them. The program then cut to a grid of blurred-out faces. It took a millisecond for Elaine to recognise that one of the faces was Joey's. At the bottom of the screen appeared the words *Rape survivor speaks out*.

Her body seized up. Joey's trial was two months away. She snatched her ticket and was making her way to the door when the man appeared at her side with two paper cups from the machine.

'I made you coffee. Come outside to drink with me.'

Elaine kept her gaze fixed on the silver rectangles in the carpet. She hoped the door wasn't far off. She hadn't even cashed out the ticket. 'I have to go, sorry.'

'Ah, come on. What do you have to do?'

'I have an appointment.'

He was falling behind. 'I seen you before.'

She stopped and turned around, squinting at him, awaiting an explanation.

'I seen you here. I lie before.'

'And what you want me to do about it?'

'Nothing. Come have coffee.'

Elaine marched back over to him and took the cup from his hand. Some of the coffee had spilt over onto his thick wrinkly fingers.

'Okay, meet you outside. I go to ladies first.'

He raised his eyebrows at her and walked away. When he was out of sight, Elaine hurried over to the TV, sipping on the coffee. She definitely didn't need the caffeine, but maybe it helped with courage. The camera was focused on the young woman in the wig. There was sound coming out of the TV but among the contorted voices of the race commentators and the jingles of the poker machines, she had to stand right underneath it to hear what the girl was saying.

'... but I don't want to be treated like a statistic. I still have a face and a life.'

'It's so brave of you. It really is. And I think what you are doing is sending out a message to other victims that they don't have to live in shame for something they had no control over.'

'Yes, and you're also sending a message to the perpetrators that you aren't letting this define you. It's truly just commendable.'

'Thanks.'

'How have you been coping through it all?'

'I've been really lucky because my family have been super supportive.'

'Now we aren't able to discuss the case in detail or reveal your identity for legal reasons, but have you been able to move on from what happened to you?'

'I don't think I will ever move on from it, especially while the legal side of things is still underway, but what I would like to say is that my life is on track. I'm happy and I'm strong and I'm looking towards the future. I would hope that anyone who has ever experienced something like this could do the same.'

'Amazing words. Thank you so much for joining us today and for sharing your courageous story. If you'd like to know more about our guest's journey you can follow the Twitter handle at the bottom of the screen.'

'And after the break we'll take a look at a groundbreaking new procedure described as the lunchbreak nose job.'

Because she had been standing right underneath the TV, she hadn't quite processed a clear image of the girl until she stepped away from the wall. The girl was small and wore the kind of blazer you'd wear for a job interview. Elaine had half expected to feel something for her, but she only felt flabbergasted that the girl had gone as public as she could.

Elaine's hand shook, which made it hard to keep the insipid coffee in the paper cup. On her way to plonk it in the bin, she realised one of the men who had been watching the races was watching her. She pulled her shoulders back and walked towards the smoking area where her coffee suitor was probably still waiting. As much as she wasn't bothered for the encounter, she couldn't find it in herself to be entirely rude.

She passed the poker machine she had been playing earlier and the genie flashed up and winked at her. Elaine swore and fished through her bag for a pen and her little notepad. She scrawled down the Twitter name that the presenter had mentioned. She would have to get Alex to help her.

The man was savouring his cigarette as though he only smoked one a day. 'I thought you weren't coming.'

'Sorry, I had to wait for toilet.'

'It's okay. I'm Valon.'

'I'm Elaine. Can I have a cigarette?'

'My pleasure. You smoke?'

'I once was smoker, yes. Long time ago.'

'I've never stopped. In Albania, you're given cigarette with breast milk.'

The first drag of the cigarette comforted her, alerted her body to something like hunger. Well, it probably was hunger; she had only eaten a few almond biscuits all day.

'Valon, do you know where to get good kebab in Ashfield?'

'I do. Finish the cigarette and we go.'

21

The plume of cigarette smoke rebounded onto Joey off the glass pane at the bus stop. He ruffled his T-shirt and stepped further away into the open for fresh air. Centrelink probably had some clause in the application that hindered people's payments if they spent it on shit like cigarettes. The last thing he needed was more strikes against him. Without a job, and with his mum on his back, he was willing to do anything to get money. Even if he didn't go to jail, he didn't want to spend the rest of his life hearing the guilt trip from his mum about how she paid for the lawyer.

When the bus pulled up, two middle-aged sisters wrapped in identical woollen scarves were sitting at the front. At first, Joey thought it was the one scarf entwining both of their necks. They were the only other passengers. He had forgotten his earphones, so he sat at the back and played a hip-hop playlist on speaker, holding the phone near his ear, dismissing the thought that it was annoying for the old sisters. One of them turned to glare.

He swore at her under his breath and stared out of the window on to Roberts Road. Everything looked ugly, speckled with decay. Cloaked in shit. A dilapidated Hungry Jack's tacked onto a servo so you could fill your car and your gullet at the same time.

Centrelink had only been open ten minutes and already there was a motley crew busting out of the weepy-blue waiting chairs. A bulging security guard winked at Joey and waved his hand in front of the automatic doors for them to open, as though Joey was invisible to the sensor.

He was incorporated into the ecosystem of Centrelink the moment he crossed the threshold. The office had its own geography, climate, native people – people brought together by messed-up parents, fibro houses, dictators, liquidators. He pressed the button on the electronic kiosk that said *Make a new claim* and a ticket spat out at him. He sat across from an old man with an eye patch who kept muttering and looking around. Next to the old man sat a skinny dude with his legs crossed at the ankles. Behind him was a lady in a business suit. There was also an Arab family eating from a Bakers Delight bag. They all looked like they had been there for years.

He panicked. Why wasn't he off at uni studying something that would make him something, dating someone, driving a nice car? The answer burnt clear as day – because he was an idiot. Because he was a weakling. Maybe what Haz had said to him that night through the window was true. Maybe he needed to start acting like a man.

The old man's sobbing dragged him back to reality. He wasn't producing any tears, just making sounds from his droopy mouth and thumping his fist into his thigh intermittently. Joey wondered why the old man was alone. Surely he had children and grandchildren who could have accompanied him. Everyone else ignored the cries, as though they knew the old man, knew what he was up to. Joey tried to ignore it too, but he pictured Tayta sitting there on her own and his heart flared. The skinny dude rolled his eyes. There was something meditative about the cries. A moody accompaniment to the office orchestra.

Joey spoke to him. 'What's wrong?'

The old man cried louder.

'Do you want some water?'

He cried louder again.

'How long have you been waiting?'

Too loud.

In what could only be described as a scene-stealing moment, the skinny dude stood up between the sets of waiting chairs, turned his palms up to the yellowing rectangular sheets of the ceiling and yelled, 'Youse know what? This is illegal, this treatment. I want the manager!'

The long-suffering employees and most of the other punters ignored him, just like they had been ignoring the old man, but Joey was intrigued.

The performance continued. 'This is discrimination. My landlord already signed the bloody form! I handed it in already-oh-why-won't-anyone-listen-to-me?'

He was shaking his legs like a baby at the beginning of a tantrum. His words were slop mixed with lament and they poured out of his mouth coated with a waning high that Joey recognised. Sweat ran through the lines on his face. Blisters on the forearms.

The guy became incomprehensible fast, whining like the mating cats that sometimes claimed the nook outside Alex's bedroom window. The security guard marched over to the clerk behind the counter, who was waving a form in his direction without looking away from her computer screen. Joey got the sense that it was all another rehearsal. That all the people in there were trying to perfect a scene they had played over and over.

The security guard took the form over to the skinny dude and spoke with a sweetness that contrasted with his physique. 'Just have the form signed by the landlord and either bring it back or upload it on the app. Do you have a smartphone? Trust me, the sooner you do this, the sooner they can help.'

The dude ignored him, reprising his hymn. 'My landlord already signed the bloody form! I handed it in already-oh-why-won't-anyone-listen-to-me? Why-won't-anyone-listen-to-me? Why-won't-anyone-listen-to-me?'

His sound had a strength to it, a penetration. It bounced around the security guard and the prams and the self-service kiosks. It rushed into the drawers in the desks, under the toilet door, and whirled around Joey's head until words, lathered in the colour of scorn, prised open his chest and throat and mouth and cracked the dude's cacophony. 'Shut the fuck up!' he yelled.

The office orchestra faltered. Joey looked at the faces around him. They were drenched in his voice. Sometimes the only thing that can break a sound is another sound. It had worked in class when a teacher couldn't get everyone to shut up. Someone would whistle really loud and the class would go quiet and the teacher would continue.

Joey kept yelling. 'No-one has to listen to your shit! Just take the fucking form and go!' His scalp itched.

The security guard came over, and that was the catalyst for the workplace song to resume, albeit quieter. The dude, having had attention diverted from him, stormed out the sliding doors.

The old man had his working eye fixed on Joey, his hands tucked tightly into the pockets of his leather jacket.

His mother met him at the front door. 'How'd you go?'

'How'd-I-go-what?'

'At Centrelink.'

'It was fucked is how I went.'

She followed him through the house to the fridge.

'Is there ever anything to eat in this house?' he said.

'Oh, sorry, I forgot you lived in a hotel. What can I get you, dear guest?' Her words were lava.

'I wish it was a hotel. At hotels you get some privacy.'

'You're an ungrateful brat, Joey.'

'And you're a fucking busy bee. You think Mrs Kyriacos makes her kids feel like they owe her something for taking care of them?'

'I don't have the fucking money and husband and mansion that Mrs Kyriacos has!'

Joey walked to his bedroom. She followed him and propped herself against the door frame. He lay on his bed with his shoes still on, which he knew would shit her. He poked at his phone without direction, willing her to leave him alone but also willing her to say something so he could fight.

She spoke with a fresh tone, as though they hadn't just had an altercation. 'So, what happened?'

Joey tried to summarise the events in his head. He dropped his phone onto his chest and fixed his gaze on the ceiling as he spoke. 'It was hell. It's full of freaks and all they told me to do, when I finally spoke to someone, was to go online and apply and I have to set up some other government bullshit account that you need ID for which I hadn't fucking taken with me.'

'Yeah, well, the government isn't going to just give you money. They're going to make you prove who you are and that you are in fact in need of it.'

'Really? Tayta manages to get it for nothing.'

For a split second, Joey was proud of the mirror he held up to his mother, and then he felt like a teeny tiny boy in his childhood bed.

'How dare you! Dragging your tayta into this. You think she doesn't deserve her pension?'

'I'm not gonna bother applying. It's too complicated.' He glanced at his mother before reaching for his phone.

She looked at the floor and then up at the spot he had been looking at. 'You know what, Joey? This is all my fault. It's all my goddamn fault.' She spoke with a *Home and Away* calm about her. 'And you know why? Because all those years ago when your other grandparents and my friends were offering help, I said no. "Let us do this for the boys, Amal. Leave them with us. We'll show them how to do this. Take a holiday, Amal. The boys aren't your responsibility alone." When those offers were coming through, I was a fucking brick wall.' She poked the wall. She was crying. 'I was a goddamn wall. Fending off support because I wanted to do this all on my own. Because I thought I knew what was best for my sons and for myself, my family. Because I thought I could be a mum and dad and sister and brother and friend and teacher. Cook, entertainer. I thought I could do it all. My way!' She was shouting now.

Alex emerged from his room and stood behind her. Joey shut his eyes.

'My whole life. My whole life I spent worrying. When I was a kid, it was about impressing my parents. When I was a teenager, it was about what people would think. When I was with your father, it was about – I spent years worrying about him in jail, for fuck's sake! And the shit you're putting me through now!'

How much shouting did Joey have to deal with? The old man, the skinny dude, his mother – their souls were trying to escape via their throats. He opened his eyes to watch her, because she was rarely like this and it was refreshing to see her be different. Alex put an arm on her shoulder that she swiftly shrugged off.

She continued, drawing deep breaths and sobbing in between her words. 'At the beginning of the year I was … I was excited. I thought, things are finally good, you know? You were going well in your job. Alex in his last year of school. Your tayta seemed chill. I was excited about …' She put her hand on her chest. 'And fuck me, look how it has all turned out.'

She nodded her head sarcastically at her own dwindling speech. Then she stood up straight, made a noise in her throat that sounded like she was agreeing with someone and walked away. Alex shook his head and slammed his bedroom door.

After a few minutes the sound of the food processer filled the house. More noise. He pictured the whirring blade in the machine mincing whatever it was his mother had put in it. He pictured her standing over it, staring into the funnel with her puffy eyes. He wished the machine would go rogue and gather the gusto to suck her in. To completely churn her up. And he wished it would pull him in from his bedroom and churn him up too. And then Alex, the furniture, the house. Greenacre, the whole goddamn country. Every single fucking thing sucked into the blades of the processer and emulsified into a useless thick sludge.

22

The kebab was a bold move for Elaine. She rarely ate takeaway, but she couldn't deny that it went down well. And then it hit her stomach as she drove back down the Hume Highway and she had to let down the windows to air her farts out. She arrived outside Birrong Boys High School early enough before school was out that she found a car spot near the gates. The lanky eucalypts in the distance were static.

Umm Kulthum was on 2ME. Elaine undid the seatbelt, reclined the chair a little and shut her eyes. She remembered watching the video of this performance on one of the first televisions in the village when she was a little girl. Umm Kulthum was provoking her audience, repeating the same line over and over again, stressing different syllables every time. The concertgoers roared for her to keep going, to repeat the same line. They were under her spell, enraptured, pleading for her to sing into eternity. Umm Kulthum was a siren, controlling the horde with the undulations of her song.

Elaine wasn't in control of a single thing.

The sounds of the young men siphoning out of the school gates prompted Elaine to open her eyes and pull the chair back up. She stared out the window at first a trickle and then a stampede of scruffy, greasy, caramel boys coming out of the gates, stealing each other's hats and shoving and fist-bumping. Some of them hopped on to old buses, some dropped down into the train station and some climbed into people movers driven by flustered mums trying to avoid all the 'no parking' signs.

Alex had been completely obscured by a big boy with a beard and was about to hop on to a bus when Elaine wound down the window and yelled out his name. He looked everywhere but her direction so she called out again and beeped the horn. When Alex caught sight of her he became taut, like a resting puppet awoken by its commander. He crossed the road clumsily, leant in through the open window and gave her a kiss.

His face was dread. 'What's happened, Tayta?'

'Baby, nothing. I was in the area and come to drive you. Come in.'

As they passed the primary school on Auburn Road, Alex said, 'It's a school zone, Tayta. You have to go forty kays.'

'Forty kays, my ayr. We driving on eggshells? Not one kid on the road.'

'Yeah, but what if one popped out in front of the car?'

'You want me to drop you here so you get the bus?'

'Maybe. I don't want to be complicit in any crime. I think we've done enough of that in our family.'

Elaine relaxed her foot off the accelerator. She hadn't discussed with Alex how he felt about his father's reappearance. Amal had given her the rundown and, for the first time in forever, she had thought to let them figure it out themselves.

'Have you spoke to Dad since?' she asked

'Yeah. Actually, we text every day. But don't tell Joey, cos he'd kill me.'

'You don't have to worry about Joey. He has other thing to care about.'

'Why didn't you go left there?'

'We going to my place. I need your help. You have your computer?'

'My laptop, yeah.'

'Good.'

At the dining table, Elaine took the little notepad out of her bag and placed it on the plastic covering the doily tablecloth. The Twitter handle wasn't a name; it was something obscure, because the girl had to remain anonymous.

She explained what she wanted Alex to do, and he didn't ask any questions. He just looked at her for a moment, spun around to his backpack and took his laptop out.

Alex leant in close to the notepad, squinting his eyes. 'Is that an A?'

'Ah, let me see. Is it A? Is it E? E.'

He tapped into the search bar and hit enter. 'What are you going to say to her, Tayta? You don't even know a hundred per cent if it is her.'

'Of course it's her. You think Channel Seven fool me? I'm gonna say sorry. Tell her Joey is good boy.'

'You know you can get in trouble for that? For contacting her.'

'Maybe. We see. This is the page?'

The two of them leant in towards the screen, their temples tight against each other. Alex clicked on the result that she was pointing at and read the bio aloud. 'Survivor. Activist.'

'That's her,' she said.

'Do you want me to read her latest tweets?'

'What's tweeds?'

'Tweets, Tayta. That's what Twitter posts are called. Here, look. Her latest one was from this morning: "Thank you to these lovely women for helping spread awareness." And there's a photo of the show's hosts.'

'Okay, what else she says?'

'Yesterday afternoon she posted this TED Talk video. It's a conversation between a rape victim and her attacker ten years after the incident took place.'

'What's Tek Talk?'

'TED Talk. Like, a video of a speech.'

'Okay. What else?'

'Four days ago, she wrote: *Being raped is not MY story. It does not define ME.*'

'Okay, enough. Send her message.'

'What? Hell no. Not from my account.'

'Make one for me.'

'Are you sure?'

'I'm sure.'

'Okay, but if Mum or Joey find out, I had nothing to do with this.'

'I told you, don't worry about them two.'

She watched as Alex followed the necessary steps to create her Twitter account. She had never had any social media. Amal had tried to get her on Facebook a long time ago so that she could interact with her family overseas, but she hadn't been bothered. There was nothing to talk about with them. Their lives had split like an old hair the second she left the village.

She still hadn't worked out what she wanted to say to the girl, but she knew in her bones that she had to say something. Her fresh Twitter handle was @Tayta_E and her profile photo was one Alex had on his computer from her birthday last year.

He pulled away from his laptop. 'It's done. You're lucky she accepts direct messages from people she doesn't follow.'

'She would be receiving lot of good messages from people. Why would anyone say no to that?'

'It's the internet. She'd be receiving lots of hate and being trolled too. What do you want me to type?'

Elaine hadn't given it much thought but she started dictating anyway. 'Hello, I am Elaine, grandmother of Joseph Harb. I see you on TV. I hope it is okay to message you. On behalf of my grandson and family I want say sorry for everything you have been through.'

'That's it?'

'No, I'm thinking. Say: you are strong girl and one day you will be even stronger woman. My grandson, Joey, is good boy—'

'Tayta. No. You can't say that.'

'Why not?'

'Because then you're making this about Joey. As if you have said these nice things to her to get to the part where you talk about Joey.'

'But this girl, she is strong, habibi. I saw her on the TV. She is strong, I know it.'

'You saw her for five minutes on TV. You don't know how traumatised she really is and the last thing she needs is the family of one of her attackers telling her he is a good person. And that's assuming that this is even the right girl.'

'So you want your brother to go jail?'

'This isn't about that! You've made it about him again. You're forgetting that she is the victim.'

Alex was shouting and Elaine, try as she might, couldn't really see what he was trying to say. She felt a little silly. Alex had moved away from the table and was looking out of the window at the old fig tree in the driveway. Youssef used to shroud the whole thing in mesh like a giant lollipop so that the birds and rats didn't feast on the fruit. Since he had died, Elaine couldn't bring herself to do the same. In fact, she hadn't eaten a single fig from the tree in a year. The creatures, on the other hand, had gorged.

The week after Youssef's death, the house had been inundated with first, second, fifth cousins who didn't know when to leave. Every day for a week the relatives had come with bags of freshly ground coffee and sweets and cigarettes and pots of fassoulia to feed her mourning family. Every night Elaine poured the food down the toilet in the laundry, dry-retching and cussing about the cook's cigarette-stained fingers or their grimy kitchen she once saw. Joey and Alex had stood behind her like altar boys as though she were executing some divine ritual. Ready to fetch the pot, hand her a tea towel, flush the toilet, grasp her elbows as they guided her back to the kitchen-bench altar. They had been so helpful that week. Unlike Amal, whose devastation at losing her father had manifested in long and loud naps.

The three of them had stayed over the entire week. Joey and Alex had shuffled through the house, shifting furniture back into place, wiping coffee spills off nesting tables, emptying ashtrays, closing blinds, and coercing seat cushions back into shape when the relatives had finally left.

Elaine walked over to Alex at the window and put her hand on his shoulder. She was so much shorter than him these days. She had to reach. 'You hungry?'

'Yeah.'

'I have malfouf in the fridge, or I can make chicken snizzle.'

'Nah, I'll have the malfouf.'

'You don't want chicken snizzle?'

'If I wanted the chicken schnitzel, I would have said.'

'I'll make chicken snizzle in case.'

She wandered over to the kitchen. Alex was neglected in all of this. She could see that now. She was glad he was texting with his father.

'Sorry for snapping at you, Tayta.'

'Don't be sorry, habibi. Give me that bowl.'

'I think you should send the apology as it is. That way you could see what she says before you say too much.'

There was no denying Alex was her favourite. So reasonable, intuitive. He was so much like her.

'Okay, baby. Send it.'

Michael and Sonia had invited Elaine over for dinner. She'd desperately wanted to avoid them in the lead-up to Joey's trial, but she couldn't think of any excuses. The trial was all Michael would want to talk about.

Their house was on a narrow street in Enfield that led to Henley Park. Michael had bought the land cheaply almost twenty years ago and they'd lived in the little bungalow for a short while before he made a tonne of money from property he owned in Queensland and redeveloped the house into a multi-level complex.

Elaine was proud of him but some of it could have been toned down. Although, probably not with a wife like Sonia.

Elaine parked the car, made her way to the intercom and pressed it.

Sonia answered the door wearing a brown tracksuit that was covered in a gold tessellated logo. She was holding one of the dogs and the others excitedly scampered around her feet. Her hair was slicked back, which was unusual for her, and she was wearing contact lenses that made her eyes green.

They kissed each other on the cheeks and then, in the very white hallway with the too-big chandelier, Charlie and Chanel appeared. Elaine was happy to see her grandchildren. She didn't see them at all as often as she saw Joey and Alex. She kissed them multiple times on their cheeks and Chanel put her arm around her and ushered her to the living area.

'Where's your dad?' Elaine asked.

'He just went to pick up dinner. He'll be back any minute,' Sonia replied.

Elaine looked over at the showroom kitchen. The giant vases with sticks. Everything was so impractical.

Charlie and Chanel caught her up on their studies. Michael returned carrying bags filled with Thai food.

The conversation flowed during dinner and then there was a moment of silence and Elaine knew it was coming.

'So, Ma, Simon's back in the picture, then.'

Elaine pushed the noodles around her plate. 'Yes, I told you.'

'Amal finally realised she can't do it on her own.'

'She did on her own this whole time.'

'Clearly she hasn't done a great job.'

'Please, can we leave it for tonight?'

'Why? Why do you always want to leave it?'

'Because I'm embarrassed enough in news and with relatives. We still need to talk about it in the home? You invite me over to question me, Michael? I've had enough.'

Her grandchildren were silent, staring at their plates. Sonia stood and started clearing up. It struck Elaine that everyone was always so silent when Michael was around.

'Chanel, habibti, what you think of the situation? You think your cousin is guilty?' Elaine asked.

Chanel looked at her father, then her mother. 'Well, I can't imagine Joey doing something like that, but he was still involved in it. And what those guys did is something that needs to stop happening.'

'Listen to your daughter,' Elaine said. 'Seventeen and is smarter than all of us. All you wanna do, Michael, is talk: talk about Joey, about Amal, about shit. Why? Is this important? You forgetting what real problem is.' She hadn't expected to unleash. She didn't like to do that in other people's homes, not even her son's. And what she was saying was hypocritical because she too couldn't handle Joey and Amal and all that came with them recently. 'Stop judging your sister and her boys. Yes, they have different life to you, but you know what could happen tomorrow? You know what situation Charlie can be in, in future?'

Michael scoffed. 'I can hands down say that Charlie will never be in that situation.'

'Charlie, what you say?' she asked.

'No-one knows what the future holds, I guess, but I will definitely avoid those situations.'

Elaine gestured towards her grandchildren. 'Listen to your kids.'

There was silence, then the dogs started yapping.

Later, as they ate ice cream in the lounge room, Chanel said, 'Tayta, can you tell me one of those stories about your grandma, please? It's been ages since you did.'

Elaine laughed. The rest of them were watching football on TV. She was glad Chanel was her only listener.

'Have I tell you how I get this?'

Elaine fished her necklace and the pendant of Mariam Our Saviour out of her blouse. Chanel held the pendant in her fingers, inspected it.

'You haven't, but I don't think I've ever seen you not wearing it.'

'I never take it off in forty-five years.'

'So how did you get it?'

'It was my grandmother's,' Elaine whispered.

Chanel came in closer to her. They created their own little bubble that blocked out all the football noise.

Elaine went on. 'The morning of my wedding, my aunts – her two daughters – give it to me in secret.'

'Why was it a secret?'

'Because they not supposed to have it. Years before, my tayta was put in the tomb wearing the necklace when she die.'

'So they took it afterwards?'

'That's right. And you wanna know something else from the day she died?'

'Yeah.'

'The priest, he didn't let her coffin in the church, and he didn't pray for her.'

Chanel gasped. 'Why not?'

'They closed-minded in the village. I don't like to say the word, but they call her a witch. Even though she have special way, she was still religious woman.'

'Tell me about something she did.'

Elaine racked her brain. 'In the war, before I'm born, there was no food in the village. Babies dying of hunger, people eating their fingernails for dinner. There's a cave in the village that go from one side of the mountain to other side, like long, long tunnel. Dark, scary. No-one ever going in there because they scared of the hyena. In my time, they block the openings to the tunnel with concrete because a little boy go missing in there. Anyway, everyone dying of hunger, no flour to make bread, nothing, and someone say they see my tayta, she was a young woman then, walk into the cave. The whole village say, "Ah, she's dead woman." The family give up on her. They think they will never see her again, and maybe they don't mind so much because it mean one less mouth to feed.'

Chanel was wide-eyed, almost in Elaine's lap.

'Two days later, a young man from the village is walking past the cave, and he fall to his knees from what he saw.' She paused for dramatic effect. 'He saw my tayta walking out of cave carrying big sack of ameh, grain, on her back.'

'What! How did she get it?'

Elaine put her hands up in surrender. 'No-one ever ask, and she never tell. And the young man who see her coming out of the cave, he end up marrying her, your great-great-grandfather.' She whispered in Chanel's ear. 'When I die, this is yours.' She held the pendant up and it twinkled in the glow of the many downlights.

Chanel buried her face into Elaine's neck, kissing her repeatedly.

23

Along with most things that had happened in the past months, waking up to a text from his father wasn't something Joey had ever anticipated would happen to him.

Hi Mate, I'll be arriving Wednesday. I'm staying at a hotel in Strathfield. Hope you're feeling okay.

The number wasn't saved in Joey's phone, but he could tell from the ordinariness of the text that it was him. And 'mate' didn't need to be capitalised.

At their last meeting, Marco had told Joey that Kyri was acquitted and didn't have to go to trial but that it wasn't public knowledge yet. Even though Marco said that Joey would still likely go to trial, he had been more confident that Joey would get off. The confidence did nothing to release the trap Joey felt caught in.

His whole predicament was deeper than his dumb parents. Deeper than Kyri and Emma moving on from him like he had wanted to move on from Boxer and co. Deeper than being left on 'read' by Ivan. Sometimes the thought of ending up in jail filled him with relief.

Hi Mate, I'll be arriving Wednesday. I'm staying at a hotel in Strathfield. Hope you're feeling okay.

What a stupid text. Joey dropped his phone back on the bedside table and put a pillow over his head to block out the afternoon sun blaring through the window.

Alex came bursting into the room holding his phone screen towards Joey, his eyes aghast. Before he could say, 'Get the fuck out I'm trying to sleep,' Alex had jumped to the side of the bed and thrust the phone close to Joey's face.

'Have you seen this?'

Joey recognised *The Sydney Morning Herald* insignia. The headline read: *Western Sydney man cleared of sexual assault*. He snatched the phone from Alex's hand and sat up.

A Western Sydney man charged with violently attacking a woman he met on a train has had his aggravated sexual assault charge dropped at the Downing Centre Court this morning. Abdul Abbas, twenty, was one of five men involved in the gang rape. During the trial, the court was told how the group of men targeted the young woman on a Bankstown train and drove her to a nearby car park where the assault occurred.

Abbas claimed the young woman had consented to the oral sex and at no point used defensive language or asked him to stop.

The woman claimed she did not agree to the sex and was forced to take drugs that clouded her judgement but admitted to replying to a text from Abbas the next day asking if she wanted to meet again with the words, 'Just u and me, yeah.'

In his judgement, Justice Francis Reynolds found the charges 'unreasonable' and said he 'could not ignore the reasonable doubt as to the accused's guilt of having committed aggravated sexual assault. The obstacle was the issue of consent.'

Earlier this month one of the co-accused was acquitted of his involvement pre-trial and a further three are awaiting their own trial dates.

Boxer was free.

The numbness inside Joey rooted itself to every nook of his organs and all the avenues of his veins. He handed the phone to Alex and sank back under the doona.

'Joey, this means you're going to get off. He did way more than you.'

'Shut the curtain properly on your way out.'

Alex didn't move. Joey turned to see what the matter was and saw him, mouth open, fingers limply grasping his phone. Joey pointed to the curtain.

24

WHAT DOES A WIDOW IN her mid sixties wear to court? What does a widow in her mid sixties wear to court to watch her grandson be put on trial? What does a widow in her mid sixties wear to court to watch her grandson be put on trial for aggravated sexual touching? Elaine attempted to ground herself and keep at bay the wooziness she had woken up with.

The lawyer had all but assured them that Joey would be absolved of the charge, considering the outcome of the other boy. It had come as a shock to her when Amal called with the news about him being found not guilty. She had cradled the idea that Joey would be safe very delicately, but she had been sure the others would pay. They had done very real things to the girl. But they weren't paying. Who would? The girl.

She had to stop herself from thinking that it was all a waste of time and energy for the girl. That it was all in vain. The interviews and the Twitter. She had never replied to Elaine's message.

The tall cupboard in Elaine's bedroom had been there since the house was built. It was so tall that she had recently bought a plastic step to get to the top shelf. She used to be able to reach it, but her skeleton had compacted. The far end of the cupboard was where all the special outfits lived. Suits and dresses and shawls she hadn't worn in decades, a floor-length coat Youssef gave her for their anniversary one year, even one of his old suits that she kept as a memento – the brown pinstripe one he wore to Michael's wedding.

She fingered the clothes. So much of it was shiny and covered in sequins and beads. Nothing she could bring herself to wear again, but she wasn't willing to decide what to do with it all. Her children and grandchildren could work it out when she departed the living world. They could come and look through the house and reminisce and cry and mourn her absence.

She pulled out the dress she had worn to Michael's wedding. It had a very low v-cut on the chest. Youssef had made her sew a piece of matching fabric on the inside to make it more 'mother of the groom'. The top portion of the dress was covered entirely in crystals and beads and so too was a strip of the hem. It had a matching bolero. She had bought it from a factory outlet in Surry Hills called Dolina. All the stylish women had gone there at the time. She had no idea it had closed down until a few years ago when she'd caught the train to Central excitedly – not that she'd needed an outfit, but she had just felt like looking in the old store. The building was still there but it had been bled of its soul, turned into a gym. The members had charged in and out as she stood, remembering the mannequins.

On Amal's wedding day she had worn her hair in a French roll with the fringe teased out. What heels had she worn with the suit? She was about to sit on the edge of the bed to think about it when she remembered what she was meant to be doing and where she was going. She shook her head, touched her empty tummy and shut the cupboard door.

She went to the everyday side of the cupboard, chose one of her regular black day dresses and pulled it over her body. In the mirror she tried to pat down the sides of her hair, which had descended into chaos during her sleep. But that's how she should look going to court. A scruffy widow going to court to watch her grandson be tried for aggravated sexual touching.

Nothing about the bricks and mortar of the court house was out to get them. The building was made of natural materials mined from the earth. She tried to calm herself, but the attempt was weightless. Not hefty enough to quash her leg-shaking fret.

The building was definitely designed to provoke fear and inferiority. Surely it was a tactic, to make criminals feel so uncomfortable that they'd comply just to get out of the room. But that wouldn't make sense for the victims.

She had sat in the same courtroom at the Downing Centre when Simon, who was now sitting on her left fiddling with a pamphlet, had been sentenced to jail for crippling the cyclist. And how odd it was that he was back, as though all that time had just been sliced away. Joey looked even more gaunt next to the snazzy lawyer, who was now Amal's boyfriend. From where she sat, she could only see the back and side of Joey's and the lawyer's heads. Alex sat next to Simon, Amal on the other side of Alex.

Amal looked surprisingly calm. She had applied the right amount of make-up, having probably expected the press to be outside, but luckily the start time had been changed, and the media mustn't have been tipped off. Still, there were what appeared to be journalists in the courtroom and a few people who looked like they'd come in by mistake and decided to stay.

In the hallway, before they were allowed into the room, the lawyer had said the victim would not be appearing, and being a judge-only trial meant that it should be somewhat simpler and faster than usual. He had added that the other men's statements were inadmissible in the trial because they were in the midst of their own legal proceedings.

Elaine had given up praying a long time ago. She tried to remember a short prayer about sacrifice as they waited for the judge but she gave up.

Alex whispered in her ear, 'It's going to be okay, Tayta.'

She squeezed his knee.

The judge entered the room and the four of them jolted up.

The presiding officer bellowed, 'The Honourable Justice Christine Lowry presiding. Please be seated.'

Elaine liked the look of the woman. Her jaw was chiselled. She may have only been a decade, even less, younger than Elaine, but she was radiant. A lot of money spent on her perfectly coiffed red hair. When this was all over, and if it was over in a good way, Elaine would go to the hairdresser and have her hair dyed. The judge sifted through some documents for a few minutes and Joey's lawyer turned towards Amal and nodded.

'Joseph Harb, you have been charged with aggravated sexual touching. The matter of aggravation is that the offence is said to have taken place in company. The charge against you is in the terms that on 15 March 2019 at Bankstown in the state of New South Wales in the company of others, you did unlawfully and indecently assault Lisa Morris without her consent. The matter proceeded before Bankstown Local Court where you pleaded not guilty and were granted a trial by judge only, in light of the media coverage of the case.'

Elaine remembered to breathe.

'The complainant is a young woman aged twenty-one years. She lives with her mother and infant brother. On the night you met Ms Morris, she was on a westbound train to her home in Cabramatta. It is alleged that she was approached by one of the men you were travelling with, Mr Abdul Abbas, and plans were made for the complainant to join your group for the night. Your first stop together was a house in Liverpool, where drugs were acquired. The group moved to a park, where drugs were consumed and you were joined by a further assailant, Mr Harry Minassian, who then drove the group to a multi-level car park in Bankstown. There, the complainant was forced to sit on the boot of the car and fellate three of the men.'

Elaine thought of the boys' ancestors, their namesakes, and pictured them ploughing the fields in their villages, unaware that their names would be uttered in the future by a smart lady in a suffocating room on the other side of the world.

'In the complainant's police statement, she did not describe herself as having performed any sexual act upon the accused but does describe having touched your penis. After the assault was over, you were driven to Yagoona station where you and the complainant left the car and entered the station. You spoke briefly with one another and proceeded to go your separate ways.'

The details made Elaine shrink. Maybe she wouldn't face anyone ever again. Maybe it was time to become an old-old lady.

The judge looked up from her papers at the prosecutor.

She lowered her glasses slightly in a magnificent way and said, 'Mr Ellis.'

He stood up. 'Your honour, we'll start by calling Senior Constable Alison Thompson to the stand.'

A blond woman floating inside a police uniform approached the stand. She looked like she had barely finished high school.

After she was sworn in, the prosecutor stood and dramatically put his finger on his top lip as though gathering his words. Elaine could tell the gesture was just for show. He was a lawyer; his words would have been gathered weeks ago. He reminded her of Jerry Lewis. It would be hard to take him seriously.

'Senior Constable Thompson, you are based at Bankstown Police Station, is that correct?'

'Yes, it is.'

'And how long have you been in the police force?'

'Two years.'

'Congratulations.'

Why was he congratulating her?

The lawyer flicked through his papers and spoke before his eyes settled on anything. 'On the morning of 16 March 2019, you were on shift at the station, is that correct?'

Elaine's shoulders slumped. This day would outlive her.

'Yes, I was manning reception.'

'Thank you for clarifying that. And Ms Thompson, at approximately what time did the complainant enter the police station?'

'It would have been between 8:10 and 8:30 in the morning.'

'And was the complainant alone?'

'Yes, she was.'

'Can you describe the state she appeared to be in?'

'She was upset.'

'Crying?'

'Not exactly. She looked pale.'

'And what happened next?'

'She approached the counter and said, "I've been raped. I need to file a police report."'

The questioning continued in this way for an hour. Elaine scolded herself for being bored. Even Jerry Lewis zoned out for a moment and had to be prompted to continue by the judge.

The story went that the constable, together with another of her colleagues – who would not be appearing at the trial – led the girl into one of the interview rooms at the station and began the logistics of the police report. The prosecutor seemed to be trying to extend the details that were entered into the report. He kept asking questions like 'Can you describe …' and 'What exactly do you mean by …' and 'How was that framed by …'. Nothing about the prosecutor's questions was leading anywhere and Elaine started to wonder if it was a tactic, a red herring, but she was dumbfounded when he started to wrap up.

She looked at the side of Joey's face, his lawyer, at Amal, but no-one was letting anything show. There was no mention of the drugs involved on the night, no detail about what happened with the other men. Just a retelling of Joey's portion – his penis in the girl's hand, their conversation at the station. Where were the prosecutor's critical points? The ones that would incarcerate Joey. The ones that had infiltrated Elaine's every thought since his arrest, cocooned her grandson, slashed at the girl's reality.

It was Joey's lawyer's turn to ask Senior Constable Thompson questions. He stood up, so schmick that the judge adjusted her posture.

'Constable, how often would you say you have facilitated a police report of this manner?'

'Ah, objection. What's the relevance of this question, your honour?' the prosecutor asked.

The judge said quickly, 'Mr Mamone, skip the question, please.'

'Sorry, your honour. Constable, is there a procedure to follow for this type of complaint?'

'Yes.'

'Where is that procedure found?'

'On the force's intranet.'

'Did you consult that procedural guide prior to interviewing the complainant?'

'No.'

'Why is that?'

'We didn't think it was necessary.'

'You didn't think it was necessary or you didn't think about it entirely?'

'We were understaffed that morning. Caught off guard.'

The lawyer laughed shortly. 'A police officer caught off guard. Why does that procedure exist?'

'To ensure we record the right information and … and for consistency.'

'How long did your dialogue and reporting last on the day that the complainant visited the police station?'

'Around thirty minutes.'

'Around thirty minutes. Would you say that was quite a short amount of time for a report of this nature – in your own opinion?'

'Well, it depends, really.'

'On what?'

'On the level of detail provided by the victim and their ability to either remember that detail or be in an emotional state to open up about it.'

'How willing would you say Ms Morris was, based on your two years of experience?'

Elaine thought she could see steam coming out of the constable's ears.

'I would say she was distressed. Hurried.'

'Hurried? Why's that?'

'She kept saying she had to get to work.'

'And she was in fact dressed in her work uniform. Is that correct?'

'Yes.'

Jerry Lewis piped up. 'Objection, your honour. I don't see where Mr Mamone is going with this.'

'Stick to the report, Mr Mamone,' the judge said.

The lawyer presented the constable with a piece of paper. 'Constable, can you please read the highlighted section?'

She looked at the judge, who nodded at her with her eyes closed.

'"Two of the guys didn't even do anything to me. They were just kind of there. One of them disappeared before we even got to the car park, or just after, I can't really remember. And the other one, Joey, he was standing real far away but then the big guy bashed him and forced him to come over and I can't remember how but his penis was in my hand. I could tell he didn't want it. And then he spewed on himself and in my hand a little."'

'Thank you. And can you read this highlighted section now, please?'

The constable looked to the judge again and this time the judge didn't nod, she stared back.

'"I was in the toilet cubicle and all of a sudden Joey was in there too. The K had worn off. He washed his face and said sorry and followed me out to the platform where we chatted briefly then I got on the train."'

'Are you aware, constable, how many more times the accused is mentioned in the report?'

She looked as though she might explode. 'No, I can't remember.'

'The answer is none.'

Elaine tried to ground herself by touching her grandmother's pendant, which she was wearing over her dress today. It was all playing out like a TV show.

The lawyer went on to ask more questions about the drugs and how Lisa described them being taken, which he was trying to highlight was willingly. Elaine hated drugs. She had seen what heroin did to Georgette's brothers and son and had decided she would hate everything about drugs for the rest of her life. And then Simon, while he was in jail. And Joey now, like his father. She shook her head.

She unfurled a little when the constable was finally released. As she passed them, Elaine saw the hairs around the constable's forehead had frizzed. She smiled at her, the same old-lady smile that she used on the cashiers at the supermarket.

The prosecution had no further witnesses. The judge called for a break. Joey would be up next.

What a silly little boy Joey was in this room. A weed in a suit.

His lawyer stood up, released one of the buttons on his jacket. 'Joseph, how long have you known the co-accused men?'

'Since high school.'

'And how would you describe your friendship? Close? Or acquaintances?'

'Not close.'

'How often would you say you saw these men?'

'Not often. Few times a year since high school finished.'

'Do you have much in common with them?'

'No. Just school memories, from the same area type of thing.'

'Would you say that applied to all of the young men involved?'

'No, I'm close with one of them, Kyri – Dimitri Kyriacos. We hang out all the time.'

'Your honour, Dimitri Kyriacos was the young man acquitted of his involvement pre-trial.'

'I'm aware. Continue,' the judge said matter-of-factly.

'Joseph, was it your idea to have an outing with your acquaintances that night?'

'No.'

'Whose idea was it?'

'I don't know, but Dimitri made me join.'

'What do you mean by that?'

'I didn't want to go. I had mentioned to him previously that I didn't want to hang out with those guys anymore.'

'How was the night framed to you?'

'We were just going to meet up and, um, smoke.'

'Cannabis?'

'Yeah.'

'How often do you smoke cannabis?'

'I've only tried it a few times.'

Elaine had to stop herself from scoffing. Amal shifted in her seat, and Alex looked at the ground.

The questioning about the lead-up to their arrival at the car park continued. He could have left when the night started to go astray. He could have stopped them. What had stopped him? Being afraid of the boys? Some bruises on his body would have been worth it. That was the problem with young men these days; they were not willing to be bruised. They were too used to being safe. Women, on the other hand; women were so accustomed to being bashed around that sometimes it didn't even hurt.

She tried to focus on her grandson in the stand, but his posture annoyed her. If only he would sit up straight, deliver his answers like they meant something, maybe the judge would find him compelling and end this thing before it spilt over to the next day. It was already two o'clock. She searched for a mint in her handbag.

'Were you sexually attracted to Ms Morris?'

'No.'

'So you definitely did not want to touch her?'

'I did not.'

'Joseph, who unzipped your fly?'

'She did.'

'And how would you describe your state of mind at that point?'

'I was … I was out of it. Limp. Couldn't really do anything.'

'Because of the effect of the drugs?'

'Yeah.'

'And what was Ms Morris like at that point?'

'She was more able, like, aware, and moving because she hadn't had as much as me.'

'Did you then place your penis in her hand?'

'No, she pulled it out.'

'Once she had your penis in her hand, did you say anything to each other?'

'No.'

'Nothing at all?'

'Nothing.'

'Was your penis erect?'

'No.'

'Where was Ms Morris looking?'

'First she looked at my face and then down towards the ground, and then I was shoved in the back and that's when I vomited and kind of came to and moved away.'

'How long did the physical contact last?'

'Like, three seconds.'

'And that was the absolute extent of the physical contact you had with Ms Morris? At no other point throughout the night did you touch each other?'

'No, that's it. Well, apart from sitting next to each other in the car.'

The lawyer spent the next half hour probing Joey about how much of his friends' interactions he had actually seen. Joey described seeing bodies together in a way but did not see the physical sexual touching. He said that he was completely removed from the scenario, at times because he was staring in the opposite direction, or because he was at the other end of the car park (around twenty metres, he said), but also due to the effect of the drugs.

Joey touched the side of his mouth and then quickly interlocked his fingers as though he were trying to take back the gesture, restrict his hands. She knew his movements all too well. She also knew that the lawyer was trying to prove two things: one – that Joey's contact with the girl couldn't be classified as 'sexual touching', and two – that the 'aggravated' description of the charge, concerning the fact that the other boys assaulted the girl in Joey's company, was void because he wasn't close enough when it happened.

'Joseph, is there anything you would like to say to the judge while you are on the stand?'

'Yes.'

'Go ahead.'

Joey read from a piece of paper. 'I want to say that I am deeply sorry to Lisa for what she went through that night and I wish I had realised at the time that she was uncomfortable and overpowered. I want to apologise to the police, the court and everyone involved for the time and emotions they have spent on this case. I know I have made some huge mistakes, but they don't include me sexually touching Lisa or trying to make her do anything. I want to get my life back on track. I want to get a job and become a contributing member of Australian society. I am young but I know my life has changed and that I will make better decisions from now on. I plan to stay sober and not partake in anything that could be classed as a criminal offence ever again.'

Elaine was unmoved. He could have done better than that. The lawyer sat down.

It was Jerry Lewis's turn. 'Joseph, you say that you are deeply sorry for Lisa.'

'Yeah.'

'So you agree then that what happened to her was against her will. Otherwise, what is there to be sorry about?'

Joey's lawyer piped up. 'Objection, your honour. That is an unfair question.'

'Mr Clark, move on please,' she said.

'You didn't really want to go on this outing, did you?'

'No.'

'Yet you were compelled to. And when you took ketamine in the park, you say it was held up to your nose for you – you didn't measure out the dose or control the administration of the drug. All you did was snort?'

'Yes.'

'And later at the car park, when you tried to leave, you were held back. Am I right?'

'Yes.'

'Were you physically restrained the entire time?'

'Not really.'

'So what kept you there?'

'Um, fear, I guess.'

'Fear of what?'

'Of what could happen to me if I didn't.'

'And what could have happened?'

'I don't know.'

'Surely you know what you were fearful of?'

'Fear of … of the guys.'

'That they would hurt you if you didn't partake?'

'Maybe.'

'So you're saying the fear of being hurt, your fear of these men who were your friends, made you do things against your will?'

'I guess.'

'It sounds like a survival tactic to me. A basic thing humans do to stay alive.'

The prosecutor looked at the ceiling and tapped his lip. He was creating space in the room for his next line. 'Do you think Ms Morris may have felt a similar way?'

Elaine's soul drooped inside of her body. The ache in her backside from sitting too long buzzed.

'I can't tell what she felt. I wasn't in her head,' Joey replied.

'What is your opinion, though?'

'In retrospect, yeah. Maybe.'

'In retrospect? Retrospect is a wicked thing, Mr Harb.'

Elaine's stomach went tight. Hunger or anger – she wasn't sure. She looked over at Amal, who was pressing a tissue she had rolled into a tight ball between her thumb and fingers.

The prosecutor asked Joey questions about his friends that required perceptive responses. The kinds of things you know about people from knowing them well, from spending a lot of time with them. Joey was sweating. He looked at his hands a lot, and over to his lawyer.

The day had been categorised by anxiety but, for the first time, a sense of dread settled over it all. Abdul Abbas had been acquitted – there was no way that Joey would be found guilty – but Abdul's charge was aggravated sexual assault. His charges had been about proving the matter of consent. Maybe Joey's lesser charge was the easier one to prove. To prove that he touched her with his penis in the company of men.

They certainly should all be punished, but Elaine didn't want her grandson to go to jail. She'd seen what it had done to Simon. Granted, he seemed to have his life on track now, but he had always been a determined person. Joey, on the other hand, would not survive in there, and even if he did, he would come out and suffocate himself and his family. Joey would always be incapable. A calf with broken legs. Like the one she had watched her father take a knife to when she was a child. Its blood had stained the mud for months.

'What was Ms Morris wearing on the night?'

'Grey tracksuit pants and a white singlet.'

'And how did she wear her hair?'

'Tied up, sort of, in a bun.'

'And was her nail polish red or green?'

'She wasn't wearing any nail polish.'

'What music was being played in the car while you were driven to Bankstown?'

'EDM.'

'Objection, your honour. What is the point of this questioning?' Joey's lawyer asked.

'Mr Clark, what are you getting at?' the judge asked.

'Your honour, I am simply trying to highlight that Mr Harb seems to remember an awful lot of detail from the night for somebody who was supposedly high on cannabis and ketamine.'

Jerry Lewis ended his questioning with that statement.

The judge called for another break, after which the lawyers would give their closing addresses and the judge would reach a verdict. The room had almost filled with journalists that Elaine hadn't heard come in. She could tell they were journalists by the way they disregarded everyone around them, tapping away at their screens.

Hobbling down the centre of the room was not how she wanted anyone in there to see her, but her legs had died hours ago. Alex linked his bony arm with hers. Simon had dashed out to the toilet as soon as the judge stood up, having nervously been sipping from a giant bottle of water during the cross-examination. Joey and the lawyer were still at the front of the room chatting, and Amal was near the doors, withdrawing from hugging somebody.

'Alex, who is that girl with your ma?'

'Oh. That's Emma.'

They approached Amal and Emma. Alex leant in and gave Emma a hug. Elaine had met her but forgot how bright the girl's face was. Emma gave her a kiss on the cheek and the pain in Elaine's back momentarily disappeared.

Amal sung her words. 'Thanks so much for coming, Em. It will mean the world to him.'

The girl flushed, cartoon-like. 'It's okay.'

'Come and join us for the break.'

'I might wait to see Joey on his way out and find you afterwards.'

Amal squeezed her hand. 'Okay, darling.'

'Good to see ya, Em,' Alex added.

Elaine was glad the break was short. In fact, the proceedings in general were rushed, like the judge had somewhere to be, or something she was itching to say. The lawyer had earlier told them this was a good sign, but it didn't do much to alleviate Elaine's stickiness. And she kept thinking about the girl at the centre of the whole thing. The victim had tried to say something about her experience, but her volume had been turned down to a whisper, not by her own hand. She wasn't even at the trial. Joey was being prosecuted by the state, the police, but the victim wasn't required or didn't want to have her say.

The judge took her seat and nodded at Jerry Lewis, who began.

'Your honour, the New South Wales police acted within their authority and judgement to arrest Mr Joseph Harb and charge him in relation to the sexual assault of the complainant, Lisa Morris. The charge they imposed was aggravated sexual touching. It is the prosecution's case that Mr Harb did in fact touch the complainant sexually with his penis, in the company of others – therefore making the crime aggravated in nature. It is the prosecution's case that, although under the influence of drugs prohibited in this state, Mr Harb's state of mind was lucid and functioning at an articulate level. It is also our case that Mr Harb was well aware of the group's intention to assault Ms Morris and that the fear he felt for his physical person, if he were to disobey his co-accused or stop the attack, is a fabrication. Your honour, Mr Harb had to have known that Ms Morris did not consent to being touched and was doing what she had to in order to survive the ordeal. This is a survival concept that the defendant has proven he is aware of and indeed tried to adopt in order to wash his hands clean of the assault. He personally touched Ms Morris with sexual intent while she was vulnerable and could not verbally consent to the touching and while his friends watched. That is the absolute and unequivocal version of events and that is why officers from Bankstown Police Station acted well within their jurisdiction and judgement to formally charge the defendant with aggravated sexual touching.'

Elaine wished he would stop saying 'Harb' and 'aggravated sexual touching'. She needed to leave the courtroom. Amal's head was in her hands. Alex's leg was shaking out of control, and Simon had his eyes closed.

'Your honour, the charge in New South Wales carries a maximum of seven years imprisonment and the prosecution implores you to sentence the defendant with the maximum penalty. Mr Harb is a sex offender and a danger to young women and should not be allowed to re-enter public spaces where he could very well reoffend. Lisa Morris was on a train on her way home to her loving family when she was groomed, overpowered and assaulted by Mr Harb and his long-term friends.'

There was silence for a moment, until someone coughed hoarsely right behind Elaine. The sound almost causing her to jump out of her seat.

'Their attack was calculated, callous, and textbook predatory. This behaviour must be reprimanded in an effort to help young Australian women feel safer in public spaces and to let those same young women know that the law, and its enforcers, are there to protect and support them from attackers like Mr Harb.'

His words shot through Elaine, through the audience, through the walls. The prosecutor had charged himself during the break, had been playing sleepy this whole time so that his final act would really sting. Elaine didn't know where to look or what to do. Joey was going to jail.

'"Sexual touching" in law means exactly what it means in ordinary English. That is to say, touching with the intent of sexual gratification – with or without the sexual organs. The accused agrees that his penis touched the complainant. Why would Mr Harb have partaken in such an act if there was no intent behind it? As the prosecution understands, the accused was not only complicit in the greater assault, but stood to sexually benefit, so to speak, from his physical interaction with the complainant and would have, if not interrupted by his regurgitation, subjected his victim to a much more serious crime.' He turned to Joey, looked him in the eyes and said, with a pause between every word, 'The consent was not there.'

The journalists' thumbs bashed away at their devices. Elaine could hear her own breathing, which was short, and the collective drum of her family's hearts.

The prosecutor sat down, nodded at his colleague and at Senior Constable Thompson, shuffled some papers. He no longer looked like Jerry Lewis.

'Mr Mamone,' the judge said.

The lawyer stood up and gestured with both hands to Joey beside him as he addressed the judge. 'Your honour, my client is a young man who was in the wrong place at the wrong time with the wrong people.'

If the prosecution had charged himself during the break, then Joey's lawyer had done the opposite. Elaine already felt unconvinced.

'Joseph Harb should never have been charged for his alleged involvement in the crime. The New South Wales police acted overzealously in pursuing an arrest and in charging my client with aggravated sexual touching. It is clear from their meagre investigation and from the inadequate police report alone that the complainant does not believe my client to be an assailant. The matter at hand that the prosecution must prove in order for a guilty verdict to be passed is whether the very negligible touching that occurred between my client and the complainant was consented to. Your honour, the police statement made by the complainant and signed by the complainant as being her true version of events states, "And the other one, Joey, he was standing real far away but then the big guy bashed him and forced him to come over and I can't remember how but his penis was in my hand. I could tell he didn't want it. And then he spewed on himself and in my hand a little." In the absence of the witness from the court proceedings we can only go off this statement and off my client's testimony to reach a verdict on the matter of consent. Ms Morris does not suggest whatsoever that Joseph forced himself on her. In fact, she states that he himself was forced by his co-accused. My client has proven himself a compelling and trustworthy witness. You have been presented with three character references from employers, friends and high school teachers purporting to his kind and caring nature. We have heard that it was the complainant who unzipped his jeans and extracted his penis for a very brief moment. Let me remind you that the consent being investigated was only in relation to that moment. Had the investigating officers questioned Ms Morris further at the time of the initial complaint, they would have recorded such detail and saved the court a lot of time and money and saved my client's family months of turmoil.'

What he was saying rang true, but Elaine couldn't help but think about how the whole thing that this girl had been through was being trivialised. And there was her glum-looking grandson.

'There is simply not enough evidence to prove beyond reasonable doubt that my client is guilty of aggravated sexual touching. There is enough evidence, on the other hand, to prove that Mr Harb was forced into a predicament that night by a group of men he did not and does not align himself with, and that he was unknowingly led into a situation he had no control over physically and mentally, in consideration of his inebriated state at the time of the alleged crime. Your honour, to find my client guilty would be an insult to the process of justice. The prosecution asks you to sentence my client to prison to send a message to young women that they are protected. Is that reason alone enough to send someone to jail? Is sending a young man to jail to demonstrate the police's duty of care to young women, when they failed Ms Morris in the first place with their mediocre investigation, enough for a prison term? The proceedings of this case should never have come this far. My client was a witness on that night. He was not a perpetrator and, in fact, his own consent in the act is something we ought to question.'

The statement hung in the air like a fart in a small room. Elaine heard the brains behind her ticking over. Elaine wondered whether the lawyer should have gone on for a bit longer.

The judge asked that they return in half an hour for the verdict. It would all be over. And if the judge ruled in Joey's favour, Elaine was going straight to the pokies.

25

They were all there: his family, the media, the lawyers, the judge. Even Emma had shown up. They had all come for him. To watch him. The star of the show. He had either played his part right and they would applaud when the judge sang, or he had flunked and would be vilified, never cast again. Either way, having his family crammed behind him, and Emma, soothed the trembles of panic that had become as much a part of him as his fingers or toes. If he was to be found guilty, Marco had almost guaranteed that he would not be sentenced to more than twenty-four months in prison. That amount of time seemed doable.

When the judge entered and everyone stood and sat for the last time, Joey felt so light that he held on to the chair for fear of floating away. He had grown to like the judge after having watched her intently throughout the day. He imagined she lived in the Blue Mountains, that she was single, had no children, no pets, but owned a comprehensive and well-curated art collection and wardrobe. He imagined she had an expensive espresso machine that was gifted to her by someone she dated briefly. He imagined she had a kindness about her, something innate that helped shed light in the dark.

Her lips parted. This was it.

'Joseph Harb, you stand accused of aggravated sexual touching. The crown alleges that you acted with awareness and that you inflicted touching of a sexual nature on the complainant without consent and with the knowledge that the touching was not consented to. The defence argues that you were coerced into the scenario and that the consent was void because you did not instigate contact. Given the testimonies and evidence I am not convinced beyond reasonable doubt that your involvement and interaction with the complainant was predatory in nature and that you forced the contact entirely against her will. Therefore I find you not guilty of aggravated sexual touching, and you are absolved of the burden of guilt.'

The journalists muttered. His mum squealed. Joey faded.

'Please be quiet. Mr Harb, it is clear that you are fortunate enough to have a strong support system behind you. Too often I have seen young men in front of me who I could not say the same for. This puts you in a good position to take charge of your life and become a successful and contributing part of society. Although you are not guilty of the crime, it was ultimately your choices that led you here today. Stay sober. Stay away from people you do not look up to. Do not become another statistic and spend your life in the prison system. You are free to leave the courtroom.'

★

His mum had over-ordered pizza. Every inch of the kitchen bench and dining table was plastered with a soggy box. Way too many for six people. Well, five. Joey didn't have much of an appetite. His father and Marco chatted underneath the pergola out the back. His mother and Alex had already started cleaning up.

They had dropped Tayta home with a headache straight after court. She'd given him a kiss on the cheek as they walked out of the courtroom but said nothing.

Joey and Emma took their Coronas to the front porch and he rolled a cigarette to share. He was barefoot, still wearing his suit pants and shirt, which he had unbuttoned and untucked. The street had the kind of calm that only ever comes a few times a year. His skin prickled. It was almost too still, as though it were a colossal photograph that he and Emma were sitting in the frame of, dangling their legs over the edge.

'What made you come?' he asked.

'Do we have to go into it?'

'Not really, but I honestly thought I'd never see you again.'

'I spoke to Kyri on Snapchat,' she said.

'Oh, yeah?'

'Yeah. He's moving to Melbourne to live with his yiayia. He's going to apply to art school. He said to say hi.'

'Why doesn't he say hi himself? You know he's stopped replying to my texts?'

'I think … I think he wants to start fresh.'

'What, and that means stop talking to his best mate? Like I'm the one who put him in that situation? If anything, I should have stopped talking to him. He's the one who forced me to go that night.' Joey held back tears.

'I think he's just trying to escape it all. And you're part of it. I don't know what's going through his head exactly but, yeah, I think he's trying to move on.'

She sure knew a lot about Kyri all of a sudden. They passed the cigarette back and forth a few times. A cat interrupted the photograph.

Emma continued. 'I knew you didn't fully do it. I was just so angry at you for … for … I just thought you would be better at not being a part of anything like that.' Her voice croaked. 'What if it had been me?'

'I would never have let that happen to you.'

'But you let it happen to her.'

That would be the card to trump him for eternity. 'Em, you remember when we were at Defqon, and you were hooking up with Boxer? I was furious because I thought I knew what he was like.'

'What are you trying to say?'

'That I thought he was a scumbag, a run-of-the-mill chauvinist. I had no idea that he could ever be capable of worse. I was dumbfounded that night and really fucking high. I still don't even know what that shit was that Lisa and I snorted. I didn't know what to do or say or anything. Sometimes I'm not even convinced I was there.'

'Joey, I need to tell you something. After Defqon, Boxer kept hitting me up on socials. I kept trying to be nice about letting him down but, in the end, I said that … that you didn't want me to hang out with him. Just to get him off my back.'

Joey vibrated. 'What did he say?'

'Nothing. He unfollowed me.'

The day, the night, their existence, it was all a tiny little blister on the arse of the earth.

'Why didn't you tell me earlier?' Joey asked.

'I don't know.'

'Well, doesn't matter now.'

'Yeah. I guess.' Emma paused for a moment. 'He wouldn't have led you into all of that as payback, right?'

'Em, honestly, I …'

There was nothing more to say. There was only the feeling of needing to disappear. His mother's laugh shot out of the house among the clinking of crockery. He suddenly thought about Ivan and his eyes felt heavier, his spine shorter. Maybe now that Joey had been acquitted Ivan might reply to him. That was the last thought he could process. His jaw clamped shut. His brain began to switch off the lights.

They went inside, Emma said goodbye to everyone, and Joey settled like dust on his bed.

26

Elaine had planned to change out of her court outfit, but it was 7:00 pm by the time Amal dropped her off so she just waited by the door until they had driven away and went straight to her car. She wanted to be in bed by 10:00 pm. She thought to invite Salma, but when she glanced over all the lights were off in the house.

At Ashfield RSL, the poker machine with the genie was switched off and had caution tape criss-crossed over it. Something about a lifeless machine in a cluster of its whizzing mates made Elaine sorry for humanity. She sat at the machine right by it.

She would play a fifty, have a drink and then go home to wash the day off her skin and lie on her back until sleep took over. A knot of men, some carrying worry beads, stood by the screens. There was also a very old couple holding hands at the bar, and a few machines away to her left were two scatty young men. They were bopping their heads even though there was no music playing. The one who was standing had his fists pushed deep into the pockets of his grey hoodie so that it was taut. The other was sitting and tapping away at the machine. When he turned at regular intervals to look around, his whole body twisted.

She angled herself so that she had her back to them and swung her handbag over her shoulder to nestle it in her lap. Ten dollars dwindled quickly and then she made thirty out of a few decent gambles. Three red hearts in a row. She knew how the machines worked. Her shoulders hung lightly, her face felt warm. She realised she was smiling.

A few moments later she was up another thirty. There was luck in the air. Joey had been let off. Already she had missed calls from relatives who had no doubt seen the news, but she would call them back tomorrow when she was less tired, when she could tell them with delight about how her grandson was innocent.

The judge had proven she had the grace and wit Elaine had assumed of her. The way she had so eloquently advised Joey about how to live his life made Elaine's heart brim with gratitude, but also made her feel entirely useless as the matriarch of the family. She could only hope he would consider the words. While the law had found Joey to be innocent, Elaine wasn't quite ready to let him off.

She closed her eyes for a quick moment and reset her thoughts. She did not want to think about the ordeal anymore. She pressed the button mechanically, gambled some very small wins, looked over her shoulder, but Valon wasn't there. She hadn't thought of him until then. Well, once or twice since their initial meeting, but not too often. She knew she had acted crazily that day. And he had been nice, offering her a coffee and a chat and paying for the kebab.

An electric screech jerked her out of her thoughts, and she put her hand to her heart. It had come from the broken machine to her right. As she looked at the supposedly dead screen, the image of the purple genie flashed up for a millisecond. She touched the pendant on her necklace and turned to see if the scatty men had noticed the sound, but they were nowhere to be seen. Coming out of the side of the machine they'd been at, however, was a payout ticket. She walked over, just to see what the amount was. Sometimes if there was only ten cents of credit left punters would hit the payout button and not take the ticket. That was probably what had happened.

She kept an eye on her own machine, held her handbag against her body and only stood close enough to read that the payout amount was twenty dollars. They would no doubt be back for it. They did not seem like the kind of people to let twenty dollars go. She went back to her machine and continued playing.

From where she was sitting, she could see the sliding doors of the club and after five minutes she saw the two men leave. They were walking hurriedly, as though they had somewhere to be. She went back over to the ticket still sticking out of their machine, whipped it out of the slot and put it in her purse. Her own payout had reached eighty dollars. Including the ticket she had just inherited, her money had doubled. She went to the bar.

The whisky was rewarding. A cap to the night. She'd play twenty and go home. She had barely set her glass down before the tracksuited men appeared on either side of her.

'S'cuze me, did you see our ticket over there?'

'Ticket? What ticket?'

'The payout thingy.'

'No, sorry.'

'Are you sure?'

'Positive.'

'Well, you were the only one around.'

Her quickening heart implored them to go away.

They went on. 'S'cuze me, we're talking to you.'

Elaine held her bag tight.

'You took it, didn't ya?'

The barman was too distracted to see her being harassed, and no-one else was around.

'Dumb old bitch.'

Elaine looked at him in the eye when he said that. He was a boy, barely older than her grandchildren. She imagined gouging his eyes out.

'Leave me alone or I call security,' she said.

'Go ahead and call them. Maybe we'll ask to check the surveillance cameras.'

'Fuck it, Jay. Let's go.'

The men walked away, muttering under their breath, headed to the smoking section. The whisky gurgled inside her. She had to get out of there. She made for the door, fumbling in her bag to find the car keys.

The Corolla was parked right at the back. She shuffled towards it as quickly as she could in her dress. She would never wear the dress again. It had been tainted by the whole day. In the car she thrust her handbag onto the passenger seat and was readying the key for the ignition when her door flung open. Where a second ago there was nobody now stood the two men, hoods over their heads.

'We know you took the ticket. Give us your cash and we'll go.'

She was stumped. Her mouth opened and closed. There was

nowhere to hide. She was already half sitting on the handbrake from fright. The men looked away simultaneously towards the entrance to the car park. A car was entering, the headlights bobbing around the dark in the rear-vision mirror. They were wimps; they would leave her alone.

She was so close to being alright, then one of them swooped towards her chest. Thinking he was going to bash her, she braced for the impact but all she felt was a sharp tug around her neck. She watched his hand retreat, and grasped in his fist was her necklace, her grandmother's pendant twinkling in the night, snatched away from her. She caught a glimpse of Mariam Our Saviour's face and implored her to come back. The men ran and jumped over the back fence.

Elaine clutched at the dashboard of the car, at the seat, at her chest, trying to find a button to press that would make her breathe again. When she did manage to inhale, she shrieked so loud that she thought she saw the trees in the car park recoil. The other car had only been doing a U-turn. She was alone, without the protection of her aunts. Without the power of the pendant.

She thought to rush back into the club, tell security what had happened. The men would have had to sign in; it was an RSL. She could take their details to the police.

Fuck the police, they wouldn't do anything.

She started the car. Fury was in charge now. The club backed on to a long laneway where the men had escaped. She headed there, mounting a kerb and driving through a garden bed in the process. She flicked the high beams on at the top of the lane and saw two figures very far off. They were mice and she was the falcon. She floored the accelerator. She would drive into them. She would drive into them, get out, find the pendant and leave them in whatever state they ended up in. Her hands were hot enough to melt through the steering wheel. She would show them what this dumb old bitch was capable of.

She hit the brakes. The car screeched to a halt just short of what she was about to collide with: a man walking his German shepherd. The man had turned towards the car, his arm shading his eyes. The dog was barking, its eyes shining green in the glaring headlights. Her heart was in her lap. She had almost run over an innocent man and his pet.

The man muttered, 'Take it easy, will you.'

For a second she entertained the thought of driving into them anyway. She flicked the high beams off and reversed back down the laneway.

After driving around the block a few times she decided to return to the club and speak with the security guard.

He said, 'I can't just give you the details. I don't even know if they signed in. There was no-one at reception for ages tonight.'

'Okay, let me see the names. I will know from the name who they are.'

'I'm sorry, I can't do that.'

'Then you are like them. You are robbing me.'

'I … I'm sorry. Make a police report and they can investigate.'

She was looking at the carpet. She let out a very short laugh and said, 'The police?'

'Yeah.'

'You know what police do?'

'Sorry?'

'The police – you know what they do? They drive around to arrest homeless people for stealing chocolate milk. They park their car in no stopping to pick up coffee and kebabs. The police … they hurt people who go to them for help. They not going to do anything for me.' Her voice cracked and trailed off.

The security guard checked his phone. She didn't know how she was still awake. And she still had to drive home. Without the pendant. Without the one thing in her life that had known her since birth.

27

Joey woke up the morning after he was absolved and realised the anxiety that had pinned him to his bed for so long had lifted like magic. It was embarrassing to feel so normal again so soon.

The first thing he wanted to do was get a haircut, but his mother had made him promise to go see Tayta before anything else, to apologise for the whole ordeal. He protested at first because Tayta was the one being weird to him, but his mum had given him a look that said, 'Don't even think about it.'

He was taken aback when Tayta answered the door. She had dark and droopy bags under her eyes, like a magician whose magic had been snatched away. He had never seen her hair that grey. She was wrapped clumsily in her bathrobe and was hunched over like an old lady, like she had aged twenty years overnight.

She unlocked the security door without saying anything and he stooped down to kiss her on the cheek. He was sure she hadn't slept. Had he done this to her? Maybe that normal feeling from earlier had been a sick joke.

He stood at the bench in the kitchen.

'You want tea?' she asked.

'Yeah.'

'Your mum at work?'

'Nah, she had already taken the day off, in case the trial …'

'And Alex?'

'Yeah, he went to school.'

The old ceramic jar that she kept the tea in must have been empty because she slammed the lid back on and went to the pantry. He would cry if that jar, with its clumsily painted fruit mural, were to break. It was stitched into the fabric of his childhood.

He looked around the kitchen. The old copper pot set on top of the cupboard, the Queensland tourism tea towel that had faded to almost white, the giant timber fork and spoon hanging over the window. They were a part of him. He thought briefly about having to dismantle it all when Tayta died.

She wasn't saying anything. This was going to be tough. He watched her scrabble with the plastic wrapping around the new packet of one hundred Lipton tea bags. She swore under her breath. He walked over to help, and had to yank it out of her hands as though she didn't want to give in.

They sat out the back side by side, facing the garden. She had put loads of sugar in his tea.

'Tayta, I came over to say sorry about stuff.' He was hoping she wouldn't want to say anything and he could deliver his little speech and leave. Knowing her, his chances were slim. 'I know I fucked up and that I hung out with the wrong guys. I'm sorry that you had to deal with it from your relatives—'

'My relatives?'

'Our relatives.' He stopped and looked at her from the corner of his eye. She had her hand over her mouth pensively, staring at the ground. He'd finish off with something lighthearted. 'I'm so glad that the judge was a nice lady.'

'Nice lady? Just a nice lady, ah? That's all she is?' Tayta paused for effect.

He braced himself for the rhetorical question onslaught. What a stupid thing to finish on. Plain stupid. But there was always a trigger for Tayta. It just so happened to be 'nice lady' this time.

'You wanna know something about nice ladies, Youssef? We are not nice. We just have … what's the word when you feel bad for stupid people?'

'Pity?'

'Pity, pity. We just have pity for everyone, mainly for men, because they are the most stupid.'

A magpie cried overhead and Tayta swore at it. She leant back in the chair, her hands resting on her lap. He had never seen her this calm before and it frightened him.

'My grandfather, he bash my mother and her sisters when they were bad. You know what bad was back then? Not clearing his mezze plates fast enough. Not ironing his trouser fast enough. And my father, he bash my mother too. And he bash me and my sisters. Sometimes, if we too loud in the morning, he make us collect small rocks from the road and kneel on them with bare knees.'

He thought he might combust. He didn't want to know any of this.

'And we never cry or try to run away or ask for help from the neighbour who see everything. And you know why?'

The question wasn't rhetorical. 'Because you were scared?'

She laughed maniacally. 'Scared? Scared? You think we scared? No. We shut up because we know same thing happening to women everywhere. We know that man's hand gonna take thousand of years to take off our throat. So we keep quiet, stay waiting. If we yell in the village, nothing gonna change. You thinking men are not so bad anymore, they don't think like this anymore, but I tell you something, Joey. Deep in the mind, any man from all time, no matter what they like to fuck – women, other men, goats – deep in the mind, they still believe woman is weaker than man.'

She stood up. Joey was empty.

She walked towards the garden and kicked with her slipper at a weed growing from a crack in the concrete until it dislodged. 'And this is why that shit happen to the young girl in the car park with you and them kleb.' She sounded like she was swallowing her tears. She bent over, picked up the weed and flung it into the garden. 'And this is why, all around the world, men always doing shit to women in car parks.'

Joey's anxiety had indeed lifted like magic earlier, and it returned like magic too.

The cash-only barber shop in the decomposing arcade in Bankstown was so small and busy that guys waiting their turn hung out near the dumpsters behind the reception hall or outside the shoe repair shop.

It was always busy. Even in the middle of the day when people were supposed to be at work, there was a disorderly queue. Customers would pop their heads in, greet the barbers in English, in Arabic, in grunts, decide to wait, or promise to return in a few hours. It was an arduous process, but the two brother-barbers cut the best fade, so the wait to spruce up before weekend shenanigans was worth it.

Most of the men had their hair cut weekly, got their beards trimmed, had their ears and nostrils waxed, eyebrows shaped. Older men usually had a hot shave. Everyone seemed to know about each other's cars, had wives who were friends, subcontracted construction work from one another.

Joey had recommended the shop to Alex but apparently, on his initial voyage, after waiting an hour in the queue, the barbers let three new customers sit in the chair before him, so he stormed out and went to Just Cuts at Centro.

One of the brother-barbers was quiet and one was loud. To Joey the haircuts were identical, but still some of the men preferred one over the other. Joey favoured the quiet one purely because he could avoid conversation. Many of the customers were brazen enough to say they'd wait for their preferred barber to free up. Joey had tried to do the same once and ended up confusing the whole shop. Since then he decided to never talk in there again.

'Cuz, you're up.'

It was the talkative one for the third time in a row.

Joey shuffled over to the chair and removed his cap, which he had taken to wearing quite low on his forehead.

'Ay, you're that bloke! You and your mates got done for getting blowies off that chick in the car park.'

Joey's blood evaporated. Everyone in the shop looked at him. If they couldn't see him directly, they stared at his reflection in the mirror. The music momentarily paused as the track switched.

'Fuck. You guys got done, bro. Ayri fiya. She must have been a sharmouta. What did she expect was gonna happen, hangin out with five blokes in the middle of the night?'

He extended his fist for Joey to bump and he obliged, shaking.

'So did you get off or what?'

'Yeah.'

'Lucky, bro. Hopefully the others get off too. You know that Haz guy grew up on the same street as my missus? She reckons he was rough as guts, but apparently his family was next-level hammered, so what do you expect? He's come into the shop a few times actually.'

As he spoke, the barber fastened the cape around Joey's neck. He flicked the clippers on and pushed the blade into Joey's temple. They were usually very fast at haircutting, but he worried the interest in him would keep him trapped in the chair longer. He gripped the worn-out plastic on the arms tightly underneath the cape. Most of the other men in the shop resumed looking at their phones or talking to each other but some were still fixated on Joey.

The barber was doing a good job of having the conversation on his own. Taking drawn-out pauses to think. Speaking with such a slow drawl that Joey was convinced he was stoned.

'You know what the problem is with this country? They don't take everything into consideration, bro.'

He switched the clippers off and turned to the men in the waiting chairs, opening his arms out wide as he spoke, pulling his neck back.

'Don't get me wrong. If someone did that to my sister, I would slit their throats, but my sister would never be in that situation in the first place, you know what I mean?'

One of the men nodded at him and the clippers came back on. Joey was a knot, pulled so tight he thought he would never come undone again.

'Obviously I don't know the ins and outs but is the woman not to blame too, ya khayi?'

Joey was glad the questions weren't meant to be answered.

No-one spoke for around five minutes and then the sound of sirens approached. The guys looked around at each other. One of them pushed his chair back, curling his neck around the door like an emu to see into the laneway. The sirens stopped moving, close by. The quiet brother grabbed a fresh razor from the counter in front of Joey and they locked eyes in the mirror.

The other one fired up again. 'No, the government now wants to take into consideration what the sluts and thieves and faggots have to say.' He made a sarcastic sound with his nose as he switched the clippers off again and turned to address his indulging customers. 'The hard-working bloke like me, like you, like him – the bloke that does his job, goes home, prays, avoids stepping on an ant – we mean nothing, cuz. Nothing, kess ekhta.' His words commandeered his arms, fingers, chest, eyebrows. He was preaching.

A response miraculously came together in Joey's gut, probed his throat, tested him.

'Trim on top?' the barber asked.

'Huh?'

'Do you want the top trimmed?'

Even though Joey did, he said, 'Nah.'

The barber switched the hair dryer on and blew away the cut hair from Joey's face and neck. He raised his voice over the hot air. 'Sometimes, boys, sometimes I reckon we're all better off getting the fuck out of here. Back to our roots, you know what I mean? Our parents came here for money, alright, but the way I see it the money has pretty much dried up and, with it, human fucking decency. I don't want my kids around all this tempting shit.'

The power in the arcade went off. The hair dryer wheezed, fell silent. The lights and music wound down like it was all just a cartoon. Eyes bounced around the shop walls. The sirens trilled, closer.

Joey ripped the cape off him and leapt out of the chair. He threw thirty dollars onto the counter and bolted.

The number still wasn't saved in his phone, but it was there. His thumb hovered over the dial button. Maybe he didn't need to know exactly what to say.

There was an answer after two rings.

'Hey, buddy.' His father's voice was bouncy. Like he'd won something.

'Ay.'

'To what do I owe the pleasure?'

Joey's voice cracked, the panic from the barber shop still coursing through him. 'Nothing ... was gonna say thanks for coming and stuff.'

'Mate, I'm your father. No need to thank me. I'm just glad we are back in each other's lives.'

Joey wasn't really bothered for the cutesy shit. 'You arrived home alright?'

'Yeah, got in about an hour ago. Sorry I left straight away. I'll come down soon, though.'

'What's it like over there?'

'The weather? It's ace. I'm about to go for a swim.'

'Nah, I meant, like, in general.'

'The Gold Coast is laidback, beaches. No drama. How come?'

'Just wondering. It's pretty shit here. I'm over all the heads in the area.'

'Maybe it's time you got out of Sydney. Went on an adventure or something.' His father had forgotten how to read people.

'With what money?'

'I could try to help you out.'

'Nah, thanks.'

'Joe, I know it's a shit time but, mate, you gotta stay positive. Things could have been a lot worse.'

They paused for a moment and Joey heard the ocean through the phone.

'Do you ever think about the guy you ran over?' Joey asked.

'Very often.'

'What would you say to him if you had the chance?'

'There'd be too much to say. But I'd start with an apology and with taking ownership of what I did.'

'Yeah.'

'What are you thinking about?'

'I gotta get out of here. Do you think I could … actually, don't worry about it.'

'Joe, I know how you feel. You can talk to me.'

'I wish I could be a fly on the wall or something and see that she's okay. That she's going to work, seeing her friends, living her life, is happy and shit.'

Another pause and Joey heard teenagers laughing on the other end. He could tell they were teenagers because he had laughed like that too. He pictured them: tanned, blue eyes, taut bodies, arms around each other. Like a Coca-Cola ad.

'I hate to be the one to tell ya this, Joey, but I know from experience that's a dangerous thought.'

'Why?'

'Well, because it makes the victim's experience about you. You want to know that they're okay so that you feel okay. It's something my therapist spoke a lot about when I was inside.'

Joey was an idiot. And now the father he never knew was telling him that he was an idiot. 'Alright, I gotta go, anyway.'

'Chin up, buddy. I'll call ya soon.'

Joey looked up at the sky to stop the tears from falling out of his eyes. His existence had no rhythm. It was a drop of oil in water. When he looked back down it started to drizzle and the parents standing on the sidelines of the play equipment in Paul Keating Park called out for their children. The park was too manicured. He longed for somewhere wild. Something wild.

'Hey.'

The call came from behind, but he didn't care to turn. If it was legitimate, they could come around to face him. He was sitting, knees crossed, his cheeks resting in his hands, staring at the grass. A pair of black Chuck Taylors appeared in front of him.

'Hey,' the person said again.

Joey looked up the body slowly. It was the quiet brother-barber.

'What's up?' Joey asked.

'Don't worry about my brother. He talks a lot of shit. Here.' The barber dropped Joey's cash in his lap.

'Nah, man, I don't want it. I got a haircut, I paid for it.'

'It's actually not finished. The back isn't blended in.'

'All good. I'll get my brother to fix it at home.'

Joey held the cash up towards the guy's waist, but his hands were firmly in his pockets. The little cut hairs on Joey's neck prickled. He needed a shower and he was sweaty and now the rain was making it worse. The notes flapped in his hand until he tired and gave up.

The guy stood there like Joey had something else to offer.

'Did you leave the shop just to find me and give my money back?'

'Nah. We had to close up. There was a fire in the building so the power isn't coming back on. Some bloke ended up with a quarter of a haircut.'

Joey tried to laugh.

'Anyway, what are you doing? You're gonna get wet. Get up,' the barber said.

He offered his hand to help lift Joey up. The hand was slender. As they walked to the edge of the park, the rain pelted down and they had to raise their voices over it.

'How are you getting home?' the barber asked.

'I don't know. Was gonna walk.'

'You wanna come over and I'll finish your hair off with my clippers? I live up the road.'

There was nothing else to do. 'Yeah, alright.'

'I'm parked at Aldi.'

'Why there?'

'Because there's nowhere else to park all day, and I'm mates with the security guy.'

The barber's shoes slapped against the puddles as they jogged to the car. The cool cats who used to scoff at TNs were now wearing them around Newtown and the guys from the area had swapped to Chuck Taylors.

The barber drove a Mazda, and the drive was less than four minutes to one of those aluminium-clad apartment blocks that cast ugly shapes on the landscape. In the lift, Joey prayed the guy had some weed, even though he didn't look the type.

The apartment stank like a sweet candle and there was an oddness to the way it was styled – too many cushions on the baby blue couch, a white throw over the armchair, a large frame with a black-and-white photo of the Eiffel Tower.

The quiet brother-barber transformed in his trendy space. His hips seemed wider, his movements longer, more liquid. And he wasn't quiet anymore. He spoke about the apartment, explained some of the knick-knacks on the kitchen bar, offered Joey a glass of white wine and when he sat on the armchair, he crossed his legs. Joey gulped the wine and looked up at the air-conditioning unit willing it to come on. The rain hammered the tiny balcony overlooking the busy road.

Joey pointed at the Eiffel Tower. 'You ever been there?'
'Nah.'
'How old are you?'
'Thirty-three. You?'
'I'm twenty next month.'
'Shit, you're a baby. Come to the bathroom. I'll do your hair.'
The vanity was covered in what looked like expensive products. Joey sat on the edge of the bathtub.

'Take your top off. The hair will get stuck to it. You can have a shower after, anyway,' the barber said.

'All good. I can shower at home.'
'Why? It's no biggie. I've got plenty of towels.'
As if the number of towels was the reason Joey didn't want to shower in the barber's apartment. 'Alright.'

He felt hungry, or nervous. Far from home. He removed his hoodie and T-shirt and hoped it would be done quick. It was only the back that needed to be touched up, after all, but it took forever, and his legs shivered.

When he was done the barber left the bathroom to get a towel and Joey slipped his jeans off and stood waiting in his undies.

The towel was thick and rolled into a neat cylinder.

'The hot water takes a minute to kick in.'

The barber left the door open and for some reason Joey thought it would be impolite to shut it. He lathered himself in the classy shower gel, washed quickly and put his damp clothes back on. The plan was to say thanks and head off but the barber, from behind his phone on the couch, told Joey to relax and wait for the rain to die down.

'Do you have any weed?' Joey asked.

'Nah, I don't smoke, man. Tried it once but it put me to sleep. I'm into other stuff.'

'Like what?'

'You ever done G?'

'Nah.'

'You wanna?'

'When?'

'Now. I got some.'

Being sober was different from not taking drugs. Joey would have some G, fake a text from someone, and say he had to go. That way he could ride the high on his own. He wanted to be alone. And he had decided to never go to the barber shop again. He'd just go back to shaving his hair off. The thought reminded him of Ivan. Of his big hands rubbing Joey's shaved head in his car. Ivan was worlds apart from the barber – he had been shameless, disarming. Arabs were the opposite. His tayta's shame, his shame, it was multi-generational, multi-dimensional, and it multiplied in the presence of other Arabs.

Aussies had shame too. Deep colonial and convict shame. And Joey was somewhere between the two.

The barber told Joey to stop drinking the wine and he went to the bedroom and came back holding a small bottle with an eyedropper. He poured a can of coke between two glasses and added some of the G to each.

As they sipped on the concoction, the barber harped on about his watch that counted his steps, counted his heartbeats, his calories, missed calls. The watch should really have a function that calculated and counted down a person's living days, Joey thought. That would be more useful.

He felt warm. The rain was unrelenting, and it was now dark. He checked his phone and feigned surprise. 'Crap, man. I gotta go. My brother is locked out of the house and needs me to let him in.'

'Oh, but you're gonna be high as real soon.'

'It's alright. I'm just gonna chill at home anyway. Thanks for, ah, fixing my hair and stuff.'

He stood up, sculled the drink and extended his arm out to shake hands, but the guy looked outside to the balcony quickly and turned back to him.

'I'll drive you. You can let your brother in and then we can come back here.'

The proposal was unexpected. And awkward. Joey dropped his hand to his side.

'I'm gonna call an Uber. It's all good.'

'Are you sure? Would be good to hang out and shit.'

'Sorry, man. I can't.'

The barber stood up and he suddenly seemed shorter, older. He walked Joey to the door and stared too long into his eyes as they shook hands.

'What's your name again?' he asked.

'Joe.'

'Joe. Alright. I'll see ya around, yeah?'

Joey's throat was locked. He smiled and walked towards the lift, being sure not to look back. It wasn't until the lift pinged on arrival that the door to the barber's apartment thudded shut. As he descended, Joey breathed out, checked his pockets for his wallet and phone and keys. Even if he had forgotten something, he would have left it there forever.

There was no calling an Uber because his account was still suspended from the time Kyri had vomited all over the back seat of a ride after a big night out. Kyri was moving to Melbourne, was going to study art. Joey was aimlessly walking in the rain in Bankstown.

Hot, dizzy and under the refuge of a butcher shop awning, he texted Emma: *What's doin? Wanna hang out?*

Emma replied immediately: *Got heaps of uni work. Soz x.*

That's all he could come up with. Who else was there? It would be dumb to call Ivan. He opened Instagram and went to Ivan's profile. He did that quite often. There was a new story update, which was unusual. In the time since they'd met, Ivan hadn't ever posted anything new. Joey's pulse quickened as he tapped on it.

The post was an old photograph of Ivan's father, smiling and holding up a glass of rakia, toasting everyone who would ever see the photo throughout time. The man looked much younger in the photo than the memory Joey had of him wedged under the garage door drilling his son. The text on the post read: *Three months without you.*

Joey's shoulders fell, his heart brimmed. Maybe Ivan was just grief-stricken and not a prick. He replied to the story: *Hey, sorry to see this. Hope you're doing okay.* There was nothing in the world he had to do but stare at the screen until the little 'read' notification appeared under his text. Luckily it only took a few seconds. Ivan liked the comment. He waited patiently for the ellipsis to appear. Surely he'd reply with a thanks at least. Nothing. It sat there, static, underneath Joey's last stupid message, *Hey man.*

The rain thrashed. The gutters rampaged, carrying wrappers and leaves somewhere. There was no-one around, not even any cars. A night to be home, but he preferred the wet.

Just as he was about to exit the chat window and aimlessly enter the deluge, the three flashing dots appeared, followed by text. *Thanks man. Pretty shit go but that's life hey. Sorry I forgot to reply to your last message. I just saw it again now. My head was all over the place cos it was like the week of my dad's funeral when you sent it and I've been off socials and stuff. You been good?*

Joey was weightless, floating. His head was about to hit the aluminium roof of the awning. It could have been the message, it could have been the G kicking in. He closed his eyes. He wanted to rip his wet clothes off and dance. He had to reply to Ivan.

All good. You wanna chat?

Ivan replied with more than Joey ever expected. *Wanna come over?*

How the hell was he going to get to Greenfield Park in the rain and high on G?

He jogged to a busier intersection and waved a taxi down. The driver opened the window ever so slightly to keep the rain out.

Joey yelled over the clatter, 'How much do you think it will cost to get to Greenfield Park?'

'Between thirty and forty dollars.'

The barber returning his cash was fate. There was only seventeen dollars in his account. He hopped into the taxi. Hopefully Ivan would drive him home later or, better yet, ask him to stay the night.

The G kept kicking in and out. When the car took off, he held on to the seat really tight, thinking he would fly out the windscreen, but when he checked the odometer they were only travelling at thirty kays. He didn't dare look at the passing lights and signs and buildings for fear they would come together and spell something out to him. He needed to ground himself.

'Busy night tonight?' he asked.

The taxi driver grunted.

The rain stopped as they approached Greenfield Park. Joey laughed and put the window down. The trees were disco balls in the night. The moon, shrouded in cloud, was a giant eye in the violet sky. It winked at him. A dance track started up on the stereo. The screen said it was 'Beachball' by Nalin & Kane.

Joey felt the music rush inside of him, change him. 'You mind turning it up?'

The driver raised the volume to blaring from the controls on the steering wheel.

People get ready, people get ready, get ready to flow.

He closed his eyes. The car could have been a ship, an aeroplane, a floating turd. He was riding something, somewhere. His muscles twitched. The closer he was to Ivan's place and to the crescendo of the track, the more he swelled against the seatbelt, swelled against the walls of the car, until he was spilling out of the window and flapping away into the night.

Acknowledgements

THIS BOOK WAS WRITTEN ON beautiful and sovereign Gadigal-Wangal land where I am a guest. I pay my respects to the custodians who have always cared for this place.

Endless gratitude to:

Western Sydney University and my very sage supervisors, Anthony Uhlmann and Sara Knox.

Incredible people who listened patiently while I answered my own questions, Patrick McDavitt and Bec Kavanagh. And Brie Hicks for your legal smarts.

Aviva Tuffield, Margot Lloyd, and the rest of the team at UQP – for placing this story in readers' hands.

www.ingramcontent.com/pod-product-compliance
Ingram Content Group UK Ltd.
Pitfield, Milton Keynes, MK11 3LW, UK
UKHW021327180426
11947UKWH00017B/1491